LIFE IN THE BALANCE

ALAN PARKINSON

CHAPTER ONE
Tuesday 17th May

Manuel Frost was on an odd day socks wise. Not that he was wearing odd socks, the very idea sent shivers up his spine. Today would be one of the days when he left the house with an odd number of pairs of socks in his sock drawer; three pairs of grey and four of black. It would seem logical to have seven pairs in total, one for each day of the week but that wasn't logical to Manuel, everything had to balance. He got through the odd days as best he could, knowing that there would be an even number tomorrow.

He put on his socks, always left sock first, then right, followed by his boxers (black today), shirt (tucked into his boxers), tie then trousers. Finally, his left shoe then right shoe.

He combed his hair into a centre parting. The curtains style of haircut hadn't been in fashion since the nineties but fashion wasn't something that concerned Manuel.

Manuel unzipped his bag and checked that his ledger was still there. He'd checked it before he went to sleep but it was best to be certain. With the relief of knowing it was safe, he was nearly ready.

He did a final check of each drawer making sure that they were as aligned as they could be. He made his bed, ensuring that everything was perfectly smooth. He straightened the laptop on the desk so it was exactly in the middle. Satisfied that everything was as it should be he went down for breakfast closing the door behind him.

"And make sure you are home on time tonight," said Barbara, his mother, "you were nearly ten minutes late last night and your tea might has well have gone in the bin."

"I was just finishing off some stuff, I don't always get to finish on time," said Manuel. "Chloe lets me leave early another night to make up for it."

"I don't want you coming home early or late, I expect you to be home on time. Probably having to stop late because of your mistakes."

Manuel didn't bother to correct his mother and started to arrange his breakfast. One slice of white toast, one slice of wholemeal, butter spread right to the edges. Tea made just the way his mother likes it. Whilst it drove him crazy, there was no point in telling her that he'd like some sugar in it to balance out the bitterness. He'd have an extra spoon in his cuppa when he got to work.

He washed up and ensured that everything was put back in the cupboards correctly. His mother had drilled into him at an early age that there was a place for everything and everything in its place. A knife in the fork section of the cutlery drawer didn't bear thinking about.

It was the same every morning, if he didn't start the day off correctly, it would bother him until he went to bed.

Once he finished with the breakfast dishes he brushed his teeth again. He brushed his teeth in order, bottom left first, top right, bottom right finishing top left. The electric toothbrush was a godsend, letting him know when he'd been brushing for exactly thirty-seconds on each section.

He straightened his tie, made sure that the short sleeves of his shirt were in alignment, put on his jacket and headed for the door. His mother cut him off before he got there and adjusted his tie some more. "Look at the state of you, is it any wonder no woman will have you?"

Manuel had long since stopped logging his mother's individual criticisms and bad vibes in his ledger. Whilst he felt the need to balance out all the rights and wrongs he encountered, he started each day with a generic entry for his mother already in the debit column. He only added her actions when they were especially bad.

In the back of his mind he knew that she was to blame for the way he was. Despite this, he was still terrified of what would happen if he moved out. *"One day I might just try it and see what happens,"* he thought.

With his backpack on over both shoulders (he never understood people who casually slung it over one) he finally left for the bus stop.

"Do you have to get up now?" Hannah unzipped her nurse's uniform and headed into the en suite where she started brushing her teeth.

"I've got to open up, perks of being the manager unfortunately." Chloe followed her into the bathroom, put her arms around Hannah and kissed her on the shoulder. "I'm jumping in the shower if you want to scrub my back," said Chloe.

"I'm going to turn in; it's been a hard shift."

"Do you want to talk about it?"

"No, you've got a shop to open. Heaven forbid your precious customers had to wait," said Hannah.

"Don't be like that, it's not my fault that you're working shifts."

"And it's not my fault that you're at work all day then studying when you get in from the shop."

"Let's not make this a thing." Chloe took hold of Hannah's hands. "We'll talk tonight when I get in. We're both free on Thursday night, we can go for a meal when I finish work?"

"Okay, sorry for being a grump, it's been one of those days."

—

"You can tell me about it, I'm sure my customers can wait for their pack of Hob Nobs."

"No, I'm fine, seriously. Have a good day at work and don't forget, they are your colleagues not your projects, you can't change everyone." She pecked Chloe on the cheek.

Chloe removed her pyjama top and headed for the shower. "Sure I can't tempt you?"

Hannah smiled and crawled into the still warm bed, slipping into the side that Chloe had just departed and fell straight to sleep. Chloe showered and did her hair in the bathroom before heading back into the bedroom where Hannah was snoring softly. She gazed at her for a few seconds then grabbed her uniform and went into the spare room to finish getting ready.

She went downstairs and had a glass of orange and a slice of toast. She didn't have time for a coffee, which is what she needed to perk her up but she would grab one on the way to work.

She lived about fifteen minutes' walk from the store. Not far enough away to bother with public transport and she quite enjoyed clearing her head on the way in. Unless it rained, the rain could play havoc with her pink spiked hair.

She'd considered toning down the hair before her interview for the Manager's job but it would have looked weird and she wouldn't have felt as confident. Luckily, they saw past the hair and the colour of her skin and she stormed the interview.

Chloe had been working at Shears for six months now and she loved it. Whilst she saw it as a stopgap, she genuinely liked the staff and most of the customers. She also believed that she could help the staff to change, whether they knew they needed to or not.

Lynn punched the alarm clock as it went off. She wanted to hit the snooze button but had learnt that she would just sleep through for the rest of the day. She wasn't exactly flavour of the month at work so being late wasn't an option.

—

She eased herself out of bed and waddled onto the landing and towards the bathroom. Darcy the cat weaved in between her calves, nearly forcing her to fall over her slippers.

"Bloody hell, Darcy, are you trying to kill me?" She glared at him but couldn't stay angry for long. She picked him up and kissed him then placed him in the bathroom sink as she sat on the toilet. She chatted away as he tried to jump down, avoiding knocking over the cosmetics piled high on the shelf.

Lynn poured herself a bowl of Bran Flakes and added some skimmed milk, she was going to have to lose this weight somehow. She knew that she should weigh her measurements of food as her diet stipulated but Bran Flakes were good for you, surely it didn't matter. She entered the serving into the diet app on her phone.

Lynn logged into the dating website but she'd had no responses. At least there weren't any cruel ones this time. She'd taken the approach of spamming nearly every male within a thirty-mile radius within ten years either side of her age. She'd stipulated right at the top that she had no time for Players so that probably scared a few off. She also asked them to stay away if they feared a real woman with curves. Tipping the scales at just over twenty stone, she had more curves than a Curly Wurly but her profile picture was from a good ten years ago. She was bridesmaid and weighed in at a far more respectable fourteen stone then.

It had been suggested that her profile was a little aggressive but she had no time for time wasters and it was better to rule them out now. If they weren't man enough to live with her curves, they weren't man enough for her.

She added three sugars to her tea and grabbed a Wagon Wheel from the biscuit tin as she logged onto the Daily Mail website, eager to pass judgement on the latest celebrity to show a bit of cellulite. The tea and Wagon Wheel went unlogged in her diet app.

—

9

Finished with her browsing she forced herself into the shower and got ready for work. She squeezed herself into her Renault Clio. The driver's seat had seen better days and the floor was littered with chocolate wrappers.

The car groaned through the gears as she headed up the road and towards the call centre. It was less than two miles and she could probably walk it but why walk when you have a perfectly good car? She also wanted to avoid the bus with the cruel taunts from school children that would inevitably follow.

As the car eventually got into fourth gear she had no intention of slowing, beeping a Lycra clad cyclist and giving him the finger for pulling out to overtake a parked car.

"Get off the bloody road, have you any idea how ridiculous you look?"

Manuel, about to go into work, witnessed the abuse, took out his ledger and made a note.

Barbara was tempted to follow Manuel out of the door and make sure he got on the bus. Despite him being in his thirties she didn't trust him to be able to do anything without her help. She sometimes wondered how he managed to hold down a job.

Accepting that she couldn't follow him 24 hours a day, she cleared her breakfast dishes and got ready for work. She had been a teacher at the secondary school for nearly thirty years now and standards hadn't improved. The children were, as they always had been, children. Unable to have a grown-up conversation and most of them were more interested in showing off to the opposite sex than learning. The teachers weren't much better.

She packed the children's books into her bag, they were hardly worth taking home to mark, she knew exactly what would be in each one. Even the ones who were trying came out with same old tired work that she saw year after year, not a hint of originality between them. She didn't however, like originality and stamped it out whenever it raised its ugly head. She had a curriculum to teach and she didn't stray from it. She hated meddling politicians who constantly wanted to change it, what did they know?

She got into her Ford Fiesta and left for work. She despaired as she passed the children on their way to school. They were constantly pushing the boundaries with uniform. Piercings and tattoos being relatively new challenges to her strict dress code. She still couldn't get her head around why the school now allowed girls to wear trousers instead of a skirt. Some political correctness monstrosity based on the ever-increasing number of immigrants taking over. She didn't approve but you can't voice opinions like that these days.

She parked in her usual spot and avoided two of the younger teachers who arrived at the same time as her. She had no time for making new friends at work, especially with people who were barely out of school uniform themselves.

She walked past some sniggering schoolchildren, ignoring their reference to one of her nicknames, Frosty Fanny. On entering the staff room, she made a cup of tea in a china cup. Unfortunately, it was with a tea bag but the teacher's budget did not stretch to a teapot apparently. She'd rather bring her own but found the last one housing a plant in the science block so hadn't bothered replacing it.

She took out the Daily Mail and read the headlines, tutting loudly. She read out a couple but didn't get a response. Either she wasn't speaking loud enough or they were ignoring her. Either way, she didn't care. Ignored in the staff room, ignored in the class room. It sometimes felt that Manuel was the only one who listened to her.

The headmaster popped his head around the door.

11

"Don't want to alarm anybody but I've had a tip off that we might be getting a call from the dreaded OFSTED. Nothing is definite but it's best to be forewarned. Could you all start preparing please? If we do get the call it could mean a few late nights and a busy weekend for us all."

"For fucks sake," said one of the teachers, "why can't they just let us get on with our jobs?"

"We all feel the same," said the Headmaster, "but it's the world we live in I'm afraid."

He left and the mumblings of discontent spread around the staff room. Barbara wasn't concerned, she wasn't going to change her ways because some snotty government inspectors were going to come and try and tell her how to do a job she had been doing for nearly thirty years.

No, if they thought they were going to get her to change they had another thing coming.

Chloe wandered up the street and gave Indy in the newsagents a wave. She grabbed an espresso in the little coffee shop; they had a kettle at work but she needed a little bit more than instant this morning.

She opened the electric shutters half way and unlocked the door, switching off the alarm as she ducked inside. It only seemed like five minutes since she'd locked up the previous night. The staff would start arriving soon. Manuel would be first, he always was; he was a creature of habit. At least he would leave her in peace when he came in and bother himself straightening items on the shelves. This gave her a small window to catch up on paperwork until everyone else came in and started regaling her with tales of their adventures from the previous night.

She'd quickly learned that the stocktaking would all be in order; this was down to Manuel's insistence that everything balanced. It made her job a lot easier having him around despite his quirks.

As soon as she'd met him she'd identified Manuel as a project; a challenging one. He was set in his peculiar ways but she believed that she could change him. She believed that she could change anyone given the opportunity.

Manuel arrived in the store and quickly straightened the tins of soup on the second shelf down.

Chloe replied to some Head Office emails and checked on stock levels then right on time, Manuel walked into the office.

"Morning, Manuel."

"Morning," he said, thinking about the cornflakes that didn't look perfect. He resisted the urge to go back out and move them.

"You have a good night?" said Chloe.

"Yes, thank you." This was already an improvement as he barely mumbled at her for the first couple of weeks.

"Do anything exciting?"

"No."

"Okay. Do anything boring?"

"What?" Manuel was confused but realised by the smile on her face that Chloe was joking. He didn't understand why people did that. "Just the usual."

Chloe was going to enquire further as to what the usual might be but the moment was lost when Stacey came bounding in full of life and full of tales of her on off relationship. "Is that kettle on Manuel? I'm parched here."

"Morning Stacey," said Chloe downing the dregs of her espresso, "I was about to make a brew. Cup of tea Manuel?"

He hadn't taken Stacey's hint. "Yes please."

"Two sugars?"

"Yes please." He took his time in the store as his opportunity to have his tea the way he liked it rather than the way his mother did. He preferred it with one sugar but decided on two to balance out the one his mother wouldn't allow him.

"What's the plans for today then?" said Chloe.

"There was a discrepancy in the stocktaking that I need to look into, the actuals and expected don't balance."

"You do realise that we do allow a small percentage for mistakes and shoplifting etcetera?"

"I realise that but I'm not happy with it. We shouldn't be encouraging crime or sloppiness," said Manuel.

"Mistakes happen Manuel, you should loosen up a bit." Chloe tugged at his tie loosening the knot slightly. She skipped off into the store, fist bumping Stacey on the way out of the office.

"Stacey, I couldn't help but notice that the cornflakes were a little untidy when I came in. Would you mind straightening them please?" said Manuel.

"Straighten them yourself, I've just come in. Why do you care so much whether the cornflakes are straight, our customers certainly don't?" She wandered back into the store not waiting for an answer.

Lynn pulled into the call centre car park and parked in the disabled bay by the door. They were rarely used and as she thought obesity was like a disability she didn't see why she shouldn't.

Frank, the security guard, had raised it with her once but got a mouthful of abuse and was accused of discrimination. He didn't care a great deal and his desire for an easy life overruled any sense of right and wrong so let her get on with it.

He hadn't seen her approaching but felt as if the sun had gone behind a cloud as she came through the door. He looked up, noticed her squeezing through the security barrier and quickly put his head down again. She once got stuck and blamed him for not opening the wheelchair access for her to walk through. He worried about the safety of the lift as she waited for it to take her up the one floor.

Lynn headed for the vending machines, got herself a cup of tea and a Twix and wandered to her desk. She mumbled a begrudged 'morning' to her team and sat down.

She made a big deal of getting various Tupperware bowls out full of carrots, tomatoes and celery. "I'm trying to be good," she said before she logged in to the phones.

She'd tried many different departments from Customer Service to Sales but she found that the Collections department was more suited to her personality. Chasing people who owed the company money was as close as she got to enjoying her work. She had little sympathy and left them in no doubt about their responsibilities.

"I can see that you failed to make your agreed payment last month Mrs Oldfield."

"I'm really sorry but my cat has been terribly unwell, I've had to pay the vet's bills."

"Whilst I'm sure that was very upsetting, you have owed us money for some time. I don't see why you thought it was more important to pay a vet. If you don't make the payment now I will have no alternative but to hand the debt over to a debt collection agency."

"But it's my cat, if I didn't pay the vet she would have died. If you had a cat, I'm sure that you would understand, she's my life," said a distraught Mrs Oldfield.

"I do have a cat but I also have the good sense to have pet insurance. You maybe should have considered that."

"I can't afford pet insurance."

"Then maybe you can't afford to own a pet." Lynn hated pet owners who couldn't afford to treat their animals properly. She was very tempted to out Mrs Oldfield on Facebook as a cruel pet owner. Maybe someone could give the cat a good home.

"Can you just give me two weeks until I get paid? I swear that I'll pay you then."

"I can give you one week from today. If you don't pay, I will be passing your details onto the debt collection agency."

"But I don't get paid for another two weeks."

"That's not my problem I'm afraid. One week or the debt collectors will be taking your cat away."

The call ended and Jeff, Lynn's Team Leader, who was listening into the call massaged his temples.

Oliver banged on the bathroom door. "How long are you going to be?"

"Can't a man have a shite in peace?" A voice shouted back.

He stormed back into his room, slamming the door. "This place is worse than bloody prison."

Oliver wasn't adjusting well to living in the bedsit but he didn't have many options when he was released three years into a five-year stretch. Moving back to his comfortable four bedroom detached certainly wasn't one of them, his wife had made that perfectly clear.

At least he was coping better in the bedsit than he had when he first arrived in prison. His natural arrogance didn't get him very far and he was soon targeted. He sought out protection and the trade-off was giving financial advice to those wishing to hide their ill-gotten gains. The anti money laundering training he had taken regularly as a bank manager was now being put to use, warning criminals on what the banks were looking out for.

He sat on his bed and sighed whilst taking in his surroundings. Along with the bed and a wardrobe he had a chest of drawers, which was also a TV cabinet for his old style 28" television that struggled to get a picture. It also housed a small kettle and one mug.

The one small window was covered in condensation and mould crept across the ceiling; the smell of damp got into everything. A small sink stood in the corner, he was embarrassed to admit that it sometimes doubled as a urinal when the queue for the bathroom was too long, a cracked mirror hung on the wall above the sink.

A small picture of his children was pinned above his bed. Children he was no longer allowed to see.

Everything about the room depressed him, he was desperate to get out and go for a walk to escape the place and all the other residents. He heard the bathroom door open, grabbed his towel and made a run for it; too late.

"Ah man, I've been waiting ages."

"I'll not be long, just got to pick the winners for today." One of his neighbours waved the Racing Post at him.

The Racing Post, one of the tools of Oliver's downfall. He looked away and stood outside the bathroom determined not to lose his place again.

"Alright mate, okay if I put the kettle on?" said Tony.

Oliver's day had taken a turn. Tony Hurbett, former cell mate and all round pain in the arse was here for his almost daily visit.

"Do you have to bring that filthy hound with you?" said Oliver.

"He can hear you, you know? Rizla's okay, I don't know why you are such a shit about him," said Tony.

"Look at him. He hasn't been washed since he was a puppy and he's slobbering all over my quilt. Get down!" He swiped a hand at Rizla, who yelped and leapt off the bed.

Following his tail for a couple of rounds, he finally settled and lay down. Tony threw him a Digestive.

"Don't be giving him my biscuits man, I've only got one pack."

"Don't be so tight, anyone would think that you didn't like him." Tony dipped a biscuit in his tea and just caught it before it broke off and dropped back in the cup. He dribbled tea down his chin in the process.

"You disgust me. You wash less than that scruffy get."

"Pass us the remote, Fifteen to One is about to start," said Tony.

"Why do you bother watching quiz shows? You barely know what day of the week it is, how are you going to answer any of the questions?"

"Have you never heard of improving yourself?"

"Improving yourself? You're watching daytime quiz shows aimed at unemployed simpletons, not doing a degree in archaeology at the Open University."

"You're worried that I'll be cleverer than you and leave you behind."

"Yeah, the thought terrifies me," said Oliver.

He heard the bathroom door open again and was once again disappointed as it closed just as he got there. Dejected he walked back into his room to see Tony settled back on the bed with his feet up.

"And you can get those disgusting Reeboks off my bed as well. Were they ever white?"

"What do you fancy doing today Olly?"

"Something that doesn't involve you and the name's Oliver."

"Don't be like that, it's not like you have anybody else to spend your time with."

Knowing this to be true, Oliver stomped out of the room to join the queue that had now formed for the bathroom.

Tony had been like a mosquito buzzing around Oliver's head ever since he set foot inside his cell. Admittedly he was a hell of a lot less frightening than the previous incumbent but he was a hundred times more annoying. He had proved useful in showing Oliver how to go on in prison; skills that he had managed to avoid learning over the first twelve months. He had also introduced him to the people who really ran the prison and who offered Oliver some level of protection.

Whilst Tony never did anything for free, it was rare that anybody found him useful so he took great delight in letting Oliver know that he knew more than him about prison life.

When Oliver was released on probation he thought that he had escaped him but when Tony followed him out of the door not more than a month later, he didn't take long to track him down to the bedsit.

Since then he had been a regular visitor with his horrible stinking dog. Oliver needed to get out of this place and away from his irritating sidekick.

"What about documentaries, Miss?"

"What about them?" Barbara wasn't going to back down.

"Surely they can educate us."

"Nothing that you couldn't learn from a book."

18

"David Attenborough makes some wonderful ones. Is it not better for us to be able to picture nature rather than just read about it?"

"They aren't documentaries, it's all computer-generated nonsense these days anyway, the man's a charlatan."

"He won the title of the Greatest ever Briton." The pupil wasn't backing down either.

"Voted for by a TV audience. If they weren't so dumbed down watching nonsense like that they would have voted for someone far more suitable. Margaret Thatcher for instance."

"Who?"

"And there you prove my point; how can you possibly not know who Margaret Thatcher is?"

"I know who she is," another voice piped up from the back of the class, "my Dad said he would happily piss on her grave."

The class erupted into laughter.

"And it's television in every household that has lowered standards to the point where people think it is acceptable to use language like that in the classroom. Go and stand outside in the corridor. I'll deal with you later."

The lad stood up without argument, a smirk on his face and left the class, high-fiving his mates as he went.

"What about the news Miss? Don't you find the BBC News is very well balanced and informative?"

Barbara wasn't prepared to admit that she watched the BBC News each night. "It may be informative but balanced it is not. The BBC has always been infiltrated by lefties."

"What's a leftie Miss?"

"Do I have to teach you everything? Go and read a history book. Learn something, educate yourselves."

She looked out at the sea of blank faces in front of her. Faces of all colours, pupils of all nationalities. Some of them probably didn't have electricity where they came from, why were they arguing so strongly in favour of television? She no longer understood pupils, she no longer understood what her job was meant to be. She was sure that she used to be a good teacher at some point in the past. Now she was a glorified security guard, teaching a pointless syllabus to uninterested pupils and was meant to live in fear of the dreaded OFSTED. She hated the job, she hated the pupils, she hated the other teachers and the ridiculous headmaster and his ridiculous new-fangled ideas. Targets before education is what it had become. Standards had slipped so low that she was faced with this rabble in front of her.

"There was a great documentary on BBC4 about the Russian Revolution last night, Miss."

"BBC4," she thought, "they can't even find enough drivel to fill one channel never mind four."

"I imagine you'll be happy to answer any questions I have on the Russian Revolution then?" said Barbara.

"We can give it a go, Miss."

It was meant to be an English class but Barbara didn't mind changing the subject if she got to prove how ignorant the pupils were. She rattled off a few questions which the pupil answered straight off. He knew his stuff.

"This is an English lesson, not history. Get your text books out."

"Do you admit that TV is worthwhile, Miss?"

"I don't admit any such thing and if you don't watch your cheek you will be going out into the corridor to join your friend. Read pages 315-325."

She gazed out of the window as the class sat silently, victims of the age-old teacher's trick of getting them to read when the teacher had run out of things to say.

Drizzle dripped down the windows and she wondered what would happen if she walked out of the class, drove to the airport, got on a plane and flew somewhere warm. Spain perhaps, a life she previously thought she might have.

It was ridiculous, Manuel couldn't cope without her and he wasn't good in the sun. No, she was stuck here. With idiot pupils, grey skies and the ominous cloud of OFSTED hanging over them all.

"Can I have a word please, Lynn?" Jeff wasn't looking forward to this, he'd been putting it off all morning.

"I'm about to go on my dinner."

"It won't take long."

She sighed and wheeled her chair over to his desk. "What's up?"

"Do you remember the call with Mrs Oldfield?" said Jeff.

"Yes, she hasn't paid yet again, I've given her a week."

"Do you not think you could have been a little more sympathetic?"

"No, why?"

"Her cat was unwell, she had vet's bills to pay."

"That's what she says," said Lynn, folding her arms.

"Not all of our customers are liars."

"Are they not?"

"No, I thought that as a cat owner yourself, you may have had a bit of empathy with her situation."

"I don't use mine as an excuse for not paying my debts."

"That's as maybe but imagine how you would feel if your cat was ill. Paying your bills wouldn't be top of your list of priorities."

Lynn knew that if anything happened to Darcy she would be left with nothing, absolutely nothing in her life. "I wouldn't care if he died. I'd buy a new one."

"All I'm asking is that you have a little more consideration for our customers. We need them to pay but there is a balance to be had."

"Okay, if you say so."

"Thanks Lynn, enjoy your lunch."

"What's that meant to mean?" She grabbed her bag and headed for the canteen. Jeff shook his head knowing that he would be having an even more difficult conversation with her very soon if she didn't buck her ideas up.

Lynn stormed into the canteen, furious that she had wasted time talking to her idiot Team Leader. He seemed to have forgotten that they were there to make money not listen to every little pissy excuse a customer could think of. There was now a queue that made her even angrier. Four size eight girls, barely out of their teens, were fussing over what salad they wanted and how many calories were in each one.

"It's bloody salad, it doesn't have any calories," said Lynn.

"Of course it has calories."

"I know what I'm talking about, I've lost nearly three stone on Weight Watchers."

One of the girls raised her eyebrows. "Which one do you go to?"

"I do my own, I'm not paying them to tell me there that there's no calories in a salad, I already know that."

"Whatever." The girls took their salads and moved on.

She opted for a ham and cheese salad and got double portions of both the ham and cheese. It was a salad, what did it matter? She also bought three bread buns so she could make sandwiches.

There were no spare tables so she sat herself at the end of a table where a couple were chatting. She didn't ask their permission and the look they gave her told its own story.

"These tables are for people who are eating, if you've finished you should go elsewhere," she said.

They didn't bother replying and turned their backs on her to carry on their conversation.

She made the sandwiches and made short work of eating them. She was still hungry so bought a Double Decker from the vending machine. That should see her through until afternoon break.

Lunchtime over she waited for the lift again to take her back upstairs. She tutted as three young girls got out of it when the doors opened.

She returned to her desk via the tea machine and was delighted to find that somebody had been to Greggs on their lunch hour and had bought cakes. It must have been somebody's birthday. She didn't bother to ask whose it was as she helped herself to a caramel custard doughnut. The rest of the team looked on, hoping for her to say thank you but knowing it was unlikely. Her mouth was still full of custard as the first call came through.

CHAPTER TWO
Wednesday 18th May

It was 6am and Indrajit 'Indy' Khan sorted out the daily newspapers. It had become a less important element of his business since the dawn of the internet but he still took it seriously. The Shears store up the road sold almost everything he did but he was still seen as the paper shop. People liked tradition and they liked buying their papers from him.

There were only a handful of paperboys working from the shop now, a sign of the times. Whilst he covered all the national newspapers, it was mainly the red tops he sold. There wasn't much demand for The Guardian or The Times around here.

He put a poster in the window. **Euromillions massive £90m jackpot this Friday.**

The lottery and Euromillions brought him a decent income. The huge rollover jackpot would keep him very busy this week. Everyone dreamed of winning their way out of their everyday lives. They knew it was futile but he didn't blame them for dreaming. He also dreamed of retiring but knew that the only way he was going to get there was by hard work. He'd had the shop for nearly thirty years now and had built a loyal customer base. He wanted to hand the shop over to his sons one day but they had careers of their own to worry about.

He was the face of the business as well. The store was known as 'Indy's' and he'd watched many of his customers grow up. Caught a lot of them attempting to shoplift sweets as children and seen their children do the same. He had an eagle eye (and a very good CCTV system) so they very rarely got away with it. They all came back as customers eventually, sheepishly trying to amend for their wrongdoing.

He opened the shutters, ready for a new day. First task of the day after opening was to hose the pavement. It never failed to amaze him what filthy animals he had living around him. Each day there would be a mix of vomit, urine and discarded takeaway food deposited on the pavement outside of the newsagent.

It would be easy to blame the increasing number of students, and they were far from blameless, but the locals always found his shop to be a convenience. Most of it was drunks caught short on the walk back from town but he knew that some of it was more sinister.

Racist attacks were rare but they were increasing. The casual abuse had intensified and he occasionally had to clean graffiti from the shutters. Sign of the times.

He dragged the hose from behind the counter and went back in and turned on the tap. He'd got the tap fitted some years ago after getting sick of pulling the hose through the store and inevitably snagging it on a display and bringing it down. It was cheaper to pay for the new tap than continuously clean up from his own clumsiness.

He gave the pavement a good clean and brushed the water into the road.

"Morning, Indy."

"Morning Chloe, early start?" The mini supermarket may have been his competitor but he got on with all the staff. No point in making enemies of them.

"Yeah, I'll never get used to getting up at this time. I'm a young lass, I should just be getting in from clubbing now."

"Have a good day, love." He waved her off as she headed up the street. He retracted the hose and put it back behind the counter.

He pushed the switch for the lights and they came to life one by one. The one on the shelving that housed the newspapers flickered but didn't come on fully. He got down on his hands and knees and fiddled with the plug in the socket. The shop needed rewiring but he had been putting it off. It was a big expense and it was only a minor inconvenience at the moment. He punched the plug, avoiding the loose wires, and the lights came to life. Satisfied with his handiwork and convinced that he had delayed the rewiring for another couple of months he retired behind the counter and waited for the early morning rush.

Grace rose at six, same as she did every morning. At eighty-four it was far too late to look for a new routine.

As she toddled into the kitchen, her first task was to feed her cat Ruby. This was her third Ruby, at ten years old she was the same age as the other two when they died. Whilst this one showed no signs of going yet, Grace had already decided that she wouldn't be replaced when she did. Grace just hoped that she outlived the cat so her feline friend didn't have to find a new home in her later years.

She poured out a pouch of Whiskas and filled the water bowl. Ruby usually went out on the wander on an evening but she was always home for breakfast.

Grace poured herself a bowl of Bran Flakes, vital in keeping her regular, and waited for her tea to brew in the pot. Apart from rationing during the war, her tea making routine hadn't changed since she was a child. Her husband was a big tea drinker when he was alive and she still made the same now thirty years after he passed.

Ruby wasn't as big a fan but still enjoyed a saucer or two when it was offered.

Once the tea was brewed, she poured herself a cup, added the sugar then the milk then took it into the sitting room where she read the previous day's Echo. She'd read the headlines the previous night with her cocoa but liked to leave the bulk of it until the day time. She scanned the obituaries, there were always one or two names she knew. As she reached her eighties, less and less of her old school friends and work mates appeared in there. Most of them were gone now. She used to have a regular social life with her friends from the civil service but as they became more infirm the outings became few and far between.

Her civil service pension along with her husband's pension kept her reasonably comfortable but she seemed to have less money these days. The vet's bills for Ruby didn't help and whilst she was happy to help a charity, she had started to feel a bit pressured to donate to everyone who knocked on the door or stopped her on the street. She did find it harder to budget these days but still refused to shop at supermarkets. She'd rather shop locally and support her local shop keepers even if it was occasionally more expensive. She liked the personal service and it was as close as she got to a social life. Her only concession to this rule was Shears. It was a national chain but the staff were lovely and they did have the stuff she couldn't find in the other local shops.

She'd read a bit more of the Echo then get herself ready for a walk to the shops. Ruby was already settled for the day in front of the fire.

Grace took the pile of unopened charity letters from the telephone table. She received so many now that she went through them once a week. Best to do it now before heading to the shops.

She sorted them into three piles. Ones that she already donated to who were asking for more, ones that she didn't donate to and thought that she should and ones that she wasn't going to donate to. There were rarely any in pile three.

27

Cancer and cats were her priority, as much as she wanted to, she knew that she couldn't help everyone so she had to choose. She made sure that she had her bank statement open at the same time so she could see how much she donated each month. There was no point helping the cats if her and Ruby were going to end up on the street. She could do without having to make those sorts of decisions.

The phone rang.

"Hello?"

"Hello Mrs Peebles, my name is Sam are you aware of how many of our ex-servicemen are sleeping rough this evening?"

"I'm afraid I don't and whilst I don't wish to appear rude, I wish you people wouldn't ring me at home."

"Just three pound a month could help someone who served our country to find a bed for the night."

"I'm really sorry, I can't help." Grace hung up and she was shaking. She hated saying no and hated being rude to people but it was the only way to get them off the phone without giving over her bank details.

She'd confided in Chloe at Shears that she was donating a lot to charity. Chloe had been good enough to sit with her and explain about the commission these cold callers were on and gave some tips on dealing with them. Grace had always considered herself to be reasonably street smart but the world was changing faster than her.

They'd agreed a strict budget for charities and Grace agreed not to donate to anyone who called her on the phone. She felt guilty but knew that Chloe was right. Chloe had also told her to bin all the letters that came through the door but she hadn't quite got around to that yet. One step at a time.

The house looked like a bomb site. Annette had just finished the school run and returned to the scene of devastation. *"How can three kids make such a mess?"* she thought.

Despite trying to get them all to eat together, breakfast dishes were strewn throughout the house. Porridge bowl on the settee, half eaten toast on the stairs. She did the first sweep of the house, collecting all the dishes and filling the dishwasher. Her stomach rumbled, she'd only had time for a quick coffee before leaving the house.

She then went through the kids' rooms putting toys back on their shelves, heaven forbid they ended up in the wrong spot. She dumped clothes in the washing basket in the bathroom; she would put a load in when she got a minute.

She caught a glimpse of herself in the mirror. Her hair scraped back in a ponytail as it hadn't been washed. The lines around her eyes would stand out if it weren't for the bags beneath them. She was tired, very tired.

She did a quick tidy round of the bathroom, still surprised at how many different places a teenager thought it was acceptable to leave a towel, and grabbed a pile of washing.

The utility room had a pile of ironing that had been there a week, she would get around to it eventually. Probably when the kids ran out of school clothes.

She put on the kettle and slipped some bread into the toaster. The phone rang in the office. She called it the office but it was only a desk in the corner of the dining room. She didn't entertain much these days so the dining room wasn't much use for anything else.

Annette had been working from home for nearly a year now. She had returned from maternity early when Oliver went to prison. There was a very real threat of losing the house, the house she had worked so hard to buy. Whilst Oliver was seen as the breadwinner, she was a very successful saleswoman in her own right and if it wasn't for her time off with the kids, she would more than likely be a director by now.

As it happened she was Senior Regional Salesperson which meant she could work from home to coordinate the salesforce and only needed to pop out to see clients when something was going seriously wrong.

Strictly speaking she was part time but she was on call 24/7. It wasn't a great arrangement but one she tolerated to keep a roof above the kids' heads.

She dealt with the call and headed back to the kitchen. The toast was now cold and she had to boil the kettle again. She took the coffee and toast back into the office and powered up the laptop; one hundred and twelve emails since yesterday. *"How can that happen?"*

She went through them, deleting as many as she could without reading them.

The doorbell rang. *"What now?"*

Working from home had its advantages but dealing with charity collectors, deliveries for neighbours who were at work and the variety of hapless salespeople who ended up on her doorstep wasn't one of them. The salespeople were usually that bad that she was tempted to invite them in for a training session.

She went to answer the door, her toast with just one bite taken out of it.

"Is your husband in?"

"My husband?"

"Yes, Oliver, is he here?"

The man standing in the doorway was well over six foot, heavily muscled, shaven-headed and covered in tattoos. Not the type of person Annette wanted on her doorstep. Another similar character was leaning on the bonnet of a BMW at the end of the drive.

"Oliver doesn't live here. He hasn't done so for years."

"This is the address he gave us."

"I'm sure he did, it sounds like the type of shit-headed thing he would do but I can assure you that he doesn't live here."

"When will he next be visiting?"

"He won't ever be setting foot across this doorstep, believe me." Annette was bright red and her voice was getting louder.

"When does he have access to the kids?"

"I'm not sure what it has to do with you but he gave up his right to see them a long time ago. Probably around about the time he started dealing with the likes of you."

He smirked and nodded, seemingly not taking offence. "Okay then, if he does get in touch can you tell him that Dale was looking for him?" Dale walked down the drive and took his mobile from his pocket to make a call, nodding for his friend to get in the car.

Annette shut the door behind her. Every bit of her was shaking. Part fear, part rage. She knew very well who Dale was and he wasn't the sort of person she wanted to turn up on her doorstep.

She grabbed her mobile and started writing a text. Oliver had given her his number when he got out of prison. He knew that she wouldn't keep in contact but she had to have it in case of an emergency with one of the kids.

She hoped to never use it but she found herself typing him a message.

You fucking bastard!!!!!!!!

Oliver's phone beeped. He didn't get many messages; it was probably Tony so he left his phone where it was as he stared at the ceiling.

He lay there for another ten minutes before reaching over and looking at the screen.

"Annette?"

He clicked on the message, it didn't make sense. He rang her straight back, terrified that there was something wrong with the kids. No answer; he texted her.

What's up? Are the kids ok? Please ring me.

He waited five minutes and with no response he tried ringing her again. Still no answer. He tried texting again.

Please ring me. Are the kids ok? Are you ok? Please ring, I am worried sick.

Another five minutes went with no response. He tried ringing again but it went straight to voicemail.

He grabbed his jacket and ran down the stairs. He would have called a taxi but he didn't have any cash. He ran all the way to Annette's; it was nearly three miles and he was out of shape. He got to the end of the cul-de-sac covered in sweat and nursing a stitch. He gathered his breath before heading up the drive.

He rang the doorbell and waited. No answer; he knocked on the door, still no response. *"Shit, maybe they're at the hospital."* The car was on the drive so that didn't make sense. Unless they went in an ambulance.

He started knocking harder on the door. He knocked on the window. A woman walking her dog gave him a funny look. He peered through the letterbox and could just make out the shape of Annette in the dining room.

"Annette," he shouted, "answer the door."

She tried to ignore him, staring at the laptop screen and deleting emails.

"Annette, what's wrong? Are the kids okay? I can't do anything unless I know what is up." He briefly considered smashing a pane in the door and breaking into the house but thought better of it.

"Annette, the neighbours are watching, please come to the door."

She pushed her laptop away and stormed to the door, yanking it open.

"Annette, thank God you are okay, where are the kids?"

She glared over his shoulder at the dog walker who hurried along dragging the dog behind her.

"What are you doing here?" said Annette.

"Your message, I panicked, I thought there was something wrong with the kids. Where are they? Are they alright?"

"They are at school and of course they are alright. No thanks to you."

"Please let's not go through all that again. What was your message about?"

"I've had a visitor this morning."

"A visitor?"

"A visitor with a message for you."

"For me, why are they leaving a message for me here?"

"That's what I'd like to know."

"What was the message?"

"He said to let you know that Dale was looking for you." With that Annette closed the door in his face.

Oliver slumped against her car. Dizzy and with acid rising in his throat.

"Shit," he thought as he rammed a handful of Rennies into his mouth. *"He knows where my kids live."*

Oliver got to the end of the road and vomited into a bush. He ignored the disapproving looks from passers-by and spat on the pavement then wiped his mouth on his sleeve. Sweat was pouring from his brow and his legs were weak. He leaned against the wall to regain his composure.

Annette and the kids had suffered enough for his crime. His going to prison was only a small part of the punishment, knowing the struggle they were going through hurt him even more. He'd hoped that keeping his distance, at Annette's request, would draw a line under the whole thing. She was struggling but she had a job and would eventually get back on her feet. Maybe find somebody else, somebody who wasn't a failure and a criminal. Someone she deserved.

But now his crimes were on her doorstep, they were never going to escape it.

Unless he did something about it.

He wiped his eyes and headed off towards the industrial units.

Oliver leaned against the entrance to the industrial estate, he knew where Dale's unit was, every lowlife in the city did even though he was meant to be low profile. He watched and waited, trying to build up the courage to go in and confront him.

His car was there; he'd upgraded the BMW since Oliver went into prison but the private registration was the same. There were various meatheads pacing around providing less than discrete security. Two Transit Vans sat in the yard, their drivers having a quick smoke whilst waiting for something.

Oliver tried to rehearse what he was going to say to Dale. Did he just go in and threaten him and tell him to keep away from his wife? It wasn't likely to work, was it? The worrying thing was that Oliver didn't know why Dale wanted to speak to him in the first place. He'd always paid his debts on time before prison, never missed one. Turned up at the pub as instructed and made the regular payment in full. Did as he was told before and during his time in prison leading to them writing the debt off. He was almost the perfect customer.

Admittedly he'd tried to keep a low profile since he left prison and did his best to avoid Dale. It was easy as Dale rarely dealt with the people who owed him money unless he really needed to. He had plenty of people to collect on his behalf. If Dale was wanting to see him, something was definitely up.

Oliver straightened himself, popped another couple of Rennies in his mouth to calm the burning acid in his gut and marched towards the gate of the yard.

A lorry swept by and straight into the yard which became a hive of activity. The shutters rattled up as it reversed in, beeping as it did so. A team of workers appeared out of nowhere and leapt onto the back of the truck. The van drivers stubbed out their cigarettes and backed up their vans, opening the back doors.

In the middle of it all stood the imposing figure of Dale directing operations.

The meatheads who had previously been loitering were now on full alert. Maybe this wasn't such a good time to disturb Dale.

He quickened his pace and marched straight past the gate and back to the bedsit.

"Get this unloaded quickly lads." Dale pointed to the lorry reversing into the warehouse.

A gang of lads were on the back of the truck and had it unloaded in minutes. Half of the tobacco coming off went straight into Transit Vans and didn't even touch the floor of the warehouse. Just the way Dale liked it.

He'd been working the illegal tobacco runs for over six months now and it was turning into a big operation. A very lucrative one as well.

Brett appeared at his side, his arms full of brown envelopes from the Transit Van drivers. "Where do you want these, boss?"

"Give 'em here. They'll have to go in the safe for now but I'm going to need to get it back into circulation as quickly as possible."

Making money was easy, spending it was another matter. He didn't want to draw unwanted attention to himself. The taxman and customs and excise were a worry. The people whose turf he was treading on were a major concern.

If he kept the goods and the money moving he had half a chance. If he got caught with a warehouse full of either, he was in trouble.

Whilst the tobacco was lucrative and reasonably low risk, these runs were merely dry runs for the real operations he had planned.

The driver of the lorry wandered over.

"Any problems?" said Dale.

"None whatsoever, didn't even get stopped. All very smooth."

"Cheers mate," he handed him one of the envelopes "you still up for doing it again?"

"If you're still handing these over at the end of it, I'm still up for doing it."

"And the other stuff?"

"Yeah, you sorted out what we discussed?"

"Yes, friend of a friend lined up."

"You've got it all planned out mate."

"This is just the start. If this all works out then we'll be moving onto bigger and better things. Let's not run before we can walk though."

"Talking of running before you can walk. I'm touching cloth here; can I use your bog?"

35

"Through there, mate."

Dale hadn't met a truck driver yet who didn't use every opportunity to use the toilet.

He put the rest of the money in the safe, locked it and opened a can of energy drink. "We need to find this Oliver character."

Chloe was working on the till with Alex who was working at Shears part time whilst he was at university. Alex looked at the queue forming and he noticed a girl who had been coming in the store recently. She was petite, slightly Gothy and despite the Goth image, she always had a smile on her face. He thought her name was Hayley and Alex hoped that he got to serve her today.

Chloe also noticed Hayley in the queue. Once she got to the front, Alex was still serving his customer.

"Sorry, I'll just be a second, my till roll has jammed." Chloe opened the till and started poking about to resolve the issue. As Alex's customer left and he started serving Hayley, Chloe's till was fixed. "Who's next?"

Alex rang the goods through the till and placed them in the carrier bag. He tried his best to look cool and in control but as he wrestled with the carrier bag, his actions betrayed him.

"Thank you, see you later." Alex handed the carrier bag to Hayley.

"Bye," she said as she looked back with a smile. He blushed.

"You like her, don't you?" Chloe had been watching.

"What do you mean?"

"Come on Alex, I've seen how you behave around her."

"She's nice." He looked over to the door where she had just left.

"We're going to talk later."

Later in the tearoom, Chloe hatched her plan. "You do realise that she drinks in The Chesters on a Friday night after work?"

"No?" said Alex.

"I think it's about time we had a work night out."

"Okay, where were you thinking?"

"The Chesters, you idiot."

"Oh, I see." He blushed again.

"I think you need a little makeover before then." She started running her fingers through his hair. "Yes a few tweaks here and there and she'll be eating out of your hand."

Manuel wandered into the tea room. "Fancy a night out on Friday Manuel?" said Chloe.

"A night out?"

"Yes, don't sound so surprised. A bite to eat and a couple of drinks with your colleagues. It'll be good for team building."

"Err, I'll have to ask my Mother."

"You're thirty-five years old, you don't have to ask your mother's permission for a night out."

"You haven't met my Mother."

"Friday night, at The Chesters. Be there, you're going to be wing man to young Alex here."

Manuel had no idea what a wing man was but agreed. "Okay then."

"We've got to do a little makeover on Alex beforehand, maybe we could do one on you."

"A what?" The horror on his face was evident.

"Never mind, one step at a time. Alex, let everyone else know. Manuel, you check in with your Mam. It's going be a good night."

Chloe loved having a project to work on.

Tony held the dregs of his joint between his filthy fingernails and managed a final drag before he threw it away.

"Ha'way, Rizla." He patted the dog on his head and he followed him into the pub.

"How many times do I have to tell you Tony, it's Guide Dogs only in here." The landlord was frustrated. He didn't mind dogs, he had one of his own but Tony's was a stinking mongrel and the customers had begun to complain.

"He is a Guide Dog; how do you think I would manage to get home without him guiding me? Isn't that right Rizla?"

The Landlord had already walked off to serve somebody else.

"Turn that up, mate." Tony pointed at the TV playing an obscure quiz show silently in the corner. The customer closest to the remote was either ignoring him or, as was more than likely, was too drunk at three in the afternoon to notice anyone other than the barmaid.

This wasn't so much his local as his regular haunt. He'd been banned from nearly everywhere in the city and this was literally the last chance saloon for him. He had to be on his best behaviour but best behaviour in here was a low benchmark. The smoking ban was enforced intermittently, drug dealing and consumption were regular events in the less than salubrious toilets and you could buy stolen goods from leggings to lamb shanks and TVs to toothpaste. The only crime was not buying a drink, or worse still, expecting one on credit.

Even by these low standards, Tony was unpopular and he couldn't blame it all on Rizla. He was regularly scrounging pints and he stunk more than his dog.

"Pint of Fosters mate and can you turn the telly up?" Tony tried to attract the attention of the landlord again.

Once Tony had paid for his pint, the landlord increased the volume slightly and placed the remote behind the bar out of his reach.

He pulled his stool to the end of the bar closest to the TV. "I'm good at this one," he said to the drunk who was barely awake.

The quizmaster read out the question, "Which of these countries uses the Dollar as its main currency?"

"America." Tony took a big mouthful of his pint satisfied that he'd got the answer.

"Egypt, Australia or Peru?"

"Eh, what's he on about? It's bloody America, every daft twat knows that." He jumped off the stool.

"Australia," the contestant answered.

"Correct."

"Correct, course it's not bloody correct. Its America man. Thick as shit." Tony had begun to raise his voice.

"Keep it down Tony, people are trying to sleep over there."

"It's a bloody fix, everyone knows its America."

"It appears that they know better than you, they're on their way to a thousand quid and you can barely buy yourself a pint of Fosters. Maybe you should get yourself on there."

"Maybe I should, maybe I should take my custom elsewhere."

"Feel free to try Tony, good luck with finding anyone who will take you."

Tony knew he had nowhere else to go. Sulking, he flopped back onto his seat and lost interest in the quiz show.

Not many people could carry off the Double Denim look. Tony certainly wasn't one of them. The jeans, baggy and shapeless were faded and dirty. The jacket, also too big was slightly darker but no less filthy. It held his cigarettes and barely covered his black EDL hoody.

"Mind if I join you?" He sat down before he got a response. Dale and Brett tried to ignore him but they couldn't ignore the smell.

"Is that you or the dog?" said Dale.

"Is what me or the dog?"

"The smell. One of you stinks, or both of you do. Do you not have running water in your house?"

"Ha'way man, there's no need to be like that."

"Can you bugger off and bother someone else Tony, we're in the middle of a conversation," said Dale.

"With him? The big lump never says a word."

"Tony, I wasn't asking. Piss off before I get him to explain it to you."

"I was wondering if you had any work. You know deliveries and stuff, I can turn my hand to owt."

"Try turning your hand on a tap and clean yourself up. You're a disgrace."

"Alright, alright. I'll come back when you're not having a quiet moment with your big friend here."

"You don't know when to shut it do you? We'll call you if we need you. Actually, you can do something for me. Do you have an address for that posh lad you were inside with?"

"Oliver? What do you want his address for?"

"None of your business, do you have it?'

"Yeah, no problem, I'll write it down. Here you go," said Tony.

"Now will you go and pester someone else?"

"Message received and understood." Tony left the table and looked around to see who else was in the pub. He spotted one of the female regulars. Part time shoplifter, part time prostitute. Full-time alcoholic.

"Alright pet?"

"Alright Tony, how's it hanging?"

"Down to my knees as always." For once he had an audience that didn't look like they were trying to get rid of him.

"Tenner," she said.

"Tenner, for what?"

"Blow job. Full service for twenty if you are feeling flush."

"Bugger me pet, I was only making conversation."

"Aye well, my time doesn't come for free."

"They are hardly queueing out of the door for your services, are they?"

"And there's hardly a queue looking to talk to you, there's a reason you know."

"Got to be careful who I speak to, I'm working for big Dale now. Got some important work coming up. Got to keep it all hush-hush."

"Oh aye? Loose lips and all that?" She shook her head and went back to her pint.

"You'd know all about loose lips, probably whistle a happy tune every time the wind blows up your skirt."

She slapped him across the face knocking him clean off his stool. Rizla started barking and the handful of customers in the bar laughed at his misfortune. He hated this pub sometimes. He wished that Oliver would join him so he didn't have to mix with the others in here. For some reason, he always turned him down.

"Too snobby for his own good sometimes," he thought.

Tony left the pub with Rizla. His attempts at scrounging a pint had proven futile and there was only so long he could nurse the one he had bought. He didn't want to push his luck too much with the landlord. People always say that being unemployed is easy but Tony found it difficult filling his days. He considered doing a bit shoplifting for some beer money but he was well known by all the security guards and it wasn't worth another stretch inside for a few pairs of boxers or a joint of lamb. He decided to wander back round to Oliver's to see if he was in a better mood.

He passed a Mercedes with a laptop case on the passenger seat. He paused.

"Don't even fucking think it." The Mercedes owner was heading back from the cash machine. Whilst he was wearing a suit, he looked like he could look after himself.

"What you talking about man? The dog just stopped for a piss. Come on Rizla." Tony hurried off, affronted that the Mercedes owner knew exactly what he was up to.

He arrived at Oliver's bedsit and the front door was open as it always was. Not much point in trying to keep out the criminals when everyone inside the building was one anyway. He climbed the stairs to Oliver's room and knocked on the door. No answer. He could hear the news on the television in the room. *"Typical Oliver watching 24-hour news, always has to be the clever one."* He knocked again.

"Ha'way Oliver, I know you are in there."

"I know you are out there, that's why I'm not answering the door," thought Oliver.

Tony tried once more but knew that he wouldn't get an answer. "Sod you then you miserable get."

He went back out onto the street and was at a loss what to do. He checked his watch. "Come on Rizla." He headed off down the road towards the dance school. They would be turning up soon.

He loitered on the street corner as various Lycra clad youngsters got out of their parent's Range Rovers and Mercedes. Some of the parents looked over at him and ushered their kids inside. And then he saw her as she skipped out of a Jaguar. He didn't want to be seen by her parents so edged behind a privet hedge and watched her enter the class. "She's a beauty isn't she Rizla?"

"Can I help you?"

Tony hadn't noticed one of the parents approaching. He towered above Tony.

"Err no, I was just…"

"Just what, looking at the little girls?"

"No, not all of them just…"

"Just what, just picked out your favourites?"

"No, it's not like that."

"What is it like then? Do you want me to call the police so we can discuss it?"

"No, please don't, it's not what you think."

A quick right hander took Tony by surprise and knocked him off his feet as he scraped his face off the wall.

"If I ever see you around here again you'll be getting a lot more than that and you'll be begging for the police to turn up."

"Okay man, I'm going." Tony left as Rizla started barking wildly. He wiped the blood from his nose onto his sleeve. This hadn't been a good day.

He sat in a shop doorway, exhausted and shocked from the assault. He had half a joint left in his pocket and struck it up.

Is this what his life had become? Covered in blood and smoking dope in a dirty shop doorway.

A passer-by threw a pound coin in his direction without even making eye contact.

"Here man, I'm not homeless." The passer-by didn't look back. Tony scraped the coin from the pavement and put it in his pocket, he finished his joint but didn't feel like getting up again. The street was getting busy with people heading to the station from work.

"Can you spare any change please mate?"

CHAPTER THREE
Thursday 19th May

Oliver went downstairs to check the post. Living in a bedsit populated by some less than honest residents meant that he had to be quick. Anything with the slightest hint of value would disappear. All he was hoping for was a single reply to the hundreds of job applications he had sent off. He knew he had no chance of getting back into the finance industry but he'd hoped that his years of management experience might count for something.

Apparently not.

There was a pile of junk mail but nothing for him. He couldn't face another visit from Tony and he planned to spend the rest of the day applying for jobs online. The only access he had to the internet was on his phone which wasn't ideal so he headed for the library.

He was a regular visitor to the library and the staff were always pleasant but he knew they were whispering behind his back. His fraud had been big news a few years back and people still recognised him. He logged onto one of the job websites and started browsing for things he might be qualified to do. He'd applied for nearly all the call centres but they all had the same question on the application. **Do you have any convictions other than spent convictions …?** Answer it honestly and he wouldn't even get a reply. Lie and the huge gap on his cv would be very difficult to explain. He'd tried doctoring his cv but on the rare occasion where he had got to an interview, he found it hard to carry on with the untruth. For someone who had convincingly lied for so long in his previous role, he found it a real struggle now. Getting caught had shattered his confidence.

He fired off twenty more applications without much hope of getting a reply. He then checked his emails. He had changed his email address since coming out of prison. His previous inbox got clogged by emails from the gambling websites he had used so frequently. He could do without the temptation. He'd tried closing his accounts but that meant logging into them and he decided that it wasn't worth the risk.

Gambling was his vice, a very costly one. He didn't care what he gambled on. Neither did the people he borrowed money from. Until he stopped paying.

His descent into criminality was rapid. A couple of favours soon turned into full scale fraud. Fraud that he did a very poor job of hiding.

His new inbox was barren apart from a few automated responses from his applications. There were some where the employer had been kind enough to tell him he had been rejected, most didn't bother.

He went back to Google and typed his name in the search bar. It always brought up the same results; it always punished him but he felt the need to do it.

When he was younger he liked having a name that was a bit different, something that stood out. Now he wished that he was called John Smith. The top searches for Oliver Durant in Google all referred to him and his crimes.

Most employers would do a quick Google search on a name before interviewing. Was it ethical? Who knows but it was common practice. The search would bring up his ashen face as he walked into court. His name forever linked with the word Fraud.

He didn't know why he still searched for his name, it always depressed him. Maybe he hoped that one day it would magically disappear or one of the other handful of Oliver Durants in the world had developed a cure for cancer and knocked him off top spot on Google. No such luck; he was destined to always be Oliver Durant, fraudster.

He left the library and went for a walk. He couldn't face spending any more time in the bedsit than he needed to. When he was in the city centre, he'd developed a route where he didn't pass a betting shop. Like the gambling websites, he didn't want to put temptation in front of him.

Once out of the centre and over the bridge, he dropped down to the river and walked along past the university and the National Glass Centre and on towards the seafront. This was his favourite part of the day, left with his own thoughts and nobody bothering him. The only problem with his own thoughts were that they often drifted back to his family, gambling and the people he owed money to. The type of people he didn't want to think about.

"Surprise!" Chloe came into the office carrying a birthday cake, Alex and Stacey were behind her.

"What?" Manuel looked shocked.

"It is your birthday, isn't it?"

"Yes, but nobody has ever got me a cake. Apart from my Mother but she only lets me have one slice. She won't be happy if I'm full when I get in."

"We're not expecting you to eat all of it, I'm expecting at least a slice for myself."

"Sorry, it's just a bit of a shock. You didn't need to bother, it's only a birthday."

"We got you a little present, it's not much but we hope you like it." Stacey stepped forward and handed him a little parcel.

Manuel ripped the paper off. "A pen, thank you; that's really nice."

"It's not an expensive one but we noticed that you are always jotting things in your notebook. Thought you were maybe writing a book. Thought we'd better be nice in case you were writing about us." Chloe winked.

"It's not a book, not about you. I wouldn't do that." His eyes drifted to the locker where his bag contained the ledger. He thought about keeping it on him all the time just in case anybody tried to sneak a look at it.

"Don't worry, you don't have to tell us if you don't want to. Come on, blow your candles out before we set the fire alarms off."

Manuel blew out the candles and Alex and Stacey took a slice each back into the store. Chloe gave Manuel his and pecked him on the cheek. "Happy birthday, hope you have a great day."

Manuel kept his hands by his side, terrified.

She left his card on the table. He opened it when she left, it took a while for him to understand it but he laughed.

Manuel's first action with his new pen was to record the cake and present as a good deed in his ledger. Whilst he didn't know how to express it, this was the first time in years that anyone other than his mother had acknowledged his birthday.

Oliver returned to the bedsit, lay back on his bed and stared at the peeling paint on the ceiling. Tony had obviously visited; Oliver had avoided him but the damp, musty smell of his dog lingered.

The TV was muted in the corner of the room and Oliver tried to clear his mind of all his troubles, lack of a job, lack of money, lack of a family.

He'd agreed to do some therapy whilst in prison, one of the ways to accelerate his release on probation. Whilst he was a reluctant participant, some of it stuck with him. He knew that boredom and stress were two of the biggest feeders of his addiction. He had to keep himself busy and stress free or he'd be straight back into the betting shops. Lying on his bed wasn't keeping busy but it was valuable time to clear his head and reduce the stress.

He heard footsteps thudding up the stairs, no doubt somebody else planning on camping out in the bathroom. He couldn't understand it, he wanted to spend as little time as possible in the filthy hole.

His door burst open.

"Knock, knock." The hulking frame already filled the room with another blocking the light from the doorway.

"Shit," said Oliver as he leapt from his bed, keeping it between him and his new visitors.

"Not pleased to see us, Olly?" Dale Benfield looked around the room.

"What do you want?"

"What sort of greeting is that?" He took a digestive biscuit from the pack and offered one to his colleague. He stayed mute and shook his head. "Are you going to put the kettle on then?" said Dale.

"Did you want something?"

"Cup of tea, two sugars."

"Very funny, how did you know I was here?" He'd tried to keep his location secret since he came out of prison and he spent as little time as possible in the bedsit.

Dale raised his eyebrows and smirked. Oliver caught a whiff of the dog again, he didn't need an answer.

"What are you doing here?" said Oliver.

"Come on Olly, you know why we are here."

"It's Oliver." He didn't like being called Olly but knew it was futile arguing with Dale.

"Of course it is, Olly." He took a little notebook from his jacket pocket. "Your name is in here, not your real name for obvious reasons but this one here, Stan Laurel. Clever eh?"

"Genius."

"As long as your name is in this little book, especially with the big numbers beside it we see here, I think we are entitled to pop in to see you whenever we like. You agree?"

"I have no idea what that is, my debt was written off when I went inside. You promised."

"And I'm a man of my word, that debt was cancelled when you kept your mouth shut."

"Then I don't understand, how do I still owe you money?"

"Well Olly, whilst me and you keep our promises, it would appear that your son Josh, doesn't."

"Josh, what's he got to do with it?"

"We'll be in touch." Dale headed for the door.

Barbara arranged Manuel's birthday tea just the way she liked it. Everything had a specific place on the table. Sausage rolls on the outside, then quiche, then the open sandwiches; tinned salmon and cucumber and egg mayonnaise.

She placed the birthday cake in the middle of the table where the rest of the birthday tea was. They had the same every year, Manuel would be looking forward to it.

Manuel came in with a big smile on his face. Barbara was waiting for him in the hallway.

"Happy birthday to my big boy," said Barbara as she handed his card over.

"Thank you."

He opened it. It was the same as every year, a painting of a steam train. He didn't like trains, he never did but it was a hobby his mother always thought he should take up.

"I've done you a birthday tea, just as you like it." She ushered him through to the dining room. She'd never asked if he liked the birthday tea, she just assumed.

Manuel took his card from Chloe, Stacey and Alex out of his bag and put it on the mantelpiece.

"What's that?" said Barbara.

"A card from my friends at work."

"They aren't your friends, they are colleagues. There is a big difference."

"They are my friends."

Barbara snatched the card from the mantelpiece. It appeared to be a picture of vegetables wearing clothes. The tagline read **Today we celebrate the day you left the vagina. Happy Birthday.**

"And this is what passes for a birthday card in your workplace?"

"It's funny."

"That is disgusting. How dare you bring such filth into the house? What if Father Russell came around and saw that. What on earth would he think of us?"

"He never comes around and what if he did? It's just a harmless joke."

48

"Harmless? It's disgusting, I feel physically sick. What sort of woman would think that was an appropriate card to give to an impressionable boy?"

"She's my friend, why can't you let me be happy?"

"Why do you always have to spoil everything Manuel?" She stormed out of the dining room into the kitchen and deposited the card into the pedal bin and then went upstairs to her room.

Oliver knew he risked the wrath of Annette but he had to find out what was going on. He waited until football practice was finished and followed the group of teenagers as they headed home. There was never a good time for a Dad to approach his son in front of his mates, especially when the Dad was an ex-convict.

"Hello, Josh."

Josh kept on walking, pretending not to hear him. His mates instinctively formed a barrier between the two of them preventing Oliver from getting too close.

"Josh, I need to speak to you, its urgent."

No response.

"Josh please. Just five minutes of your time and then I'll leave you alone."

They quickened the pace and Oliver tried to keep up.

"Josh, I'm willing to have this conversation in front of your mates but I don't think you'd want that."

"This isn't a conversation," said Josh.

"He speaks, at last. Come on son, just hear me out."

"He doesn't want to speak to you." The biggest of Josh's friends squared up to Oliver.

"None of your business sunshine, I remember when you were running about in a shitty nappy. Think you're the big man now?"

"Think you're the big man because you've been in prison? You're a joke, he doesn't need you."

"It's okay mate, ignore him," said Josh as he put his arm around his friend, "he's not worth wasting your breath over."

"Josh, please don't make me do this in front of your mates."

"Does Mam know you're here?"

—

"No, and I think it's in your best interests if she doesn't find out."

Josh shrugged.

"Josh, it's about Dale Benfield."

Josh slowed his pace, "Go on lads, I'll catch you up."

Manuel went to the pedal bin to retrieve his card. When he picked it out he noticed the remnants of another card. He took it out of the bin and spotted the other bits. He didn't piece them all together but he did enough to see that it was a birthday card to him that his mother kept from him.

He hadn't noticed his mother had come into the kitchen behind him.

"What are you doing?" said Barbara.

Manuel looked up from the pedal bin. "Getting my card back."

"Who said you could?"

"I don't need your permission, it's my card."

Barbara tried to swipe the card from his hand but Manuel was too quick. He pushed it into his pocket. "Maybe you should take one of the other ones from the bin." He threw the torn pieces of card onto the floor.

Barbara thought about picking them up but she knew there was no point. "I was protecting you, those people aren't worth knowing."

"It's not for you to decide. They are my cards."

"They are my family and I'm telling you that they aren't worth knowing."

"I'd like to find out for myself. Were any of them from my Dad?"

"Your Dad? Don't be ridiculous."

"Why is it ridiculous? He could have been sending me a card every year for all I know."

"He didn't want to know you as soon as he knew I was pregnant. He's not going to want to know now."

"I'd like to know him."

"Maybe you should get yourself over to Spain and find him. You'll do a better job than me."

"Spain, is that where he is?"

"Who knows? It's the last place I saw him."

"I'm half Spanish?"

"Who knows, who cares? I'm your mother that's all you need to know."

"I care, I want to know who he is."

"You don't know what you want. Foreigners aren't to be trusted but you won't listen, you still have to listen to that Chloe character."

"She isn't foreign, she's from London," said Manuel.

"Come off it, I've told you, she'll be lying."

"Why would she?"

"Why would anyone?"

"You would know."

"Don't start Manuel, I'm not in the mood."

"All I want is to find my Dad. Is that so wrong?"

"I'm afraid I can't help you there, you'll have to find him yourself."

"Maybe I will."

"You couldn't find your way to the end of the street without asking for directions. Grow up and accept that this is your life. You aren't going anywhere, you're not going to amount to anything, no matter what your deviant friend says. She will dump you as soon as she finds a new toy to play with." Barbara was now towering above Manuel as he crouched by the bin. She kicked the card remnants across the floor. "Tidy this mess up."

Manuel swept up the card as his mother stormed out of the room again. He was going to gather all the pieces together and see who the cards were from but decided against it. *"What's the point?"* he thought.

His mother wasn't going to help him and what would he learn anyway. It didn't appear like any of his extended family would know who his Dad was. He had to accept that his mother was the only family he had and she was enough trouble on her own, why would he want to add to it?

He took the card from Chloe from his pocket and read it again. At least somebody cared. He then took out his ledger. He wasn't sure where his mother's actions fitted on the good or bad scale. Keeping the birthday cards from him had been cruel and selfish but maybe she genuinely believed that she was doing it for the right reasons. *"Who knows what's going through her mind?"* he thought.

He went into the sitting room. His Mam was in the armchair reading the paper. He picked up the remote control and switched on the television. He started flicking through the channels in search of something worth watching. He settled on The Simpsons on Channel 4, he'd heard people talking about it at work, saying how funny it was but he'd never seen it. He placed the remote on the arm of the settee and settled back to watch it.

Without speaking Barbara snatched the remote and switched it onto the BBC news. She placed the remote down the side of her armchair, out of the reach of Manuel, and went back to reading her newspaper.

"Why did you have to say that in front of my mates?" said Josh.

"I tried to warn you."

"What do you know about Dale Benfield?"

"Enough to know that you shouldn't be mixing with the likes of him," said Oliver.

"And you are in a position to pontificate about who I should mix with?"

"Not pontificating, I'm trying to protect you."

"Bit late to be worrying about that. Dale Benfield is my business, nothing to do with you."

"He's made it my business now. He's a very dangerous man and he's threatening to hurt both of us."

"I'll take my chances."

"You don't get any chances with the likes of him. Why do you owe him money?"

"Like I said, none of your business."

"Please tell me it's not drugs."

"What do you take me for?"

"Not gambling, surely?"

"Don't judge me by your own low standards, I'm nothing like you."

"So why do you owe him money?"

"Because of you and your pathetic attempts at being our Dad."

"I don't understand."

"You never will. Have you any idea how hard it's been for Mam since you went inside?"

"I imagine it has been tough."

"Tough? You haven't got a clue."

"I'm here now, I'm trying to help."

"The best help you could be is staying away from us like you're meant to."

"Tell me why you owe him the money and I'll fix it."

"You're pathetic."

"Just tell me, Josh."

"If you are so desperate to know, the money was for Christmas."

"Christmas?"

"I was sick of seeing my sisters going without presents for another Christmas. How do you tell them that Santa doesn't like them as much as the other kids? I borrowed £500 to buy them some proper presents. Mam found the presents and made me take them back."

"Does she know where you borrowed the money from?"

"No, she said she didn't want to know if I paid the money back as soon as possible."

"And did you?"

"Yes."

"So why does he still say you owe him money?"

"Because by the time I went to pay him, he'd already added the interest. I couldn't afford that. For every missed payment, he added more. I'm fairly sure you know how criminals operate."

"Josh I'm sorry."

"Yeah well, sorry doesn't help."

"I'll sort this, I promise."

"Keep out of it Dad, I'll sort it myself."

"How are you going to be able to pay him off, you are still at school?"

"Because I work for him. Are you happy now? I work for Dale Benfield because you are a shit Dad."

"Why did you have to tell Dale where I lived?" said Oliver.

"He asked me," said Tony.

"And that's good enough reason to drop me in it?"

"He was going to smash my fingers with a hammer, it's not like I had much choice."

"He was going to smash your fingers?"

"Yes, you don't think I would just give you up like that?" Tony rubbed the side of his nose with his index finger.

"What sort of maniac goes around smashing people's fingers with a hammer?"

"Dale Benfield."

"I could do without having him in my life. Part of my probation is not consorting with criminals."

"You're consorting with me."

"Real criminals," said Oliver, "you barely even register."

"Hey man, you can hurt my feelings you know."

"I can't be dealing with him Tony, I can't. He's bad news. Christ knows what he has planned for me."

"Don't think you have much choice. You either pay him what your son owes him or you do what he says. Only other option is to disappear."

"What do you mean disappear?"

"That depends," said Tony, "you can go into hiding, but if he finds you, he'll disappear you and your family for good."

"Fucks sake," Oliver threw the pillow across the room. "I need a way of paying him off."

54

"And how are you going to do that? The only way you can make money is by working for him. If he finds out that you've got any other earners on the go he's going to tax you before you've had a chance to pay him."

"What if he doesn't find out?"

"He always finds out. What's he going to say when you turn up with a bag full of notes? He's going to ask questions."

"I don't have to tell him."

"It's the world you live in Oliver, whether you like it or not. When you crossed that line, and borrowed money off them that was you in for life."

"I could tell them I've won the lottery."

"There's more chance of you winning the lottery than there is of you escaping Dale and his mates."

"Once I've paid them I'm out of here."

"It's never going to happen," said Tony.

"Just because you've never escaped this life, doesn't mean that I can't."

"That's just it, you might be the man with the degree and all the financial qualifications but I've been around these people all my life. You can't win."

"Who says I can't?"

"What happened when you went to prison?"

"What do you mean?"

"They said they'd take care of you if you kept your mouth shut."

"Yeah, what about it?"

"You surprised everyone by keeping your end of the bargain and what did you get in return?"

"They cleared the debt."

"And what happened next?" said Tony.

"What do you mean what happened next?"

"They cleared your debt as promised, then they got their claws into your son. The cycle never ends."

Oliver knew that he was right. "I have to do something. I can't live my life like this."

"There's only one way out. We have to do a one-off job that is so big that we can disappear for good," said Tony.

"We?"

"You don't think I would leave you to do it on your own."

"I can't think of this at the moment. Right now, we just need to start earning some coin to keep Dale at bay."

CHAPTER FOUR
Friday 20th May

"Like to help bairns with cancer?"

"Fuck off!"

"Charming." Tony's latest scam wasn't going so well. A bucket with a picture out of the paper taped to it, a dodgy laminated ID and the front to try and carry it off was all he needed to get started. He'd done it before and it could be a good earner but you had to pick the right time and place. Match days, weekend of the Airshow, big crowds with their pockets and wallets loosened with alcohol, they worked fine. Wednesday morning on Chester Road not so well.

The match days had their own risks, bigger police presence, the chance of someone pissed up and pissed off giving him a clip. A fuck off was about as much as he could expect today, and it was about as much as he had got. He'd be lucky if he'd made a fiver.

He should have gone into town but he couldn't be arsed. He loitered outside of the post office, hoping to catch some pensioners coming out with their pensions. After half an hour, he realised that perhaps they no longer get their pensions from the post office. Maybe they didn't like dogs. "You're costing me money, Rizla."

He wandered to the Chesters but it was too early to get anyone who'd been drinking, this was a big waste of time. He headed back up towards the hospital, a big risk strategy.

"Like to help the bairns with cancer?"

His bucket rattled as a few pound coins went in. A hurried mother shepherding her children towards the hospital, possibly to visit a sibling. Another pound coin dropped in from an elderly couple. His strategy was paying off.

"Oi, what are you doing?" A six foot two, heavily muscled beast was striding toward him. Tony tried to make a quick exit but got caught in a tide of nurses who had got off the bus and were heading in for their shift. A hand grabbed him by the shoulder. "I said, what the fuck are you doing?"

He decided to front it out. "Collecting for the bairns' charity, you not want them to go to Disney?"

"Bairns' charity my arse. My bairn's in there seriously ill and you are out here scamming people. You are scum."

A right hander caught Tony on the cheekbone and knocked him to the ground. He still held on tightly to the bucket. "What did you do that for?"

"If you don't do one now you'll be lucky if you can crawl into hospital."

A crowd had started gathering and Tony could see the security guards approaching across the car park. He crawled backwards, dragging his bucket. A couple of coins dropped out, he didn't dare reach for them and scrambled to his feet and exited out of the gate. Today hadn't been a success.

He headed off back down Chester Road, feeling the lump forming on his face and decided to give up and head home.

He was passing Shears and he saw a girl in her twenties, purse already in hand heading into the store. No harm in asking.

"Spare some change for bairns with cancer?"

"Yeah okay." She opened her purse but then gave Tony another look and had second thoughts. The scruffy clothes, the bruised face, it wasn't the best look for a charity collector. "No, sorry." She went inside.

He followed her. "Come on love, it's to send them to Disney. Surely you want the bairns to be able to see Mickey Mouse before they die?"

She quickened her pace.

"Get out."

"What?" Tony hadn't seen Chloe approaching.

"Get out and take your bucket with you unless you want another black eye," said Chloe.

"And you're going to give it to me?"

"I will if I have to." She might only be slim and five-foot-tall but Chloe could be intimidating when she wanted to be.

"What about the bairns with cancer?" Tony had convinced himself that he was doing good, he hadn't convinced anyone else.

"I'll give you five-seconds to get out or I'll take your scrawny little head off your shoulders." Chloe advanced, her fists clenched.

"Alright keep your hair on."

Humiliated at being bullied by a tiny lass, Tony trudged out of the store. "Come on, Rizla." They crossed the road and he sat on the wall, lighting a cigarette. "Poor bairns dying of cancer and nobody wants to help them. What's the world coming to?"

He counted the money in the bucket, barely enough for a pint. It wasn't worth walking into the town and he was barred from all the pubs around here. What a waste of a morning.

He considered his options. Buy a couple of cans? He couldn't go in Shears now and he didn't want to go in the newsagents to give that Paki his hard-earned money. He might as well head home for a nap.

"Come on, son." He yanked at Rizla's lead and dragged him away from whatever he was sniffing on the wall. He noticed a well-dressed elderly woman come out of the butchers and head up the road. Maybe this was his one last chance.

"Come on Rizla, be on your best behaviour, we're going to turn on the charm and get ourselves a few quid." He waited for a gap in the traffic and ran across the road with the intention of blocking her path.

Grace got herself ready for a trip to the shops. It took a lot longer these days but she didn't see that as an excuse, she would always be well turned out. She had to laugh when she saw the youngsters popping to the shops in their pyjamas. She wished she had their confidence. A little bit make-up, her hair in a bun and a smart skirt and jacket, she was ready to go out.

"See you soon Ruby." The cat looked up but barely purred, far too comfortable. Grace grabbed her shopping trolley and trundled down the garden path.

"Morning Grace," said one of her neighbours. They were a nice family. She wouldn't call them friends but they were always polite and she knew she could call on them if she ever had a problem. They were a busy young family, she didn't like to bother them much.

She popped into the butchers.

"I'll have a nice piece of liver please."

"Liver and onions tonight is it Grace?"

"It is Harry, you can't beat a bit of liver."

"Indeed, sixty-three pence do you?"

"Yes, that's lovely Harry, thank you."

"Can I get you anything else love?"

"No thanks, I'll see you tomorrow."

"Okay, take care."

Grace stepped gingerly out of the shop and headed up the street towards Shears.

"Kiddy's cancer, love?"

"I'm sorry?" Grace was taken by surprise by the young gentleman shaking a bucket at her.

"Money for the bairns with cancer." He pointed at a blurry picture of some children that appeared to be on a hospital ward, some with bald heads.

"The poor dears." It's terrible that she'd got to 84 yet there were children who were struggling with cancer. She went for her purse.

"Thanks love, we're hoping to send them to Disney."

Grace looked in her purse, she only had about forty pence in change, a ten pound note and a five-pound note. She hesitated.

"It'll cost thousands, the sooner we get the money, the sooner we can send them. You know, before it's too late." Suitably embarrassed, she put the tenner into the bucket.

"Thank you love, you're a saint." He walked off down the road as Grace stepped into Shears.

Chloe noticed her coming through the door and rushed over to grab it for her.

"And how are you this fine day Mrs Peebles?"

"I'm very well thank you Chloe and will you please stop calling me Mrs Peebles?"

Chloe laughed, "Of course Grace, we aim to please in your local Shears store."

They'd been through this routine almost daily since Chloe had started working there. Grace wondered how Chloe managed to stay so enthusiastic. Truth was that Chloe liked Grace, one customer who was polite and never gave the staff any problems.

"And how's that lovely girlfriend of yours?"

"Oh you know, she can be a little grumpy at times but she does look good in a nurse's uniform." Chloe winked at her.

"My other half was always grumpy Chloe, but he didn't look as good in a nurse's uniform." They both laughed.

"Anything you need, I'm just over here."

Grace went towards the cat food and picked up two packets of Whiskas and then to the vegetable aisle.

"Morning Manuel love," said Grace.

"Morning." He looked away sheepishly.

"Looking very smart there, I bet you have all the female customers after you." She punched him playfully on the arm. He went red.

"I wouldn't know about that."

"Maybe Chloe's Hannah has some nice nurse friends," Grace straightened one of the tins of soup for Manuel, "you should ask her."

"Maybe."

Manuel would normally hate this sort of conversation with his mother but he knew that Grace genuinely meant well. He never spoke to customers, in fact the he wasn't sure whether Chloe really wanted him to. But Grace was different, he felt comfortable talking to her.

She walked around the shop and picked up the bits and pieces she needed. She placed the gravy granules in her basket, she was far too old to be making it from scratch, a couple of potatoes for some mash and an onion. She also picked up her treat, a cheap bottle of sherry. She didn't really drink in the house but she occasionally liked a little glass every now and then after her tea. At her age worrying about health concerns due to alcohol wasn't something she had to care about.

Grace emptied her basket onto the conveyor belt. Chloe rang it through.

"That'll be twelve pound and four pence please Grace."

Grace went into her purse and looked at the loose change rattling about in the bottom alongside the five-pound note.

"I'm sorry love."

"What's up?"

"I forgot, I don't have enough, I gave ten pounds to that nice gentleman collecting for the kiddies."

"Not the man with the bucket?"

"Yes, why?"

"Nothing." There was no point in embarrassing Grace. "How much do you have?"

"Not much, maybe I can put the sherry back. I was being a bit a little extravagant" Grace was getting flustered.

"Let's have a look, there's nothing wrong with a bit of extravagance every now and again." Chloe counted the pennies in the purse and realised that putting the sherry back wouldn't make any difference.

Chloe pressed a couple of buttons on the till and produced a receipt, slipping the money back into the purse. She put the sherry into a carrier bag along with the food and the Whiskas.

"There you go Grace, have a nice day. We'll see you tomorrow." She winked at Grace who looked back, confused.

"Right, yes, thank you Chloe, thank you. You're an angel."

She headed for the door as Chloe went into her own purse and put the money into the till.

Manuel looked on impressed. He already had his ledger out and was adding something into the credit\column.

"You sure about this boss?"

"Too late to back out now mate. If we want to make the step up, these are the people we need to be dealing with." Dale indicated and pulled onto the slip road.

"I know that but this is a big step, once you are in with these guys, there's no backing out."

"I've thought it through, Brett. We're doing well and soon we will make our move to secure Sunderland for ourselves but it will be a lot smoother with Manchester behind us. This deal is our opportunity."

"I get that but aren't you a little bit nervous?"

"Shitting it mate, shitting it but it's the only way. How far to go till the turn off?" The motorway had become winding country roads, clear of any other traffic.

"Another five miles or so I think. Can't tell with this bloody atlas. Why can't we use the Sat Nav?"

"We don't want any record that we've been here. Same reason that we're not meeting in a service station. Less witnesses, no cameras."

"That doesn't fill me with confidence."

They sat in silence for another five minutes then the turn off appeared ahead. "Turn left here Dale," said Brett.

They turned into another country lane and after another five minutes they came to a boarded-up pub, a faded Vaux sign hanging from the front. "Here it is," said Dale.

"Didn't know they had Vaux pubs out here."

"They don't anymore." Dale pulled into the car park and as expected they were the only car. He switched off the engine and waited.

"Nice place for a hit," said Brett, trying to joke but his laughter was betrayed by the nervousness in his voice.

Ten minutes later and right on time a BMW pulled into the car park. The two characters who got out weren't who they were expecting to see.

"Who's that?" said Brett.

"Don't worry, it's only precautions." Dale got out of the car and Brett followed.

The taller of the two men from the BMW, who was wearing an earpiece, pointed at Dale's car and Dale instinctively knew what he meant. He placed his hands on the roof and spread his legs, Brett did the same.

They were patted down in silence then the man with the earpiece spoke into a microphone in his sleeve. "All clear."

A black Range Rover with tinted windows swept into the car park. The driver got out and opened the rear door. A well dressed, thick set in man in his fifties got out. There was no mistaking Harry Clifford, his reputation went before him.

A third man got out of the back of the Range Rover. Equally well-dressed but he did not sit well in the clothes. Small and wiry, his face showed no emotion. He made no attempt to approach them.

Harry greeted Dale with a broad smile. "Dale, nice to finally meet you." He offered a firm handshake.

"Nice to meet you Mr Clifford, this is my partner…."

"Brett, yes we know all about you." He shook Brett's hand as well. Brett glanced at Dale. "We do our research, we need to in this game."

"Of course."

"Sorry to drag you out here Dale but I like to do these things in person."

"I understand."

"I trust that everything is in place after your meeting with my associates?"

"Yes, we're ready to go as soon as you say the word."

"Consider this my word to go ahead as planned."

"Thank you, we won't let you down."

"I know you won't," said Harry. "I'm aware that my associates have explained this to you but it's always worth reiterating. I trust that there is no paperwork that could in anyway lead to us?"

"No, we don't have any paperwork relating to this side of the business held on the premises. It is stored in a secure location off site that is only known to me and Brett. We've encrypted the documents so they don't make sense to anyone but me." He knew he was stretching a bit calling Oliver's bedsit a secure offsite location and he worried a little about how much Harry knew about them.

"That's good to hear." Harry didn't appear to be concerned.

Dale, however, was slightly concerned by the third mystery man who had been staring at him throughout. "Can I ask who that is?" said Dale nodding towards him.

"You don't need to know and quite frankly, you want to hope that you never need to find out."

The man, who had previously not shown a glimmer of emotion, smiled an almost toothless smile with one solitary gold tooth nestled under his top lip.

"Good luck Dale, speak soon."

With that the meeting was over and the cars departed as swiftly as they had arrived.

Dale exhaled loudly, as if he had been holding his breath the whole time. Maybe he had. "This is it Brett, this is it."

Buoyed with conning the old woman out of a tenner, Tony bounced down the street with a bit more of a skip in his step. The smile on his face must have had a positive impact on the punters as well because a couple of them threw some coins in the bucket without him even needing to ask. Maybe today wasn't turning out as bad as he thought.

He passed the bookies and the mobile shop and even walking past the Halal shop couldn't put him in a bad mood. He was looking forward to making more money than Oliver for once.

Even when he was in such a good mood, he was always on the lookout for an opportunity and one presented itself right in front of him.

A Mercedes was parked outside of the printing shop with its boot open. The owner was heading back into the shop and two boxes were asking to be taken. Tony didn't need a second invitation and swiped one, putting it under his jacket in one swift movement. He took a right down the back lane and didn't bother to look back.

The car owner came out of the shop and placed another box in the boot, checking the street for Traffic Wardens. It took a moment for him to notice the box was gone, then another as he thought about whether it had been there in the first place. Unsure, he wandered back into the shop to confirm how many boxes he had picked up. By the time he was one hundred percent sure it had gone, Tony had disappeared.

Oliver and Tony arrived at the bedsit at the same time, both carrying buckets.

"How'd you do?" said Tony.

"Not so good," said Oliver, "a few quid."

"I made loads, like stealing kets from a baby. I got this as well."

"What's that?"

"No idea, just a box I swiped from a car. Could be anything."

"Is there anything you won't steal?" said Oliver.

"No"

"We might as well get it open and see what we've got."

Tony took his front door key from his pocket and tore along the Sellotape, ripping the box open. "Let's have a look. Well that's fucking shit," said Tony.

"What is it?"

"Business cards, thousands of them. What use are they to us?"

"Where did you steal the box from Tony?"

"Outside of the printers."

"And what did you think would be inside it?"

"I didn't think, I just took it. What a waste of time." He grabbed the box and went to throw it in the bin.

"Don't be so hasty, Tony. We might think of a use for them yet."

Tony's pride and good mood were dented and he tried to restore it. "Come on, let's see how much you got in your bucket."

"I don't like this one Tony, bairns with cancer, it's not right."

"Doesn't matter what the charity is, people are happy to pay to get rid of the guilt of being too busy too care. They go away happy thinking they've done something without having to make an effort. We make a few quid. Everyone wins."

"Except the kids with cancer," said Oliver.

"They're fucked anyway, money's better off with us."

"You can't say that." Oliver couldn't bear the thought of either of his kids having cancer.

"It's a tough old world out there Oliver. You have to look after yourself because nobody else is going to do it for you."

"It would be different if you had your own kids, Tony."

"I do..." His voice trailed off. He tipped the contents of his bucket on the bed. "Ha'way, let's see what you've got."

Oliver tipped out his bucket as well. About half the contents of Tony's and nowhere near as many notes.

"Better than nothing I suppose."

"You've got to up your game Oliver. You're not going to escape Dale bringing in a couple of quid at a time."

Tony started counting the money as Oliver stared out of the window at the passing traffic. He slipped some notes in his pocket when Oliver wasn't looking. Only fair as he'd made the most money.

"Here we go," said Tony, "fifty-fifty as agreed." He handed Oliver two notes and a pile of coins.

"How come I get all the coins?"

"I made all the money and I counted it out, there has to be something in it for me."

Oliver knew that Tony will have squirrelled away a few quid but couldn't be bothered to argue. He pocketed the cash and would bag it up and take it to the shop later. They were always looking for change.

"See you later, Tony."

"Where you off to? I thought we could go for a pint to celebrate."

"Somehow defrauding dying kids doesn't feel like worth celebrating." He trudged out into the street, despairing at how low he had sunk.

Chloe dragged Alex along to the barbers, they'd popped out for an hour and left Stacey in charge. "Don't worry, it won't be anything too drastic."

His hair didn't have a style, it grew where it wanted. It would never occur to him to apply any sort of product to it. When it was Alex's turn Chloe gave instructions to the barber.

"Who's that, your Mam?" said the barber.

"Worse than that, my boss. She's very determined."

"I can tell. Does she take this level of interest in everything you do at work?"

"It's not about work, it's all for a girl," said Chloe, "far more important."

"Don't worry son, when we're finished with you you'll be beating them off with a shitty stick. Were you wanting something a bit like your friend's?"

Alex looked at Chloe's pink spiked affair and whilst he was too polite to say, the look of horror on his face said it all.

Chloe laughed at his discomfort. "Keep it smart and simple, one step at a time."

When the barber was finished, Alex was delighted with the transformation. Chloe paid the barber with a generous tip then grabbed Alex's hand, "Come on, we're not finished with you yet."

She took him into town and got him a new outfit. Again, it was nothing too drastic but it was enough to show that he had tried.

Alex was first to arrive in the Chesters. He got a drink and sat in the far corner, he could see Hayley and her workmates drinking at the other end of the pub. He wished the others would turn up soon. Stacey soon arrived and they were finally joined by Chloe and Manuel when they closed the store. They ordered some food and while they waited for it to come out, Chloe took the time to give Alex an intensive training session.

"Choosing a table a little bit closer to her might have been a start. Never mind, we'll work with what we've got. It's all about being confident and taking your opportunities."

The rest of the group chatted whilst Manuel listened intently to the advice Chloe was giving to Alex. It was all alien to him but maybe there was some sense in it. After they'd eaten and Chloe had treated them all to a shot, it was time to put her coaching into practice.

"Your round Alex," she said.

"What?"

Chloe pointed to the bar where Hayley had gone to buy a round.

"Oh, right." Alex leapt from his chair.

"Don't come back without her phone number."

Alex headed off to the bar and his workmates tried their best not to make it obvious that they were watching his every move. Chloe looked over to Hayley's workmates who were doing the same. "*Easy money.*" She thought.

They could see Alex and Hayley talking and even noticed Hayley laughing a couple of times.

When Alex returned with the drinks Chloe could barely wait to find out what had happened.

"How did it go? Did you get her number?"

"No."

"No? What do you mean no? I saw you talking, you were great together." She was beginning to doubt her own skills.

"It's better than that," said Alex, "they're off into town after this drink and she's asked if I want to join them." He grinned from ear to ear.

"I told you." Chloe was delighted. "Can't believe you would abandon us just like that mind. Our company not good enough for you?"

"It's not that, I err, just thought…"

"Don't worry, I'm pulling your leg. Have a good time and I want a full report tomorrow."

Manuel marvelled at how well Chloe's coaching had worked. He took the ledger out of his bag and discretely made an entry into the credit column. Chloe had single-handedly managed to balance out his mother's misdemeanours.

CHAPTER FIVE
Saturday 21st May

It was rare that Manuel went into town, especially without his mother, but this was one of his rare treats. He felt the vouchers in his pocket and went into WH Smiths. Whilst his mother hadn't forgiven him for the birthday card, she had still allowed him his present.

His mother didn't believe in presents for birthdays and Christmas. Far too much fuss buying and wrapping them. She did however purchase him vouchers for WH Smiths with strict instructions as to what he could buy.

Books were fine if she approved them first, magazines were not. Magazines were for the lazy and the illiterate. On no account was he to spend the vouchers on sweets or chocolate and any board games had to go through the same vetting process as the books.

He didn't mind the restrictions because the one thing he had free-reign over was stationery; and Manuel loved stationery.

Pens, rulers, notepads. He could look at them for hours. WH Smiths was his favourite shop, not that he ventured into many others.

He looked at the notebooks. They came in numerous fancy designs now, Star Wars, football, various cartoon characters that he had never heard of. Whilst they were all interesting, they weren't for him. His mother probably wouldn't approve of them anyway but he was happy with a plain old black notebook with a red spine. He picked one up knowing that he was going to purchase it. He took comfort in the familiarity of its feel.

He already had a box of sticky labels so he could label each notebook.

He picked up the Dymo label maker, as he did each year but put it back. It was the dream item but too extravagant for his tastes.

He looked through the pens. He'd never had a fancy for a fountain pen and whilst he loved the Parker ballpoint his colleagues had bought him, he didn't want his mother to think of him as a show off so he kept it hidden.

He selected a pack of six black biros. It was the same as he bought every year. He normally had a treat, a ring binder, a ruler. One year he even bought a retractable pencil but found no use for it.

He went to the till knowing that the cost of the pens and notebook wouldn't be anywhere near the value of the ten-pound voucher so he grabbed a couple of word search puzzle books.

He would give them to his mother.

The same as he did every year.

Oliver hated this place. It reminded him of exactly where his life went wrong. He stepped into the pub. It stunk of stale beer and even staler sweat. Its occupants clothed in either tracksuits or dirty denim and some of them hadn't even bothered to get out of their mobility scooters. There was a sign on the door saying to leave them outside but everyone knew they would be gone in minutes if people abided by the rule.

He ignored the bar with its basic offerings of John Smiths or Fosters and headed to the back of the pub, the carpet squelching underfoot as he did so. The patrons of the pub ignored him as he had ignored the bar, he was of no interest to them. They carried on with their dominos or watched the horse racing on one of the TVs dotted about. A different race on each.

The walls were decked out with pin boards covered in today's Racing Post, the pub effectively a bookies with alcohol.

A fruit machine chimed in the background then rattled with pound coins as someone won back a fraction of what he had probably put in. Just enough to keep him thinking he would win again. Oliver watched as he started feeding the pound coins straight back into the machine.

Whilst he had always been nervous entering this place, nervous that the gambling bug would strike again. It did nothing but depress him. As much as he wanted to look down on the customers in here, he knew he was just like them, lower even, he'd been to prison.

"Welcome back, Oliver."

Oliver snapped out of his daydream. "Err yes, I want to pay some of my son's debt." He handed over a handful of cash he'd got from the charity scam and it was recorded in a little notebook.

He hated this interaction, he'd much rather set up a standing order but that wasn't the world he lived in anymore. Cash payments in back street pubs to people who would hurt you on behalf of people who would hurt you even more if you didn't pay on time. He didn't get a receipt, didn't like to ask how much he still owed, just trusted that they would tell him when the debt was paid but he knew that day would never come. He would keep a record himself back at the bedsit but you were never out of debt with these people.

"Did you want anything else?"

'Err no, just thinking." He considered asking what Dale had planned for him but thought better of it. Dale deliberately steered clear of the pub where the collections took place and in theory, his customers shouldn't even know who they were borrowing from.

"You're making the place look untidy." He was shooshed away to the laughter of the others around the table.

"Bye." He walked off.

"We do have a game of poker later if you want to join us."

"Not my thing, thanks." He didn't have the stake money even if he did play and he certainly wouldn't want to be borrowing it.

"Or you can stop and have a pint with the lads if you want." They all laughed again.

"No, you're alright." He knew they all thought he was a joke. Criminal types tolerated other criminals if they were from the same background but a respectable, upstanding member of the community who had fallen on hard times, they were neither part of the criminal community nor the respectable one they were so used to.

He walked out of the pub into the drizzle and the exhaust fumes but felt a lot cleaner for it.

He checked his trouser pockets and pulled out a handful of coins, the only ones he had left. He popped into the newsagents and bought a packet of Rennies. His stomach was getting worse, he knew he should go and see the doctor but he couldn't be dealing with any more bad news or complications in his life.

Drizzle, debt and Rennies for lunch. Not the life he had dreamed of when growing up.

CHAPTER SIX
Monday 23rd May

Manuel was second in line at the bus stop when it pulled in. Despite getting the bus each day he didn't bother buying a pass, he preferred to pay the exact fare daily. After barely soliciting a grunt from the driver, he looked up the aisle. A quick count showed that there appeared to be more people sitting on the left so he sat on the right.

A group of school children sat in front of him. The language from them was cutting and their tales of sexual exploits were shocking but it was something he had become accustomed to. He tried to look out of the window and ignore them, pleased that he'd managed to walk past them without comment.

About five minutes into the ten-minute trip he noticed that one of them had a marker pen and was writing his name on the back of the seat. Manuel looked up to see if the driver had spotted them in his mirror but he was too busy trying to negotiate his way through the rush hour traffic without killing a cyclist to notice some teenage vandals. Manuel gripped the seat rail, his knuckles turning white. He wished he could say something but instead he removed his ledger from his bag and added an entry into the debit column. Vandalism wasn't one of the worst crimes but it was still a major irritant. He gave it a two out of ten and hoped he witnessed a good deed before the day was out to balance the books.

Satisfied that the deed had been recorded he relaxed and hoped that the rest of the trip passed without incident.

The rest of the day passed uneventfully but the morning's vandalism ate away at Manuel. He looked at his ledger on the bus on the way home. Whilst it was only two points, he needed to balance the books. The bus idled at a red light as Manuel gazed at the overgrown garden in the house opposite. Weeds grew everywhere, empty crisp packets, their colour faded in the sun, sat trapped on the thistles. Empty fast food cartons littered the lawn. The garden contrasted sharply with the two either side. Maybe it was a pensioner who couldn't cope with the gardening anymore.

This was his chance, this was how he would balance the books. Relieved, Manuel returned the ledger to his bag, sat back and enjoyed the rest of his journey.

On arriving home, his tea was on the table as usual. Sausage, mash and peas tonight. One sausage either side of the plate. Mash at top of the plate, peas at the bottom. Start on the peas, eat the left half of the mash next, then the right. Left sausage then finally the right. Everything must be done to keep the plate balanced.

"Do you have to take so long eating your food?" His mother shook her head, conveniently forgetting that it was her who taught him that he had to eat his veg first.

He was trying to hurry tonight as well, he had things to do. After his tea, he would have to sit with a cuppa and watch the local news with Barbara. This was their routine.

She opened the biscuit tin and offered it to Manuel. "Just the one, don't be greedy."

He hadn't attempted to take two custard creams since he was a child and was severely reprimanded. Why she felt the need to remind every night he didn't know. *"Would the world really end if I had two?"* He didn't know the answer but suspected that it might.

He cleared the plates and did the washing up ensuring everything was dried and put away. He didn't like mess.

He pretended he was going to bed to read his book with his cup of tea and waited for his mother to finally retire for the evening. She had a routine involving an eye mask and ear plugs. She claimed the ear plugs were necessary as she could hear him snoring through the wall. Always his fault.

Half an hour later, when he was convinced that she was asleep, Manuel put on his dark jacket and hat and sneaked out of the back door. He took some tools from his mother's gardening shed and jumped over the fence.

The house he had spotted was at least twenty minutes' walk away but he didn't want to be seen on public transport. He used the back lanes as much as he could and hoped that he couldn't be seen. Once he arrived at the house he was relieved to see that there were no lights on. The neighbouring houses were also cloaked in darkness.

He got to work. It wasn't easy with only the street lamp from down the road to work with but he didn't think it would take more than an hour. After half an hour, he had made more progress than expected but he heard voices. Loud voices. It was mainly a student area and with a pub along the road, this was a popular thoroughfare for drunken revellers. The noise they were making had given him early warning and he hid behind the wall. The noise got closer and he waited for it to pass. As the last voice was passing something hit him on the head. An empty kebab wrapper, covered in chilli sauce. He wiped the sauce from his face and thought about entering the misdemeanour in the ledger. He'd probably done enough with the garden to even it out and he was going to tidy the wrapper anyway so didn't bother. He got back to work.

He heard the door go behind him. He was frozen with fear. How on earth was he going to explain this? He didn't dare look around.

Something stroked his leg. He nearly leapt out of his skin.

A bloody cat; the door he had heard was a cat flap.

Shaking, he decided that he had done more than enough to balance the books and it was time to leave. Just as he was putting the weeds in the wheelie bin he noticed the cat having a big shit in the middle of his newly cleared lawn.

Animal behaviour did not register on his ledger. He was going home to bed.

CHAPTER SEVEN
Tuesday 24th May

"Are you going out for an explore, Darcy?" Lynn stroked the cat as she struggled to bend down to pick up the charity envelope that had been put through the door. She threw it straight onto the pile in the corner that she would one day throw in the bin. "Charity begins at home."

She opened the door and put on her Gucci sunglasses even though the sun was barely out. She soon took them off when she was greeted by a sight that she couldn't quite believe.

The garden that was a total mess when she came in from work the previous night was almost spotless. Weeds and rubbish were all gone and whilst the lawn needed a bit of attention, it was no longer overgrown. There was a cat turd in the middle of it and she glared at Darcy but other than that it was perfect.

She looked up and down the street expecting some hidden cameras. Lynn then went back inside to see where the charity envelope was from. Maybe it wasn't asking for donations. Maybe there was a charity that went around secretly helping those with slow metabolisms.

Totally bemused she shuffled to the car and drove to work.

She logged onto the phones with a little smile on her face, a rare event. She was even polite to customers, a rarer event still. She racked her brains but couldn't think who would have taken the time and effort to tidy her garden without telling her. She looked around her team and despite the secret wish that her appreciation of Sean was mutual, she thought it unlikely.

Then she thought a bit more. Maybe it wasn't as benevolent as she'd assumed. Maybe it was a scam. Her customers tried to scam her every day, it was her job to catch them out. The more she thought about it, the more it made sense. It was probably gypsies who would leave her with a big bill when she got home tonight.

Her mood changed and the customers bore the brunt. She didn't care if her calls were being monitored, she wasn't giving an inch for the rest of the day.

She had worked herself into a frenzy by home time and stormed out of the door in a foul mood, ignoring the cheery "Good night" from Frank on her way out. She screeched out of the car park and left for home.

Lynn bumped her car onto the pavement outside of Shears. It was double yellows but she didn't see why she should walk when the disabled got away with their blue badges. Was her metabolism not a disability? She squeezed through the double doors, elbowing the old woman out of the way and headed straight for the ice cream aisle. She needed some comfort food.

She stomped around the shop filling her basket with mini rolls, party bags of crisps, sausage rolls and the ice cream. But she wasn't eating alone, she didn't forget her closest friend and bought a nice piece of salmon for Darcy; only the best for the man in her life. She barged to the front of the queue.

Stacey rang the goods through the till.

"Ooh, I love that Ben and Jerry's. Cookie dough is my favourite, have you had it before?"

Lynn took a moment to think about whether the girl on the till was trying to be funny about her weight but decided that she probably didn't have the brains to use wit. She wouldn't usually interact with the girls in the shop but she wanted to test her theory about the gypsies on her.

"I've had a stressful week, I need the ice cream to keep my blood sugars up. Bloody gypsies have tidied my garden without my permission."

"Gypsies?"

"Yes, if it's not bad enough dealing with thieves on the phone all day, I now have them raking about in my garden."

Stacey nodded and oohed and aahed politely during the conversation, keeping an eye on the queue that was growing behind Lynn.

"Could have been the neighbours," said Stacey.

"What?"

"The neighbours, maybe they thought the garden could do with a bit of a tidy, you know keep them in line with the others in the street. Didn't your Hannah do something like that once?" Stacey invited Chloe to join the conversation.

"Yeah, we had an elderly neighbour who couldn't keep on top of her garden. My girlfriend asked if she needed help and tidied it up."

Lynn looked Chloe up and down. "Maybe you should think about keeping your opinions to yourself. Maybe if you spent less time gossiping the queues wouldn't be so big in here." Lynn grabbed her shopping bags and stormed towards the door. "Lesbians have no business being in other ladies' gardens."

As her car screeched away from the kerb Manuel watched on from the shelving where he had been rearranging the cakes. He removed the ledger from his pocket and made a note of something he needed to look up.

CHAPTER EIGHT
Wednesday 25th May

Manuel went about his usual morning routine but Barbara treated him with more suspicion than usual; she knew he was up to something.

He'd been acting strange for the past couple of nights and she needed to know what he was up to.

As soon as he was out of the door, Barbara darted upstairs to inspect Manuel's room. She checked under the mattress, under the bed and in his sock and underwear drawers. No pornography or drugs as far as she could see but you could never be sure.

She switched on his laptop, checking his Internet history. She wasn't comfortable with him having his own laptop, let alone connected to the Internet. She'd agreed it on the understanding that it was not password protected although she wasn't entirely honest about how often she checked it.

She knew he wasn't clever enough to hide his history from her but she'd never found anything of note.

Until today.

At 20:53 last night there was a Google search.

One word.

Lesbians.

She felt faint and grabbed onto the desk to steady herself. She didn't need to look at the results to know what they were.

There was going to be hell to pay for this, he was going to wish he had never been born. All he ever did was let her down. He was just like his father.

Oliver wandered along the road without anywhere to go. There was only so long he could spend in the bedsit.

He found himself walking through the city centre. He learned quickly to look away when he passed the bookies, of which there were many. The temptation to gamble was always there and once he had successfully managed to negotiate his way past all the bookmakers, he sat on the wall opposite Mr Khan's paper shop and did some people watching.

Not being a natural criminal it had been quite an education working with Tony, learning how to spot an easy mark. He wasn't looking for a victim but he enjoyed watching, trying to guess everybody's stories.

The newsagents was very busy and he couldn't put his finger on why. Then he saw the sign in the window.

Euromillions jackpot £130m this Friday.

"£130m, that would solve a lot of problems," he thought. *"Don't even think of it Oliver. I'm stronger than this."*

It was a mark of how far he had come, or how far he had fallen that instead of thinking about how he could gamble he soon moved on to thinking about how he could scam the Euromillions.

If it was that easy, somebody would have done it by now but there must be a way. Where there was money, there was always a way to scam it.

He realised that despite all his years of gambling, he'd never bought a lottery ticket. Scratch cards, yes, he'd bought hundreds but the lottery didn't give him the instant gratification that other forms of gambling did. He wasn't even sure how to put a ticket on. He decided to take a closer look.

He left the wall, crossed the road and headed into the shop.

"Afternoon," said Indy.

"Hello," said Oliver as he scuttled towards the back of the shop and picked a random pack of food off the shelves. He then edged himself back down the aisle so he could see the lottery display and he watched the customers as they filled in a ticket. He then went to the display itself so he could get a closer view of the tickets and watch Indy as he put the tickets in the machine. Maybe there was a scam to be had here.

Indy was no idiot and was also watching Oliver. He wouldn't last long in this business without knowing who the local criminals were and Oliver's face had been splashed all over the papers some years back. He'd been acting suspiciously since he came into the shop and Indy wanted to know what he was up to.

"Are you okay there mate, do you need any help?" No need to be aggressive or accusatory.

He took Oliver by surprise, "Err no, I'm just trying to work out how to put one of these tickets on."

"The Euromillions? You after the £130m then?"

"It would be nice."

Indy showed him how to fill in the ticket. "That'll be two pounds fifty please."

"Two pounds fifty?"

"For the ticket."

Oliver realised that he was going to have to buy it whether he liked it or not.

"This isn't really gambling, is it?"

He took his ticket and left the shop as two others joined the queue buying numerous tickets at a time. He was still trying to work out how to beat the system. Then it came to him.

"I don't have to beat the system at all."

Oliver stared at the Euromillions ticket in his hand. He'd sworn that he would never gamble again but this was by accident, it wasn't his fault. He knew the ticket wouldn't win, he wasn't stupid but he studied it carefully. *"Surely there's a way I can make this into money."*

The selected numbers, he went for a lucky dip rather than using his prison number, were prominent at the top. The date of the draw, barcode and other related information were at the bottom. A plan was slowly beginning to form in his head. He went over to the sink and slowly dribbled some water over the bottom half of the ticket then crumpled it. He then put it on the radiator to dry.

He put the TV on but dozed through Bargain Hunt. When he woke, he retrieved the ticket from the radiator. It had turned out just as he expected. *"Perfect."*

The numbers were clearly visible but the date and barcode were illegible. This was too easy. All he had to do was wait until the numbers were drawn, buy a ticket for the next draw with those winning numbers and alter it so the date was removed. A winning Euromillions ticket.

"Of course it's too easy," he thought, *"this is the type of ridiculous shit that Tony would try and pull."*

He crumpled that ticket and threw it across the room, slumping back onto his bed. Camelot weren't idiots, they'd have all sorts of safeguards in place for this sort of stuff. A known criminal who had managed to wash just the bottom half of his ticket turns up claiming to have a winning ticket? It was a ridiculous idea and one that would end up with a one-way ticket to prison. If he'd started thinking like Tony, then he really was at rock bottom. He punched the headboard on his bed then reached for a handful of Rennies to fight the acid building in his stomach.

"Fucking idiot," he said to himself.

"Hold on, a fucking idiot is just what I need."

As long as there were people like Tony in the world, there was money to be made. He scrambled off the bed and picked up the scrunched-up lottery ticket. Maybe there was a way to make money out of this.

Oliver strode back down to Indy's shop. The winning numbers from Tuesday's Euromillions were showing on the counter. The jackpot hadn't been won but this was the beauty of his new plan, he wasn't going to claim to win the jackpot, that was too obvious. He filled in his numbers and went to the counter.

"Caught the bug?" said Indy.

"What?"

"Back in buying tickets again so soon?"

"Yes," Oliver wasn't overjoyed at being recognised, "my Mam said she wanted one."

He got home and went through the same process of washing the ticket and leaving the numbers showing. Now it was time to test his theory.

He donned his court suit and headed out of town, this wasn't a scam he wanted to pull close to home.

He loitered outside of a newsagent until he spotted someone who looked like they could be a mark. A young mother with a pushchair coming from the cashpoint seemed ideal. He put on his best disappointed face and approached her.

"Excuse me love, you couldn't help me out here please?"

She looked a little wary but the suit gave her some level of reassurance. "What's up?"

"Had a bit of luck on the Euromillions last night. Been using the kids' birthdays for years without a sniff," he waved at the child in the pushchair, "but last night they finally came up trumps."

"Congratulations."

"Not all five numbers and the two stars unfortunately, that middle child has always been the awkward one."

She laughed. "That's a shame."

"But I did get four numbers and a star, that's just over £150."

"Well done, that's still a nice little amount."

"Only problem is, my wife in her wisdom decided to wash my jeans with the ticket in," he produced the ticket from his pocket and showed her, he then pointed to the winning numbers in the window, "the numbers are still clearly showing but the miserable bugger in there won't cash it in because he can't scan the barcode."

"Bet you could kill her."

"Least said about her the better. Anyway, all is not lost, he reckons that the Camelot offices in Sunderland will cash it in no problem, just need to tell them when and where I bought it and they'll check their records."

"That's lucky."

"It would be if I had time to go there, I've got an important meeting now and I'm backed up all week. I don't see when I'm going to get the chance."

"I'll take it, we can go halfies." A big smile came across her face.

"You can read my mind. Here's my business card," he handed over the card and the ticket, "give me a bell when you've cashed it in and I'll collect my half. I can trust you to phone me, can't I?" He winked at her.

"Eee, what do you think I am, of course you can."

"Only joking, are you sure you don't mind? It is putting you out of your way to have to drive through there and then come and find me to give me my half."

"No, it's fine." She didn't sound so sure when she considered the logistics of two trips to make £75 but it was still worth it.

"No, I'm being selfish, I haven't thought this through," said Oliver. "How about this? You give me £50 now and the ticket is yours. You make £100 and you don't have to make a second trip. Seems a bit more worth your while then."

"If you put it like that it does sound more reasonable. Are you sure you don't mind? It's your ticket after all."

"No, don't mind at all, I was being greedy. If my business meeting comes off as planned today I'll be popping the champagne corks anyway."

"Really?"

"Yes, can't say too much about but could be securing a government contract worth a few hundred thousand." He checked his watch. "But if I don't get there soon I'll be in trouble."

"Yes, don't let me keep you." She went into her purse and produced £50, still fresh from the cash machine.

"You've got my business card if there are any problems. Just tell them you bought it in this shop on Tuesday lunchtime, about twelve thirty."

"Tuesday lunchtime, twelve thirty. Got it. Good luck with your business meeting."

"Thank you, you're an angel. Make sure you buy him something nice with the winnings." He waved at the child again. The child didn't wave back.

Oliver got back to the bedsit buoyed with his new idea. It had worked a charm. First time as well. He wouldn't always be so lucky but three or four of them after each draw and he would make a tidy sum. He would have to vary the location of the scam so there would be travel costs and Camelot would soon get suspicious of people turning up on their doorstep with dodgy tickets but at £50 a time the mark-up was incredible.

He put the kettle on and smiled for the first time in a long while.

"What are you looking so happy about? And why are you wearing a suit?"

No matter how happy Oliver got, Tony was never far away to spoil his day.

"Nothing, was just trying it on. I was happy that it still fitted," said Oliver.

"You've got a scam going, haven't you?"

"No."

"Yes you have, and you weren't going to include me."

There was no point in lying. "You wouldn't understand."

"I'm not stupid, try me."

With a sigh, Oliver tried his best to explain it to Tony. As expected, it didn't go well.

"It sounds canny but I don't understand why you don't just walk into Camelot and claim the jackpot. Why settle for £50 when there's £150 million up for grabs?"

"Because Camelot would have us sent straight to prison."

"They would for £150 as well, might as well go for the big one."

"But we're not going to Camelot. The mark is."

"But they have your business card."

"It's not my business card you idiot, it's the ones you stole."

"How do they get in touch to give you the money?"

"I give up, and you wonder why I didn't tell you."

Barbara waited at the dining table. She hadn't been able to concentrate all day at work and had thought about confronting Manuel in the store but managed to restrain herself. Just because he was a deviant, it didn't mean she had to ruin his career. She would not be airing this dirty laundry in public.

As soon as she heard the key in the door she was out of her seat and waiting in the hallway ready to confront him. Manuel had no idea of the maelstrom he was walking into.

"Come here you filthy little man." Barbara grabbed Manuel by the ear and dragged him into the dining room. "What do you call this?" She pointed at his laptop.

"Err, I don't know. What's wrong?"

"What's wrong? I'll tell you what's wrong. Filth, utter filth. I can barely bring myself to say the word. Pornography, under this roof, pornography. "

"Pornography?"

"My God, what are the women at the church going to say?"

"Say about what?"

"About your dirty little habits."

"What dirty little habits?"

"Don't pretend you don't know what I'm talking about; and not your usual common or garden filth. Oh no. You pathetic little specimen, you had to go for the worst possible kind."

"But, but I don't understand," said Manuel.

"Lesbians, that is what I am talking about. I can barely look at you, you depraved little beast." She finally let go of his ear and pushed him away.

"Oh, that?"

"Yes, that; have you anything to say for yourself?"

"I was curious."

"Curious? Curious? People get curious about how electricity works, how clouds are formed, not curious about ungodly acts between two women."

"It's not what you think. You always said that I'm no good talking to people, I thought I'd do some research so it was easier to speak to Chloe."

"Chloe, the black woman from work?"

89

"Yes."

"You want to strike up a conversation with someone from work and the first subject that comes to mind is lesbians?"

"Yes, sort of. I heard one of the customers saying that Chloe was a lesbian. I thought it would be easier if I knew what they were talking about."

"Chloe is a lesbian?"

"Yes, she has a girlfriend."

"My God." Barbara had to sit down.

"Have I done something wrong?" said Manuel.

"It's all clear now, it's all her fault. She's trying to corrupt you."

"Chloe?"

"Yes, Chloe. She's black and a lesbian? That's just attention seeking in my book."

"She's okay Mother, she always looks out for me."

"She'll be wanting to turn you into one of them."

"A lesbian?"

"You know what I mean. I can't even think of it. I feel physically sick. I don't want you to speak to her again."

"I have to speak to her, she's my boss."

"And I wonder how she got that job."

"Interview?"

"Quota filling, that's what it will be. I'm tempted to write to the Mail."

Manuel was more confused now than when he was when he had been grabbed by the ear. His mother looked like a broken woman. She was just staring into space now.

He took this as his chance to disappear upstairs to his bedroom. He didn't bother trying to take his laptop.

Barbara sat for a while not sure what to make of the conversation. If there was one thing she knew about Manuel it was that whilst he may have his secrets, he was a hopeless liar. He was telling the truth about this Chloe character.

—

90

She was going to have to go to Shears and talk to Chloe. Whilst the thought of some young lesbian undressing her with her eyes turned her cold, Manuel needed protecting; protecting from himself as much as anybody else.

Yes, Chloe was going to get the biggest talking to of her life.

"I'm sorry Father, Barbara Frost is on the phone again." The housekeeper held her hand over the mouthpiece.

"Christ on a bike, what does she want now?" Father Russell put the TV on mute.

"Said it was confidential, something to do with her idiot son Manuel."

"Does she not know that Eastenders is on?"

"I'd be surprised if she even watches the telly, too busy sticking her neb into other people's business."

"She's not going to go away, is she?"

"She'll turn up on the doorstep if you don't speak to her."

"Give me the phone, I'll have to catch up on iPlayer."

She passed the phone to him and went to busy herself just outside the door in the hope of overhearing the conversation.

"Hello Barbara, how can I help?"

"Hello Father Russell, I'm sorry to bother you. I really need to speak to you about Manuel."

"How is the young man?"

"Troubled."

"Anything in particular or was this a general observation?" He took a sip of the wine he had been enjoying before the call.

"He has an unhealthy interest in, oh I can't bring myself to say it."

"We're all friends here Barbara, you can tell me." He saw Kat Slater on the screen screaming at someone, he knew how she felt.

"Lesbians Father, lesbians."

Father Russell sat up and put the TV on standby, she had his interest now. "Lesbians you say, what sort of interest?"

"The Internet, I searched his Internet history. I was mortified to see what he had searched for."

91

"Can you remember what the sites were called Barbara?" He frantically started looking for a pen and paper.

"I'm sorry?"

"The websites Manuel was accessing; can you remember what they were called?" Whilst Father Russell was well acquainted with lesbians on the Internet, he was always open to new suggestions.

"I'm sorry Father I don't, the very thought of it turns my stomach. I switched his laptop off in disgust."

"Do you think you could bring yourself to look again, Barbara?"

"I'm not sure I could, Father. I'm sorry, why do you need to know?"

"Some sites are better than others. So I've heard. Worse than others I mean. It's for penance purposes, I'd need to know how bad they were before I decide on his penance."

"Are they not all a sin against God? It's unnatural Father; disgusting."

"Quite." Disgusting was exactly the label he'd put on the film he'd watched last night. He could do with finding a few more like that. "Shocking Barbara, shocking."

"What should I do Father? I'm at a loss."

"Would you like me to speak to him Barbara?" If she wasn't going to offer up the information, maybe he could ask the filthy bugger himself.

"Would you Father? He needs guidance. He needs to keep away from this Chloe woman, she's a bad influence."

"Chloe?"

"She's one of them."

"A lesbian?" He was interested now and sat up straight in his armchair.

"Yes Father, can you believe that they let them have jobs with responsibility these days?"

"How do you mean?"

"She's manager at Shears where Manuel works. Can you believe that they would put that woman in charge of my Manuel? They should know how impressionable he is."

"We live in a world of equal opportunities, Barbara. Everybody is equal in the Lord's eyes."

"And don't I know it Father? Who ever thought of a black lesbian? Ridiculous."

"A black lesbian?" He'd already decided that he was going to visit Shears to see Chloe. If she was anything like the ones he had seen in the films he'd downloaded he would become a regular customer.

"Yes, Father. Disgusting, isn't it?"

"I hope so."

"I'm sorry?"

"I mean yes Barbara, disgusting."

"I'll get Manuel to speak to you on Sunday after mass then?"

"Manuel?"

"Yes Father, about his addiction to lesbians."

"Yes Barbara, I need to speak to Manuel quite urgently."

"I knew I could rely on you, Father."

He hung up and forgetting about Eastenders, he headed for his bedroom and his laptop.

"Just going for a little quiet contemplation." He told the housekeeper. She knew exactly what he meant.

CHAPTER NINE
Thursday 26th May

Barbara sat in the staff room stewing about how she was going to confront Chloe. The talk with Father Russell hadn't been a great deal of help. He was one of those modern priests, too inclusive and guitar twanging for her liking.

She knew she had to confront Chloe but didn't know whether to do it publicly in the store or wait until she finished her shift. She sounded like the type who needed to be publicly shamed, her colleagues needed to see her for what she was. Even thinking of her made Barbara's blood pressure rise, who did she think she was spreading her wanton ways to Manuel? He was far too impressionable to be dealing with lesbians. *"Chloe must be impressionable as well if she hasn't grown out of it by now,"* she thought.

"Cup of tea, Barbara?" One of the other teachers was heading towards the kettle.

"No, I have one." She hadn't considered to offer when she made her own.

She logged onto the Daily Mail website and tutted. More immigrants coming into the country to claim benefits. *"As if we don't have enough benefit scroungers of our own."*

She clicked on the comments section. The vast majority matched her own views but that didn't stop her adding one. Strictly speaking she shouldn't be using her work laptop to post controversial comments however she didn't see it as controversial and her job was to educate. Why shouldn't she educate the ignorant masses on the dangers that foreigners bring to this country?

94

Commenting on the Mail website was therapeutic and she had calmed down somewhat. She went through the afternoon on autopilot, grabbed up her bags and headed for the car park.

Barbara parked in the pub car park, ignoring the notices telling her it was for patrons only. She locked the door and stormed over to Shears. She didn't wait for the customer who was leaving the store and barged straight in past her. It wasn't difficult to spot Chloe. Her shocking pink spiked hair stood out even amongst all the Day-Glo sales stickers.

Chloe spotted her out of the corner of her eye and made a mental note to keep an eye on her. Despite her short time in the role, she had quickly learnt to spot the customers who were trouble. This one was going to be a complainer or a shoplifter. She was soon to find out which one.

"Can I have a word please?" said Barbara.

"I'll just be a minute madam while I serve this lady."

"I haven't got all day."

Chloe decided not to respond to the provocation and served her customer as quickly as she could.

"Stacey, can you take over here for a minute please?" She stepped out from behind the till. "My name's Chloe, how can I help you?"

"I know perfectly well who you are."

This knocked Chloe slightly. She had never seen this woman before but she seemed certain that she knew Chloe.

"Okay, how can I help?"

"You can stop corrupting my son for a start."

"I'm sorry, I don't think I understand." Chloe was beginning to wonder if the woman had got the right person and if she even had the right shop.

"My son, he's turned into a sexual deviant and it's all your fault." The whole store had stopped to watch the sideshow. Whilst Chloe was convinced that it was mistaken identity she decided on some damage limitation.

"Would you like to come through to the office so we can discuss it?"

95

"No I would not. Heaven knows what sort of things you get up to in there. I'd like to have this conversation in front of witnesses. I don't want you working your witchcraft on me."

"I beg your pardon, witchcraft?" Chloe didn't like where this was heading.

"That's what your type get up to, isn't it? Ungodly acts."

"Hey, there's no need for that." Stacey shouted over from behind the till.

"It's okay Stacey, I've got this. I'm sorry madam, I don't know what you are talking about and I'm pretty confident that I haven't corrupted anybody's son, it's not my thing."

"Not your thing?"

"I get on the other bus, your son, whoever he is would be safe with me."

"I'm not here to discuss the benefits of public transport and I'm sure I wouldn't trust you with my son whatever bus you got on."

"I'm not sure you understand."

"I'm not sure you understand. Look at the state of you with your pink hair and piercings. Did you not get enough attention when you were a child?"

"Look, if you have a specific complaint I'm happy to listen to it, in the office. If you don't, then I'm not willing to stand here and listen to personal insults and I'm going to have to ask you to leave." The other staff on the floor were now behind Chloe silently backing her up.

"You keep away from my son or you won't be hearing the end of this."

Chloe was lost for words and shook her head. She heard a voice behind her.

"Mother?"

"Manuel?" Chloe and Barbara said in unison.

"What are you doing here?" said Manuel.

"Trying to save you from this evil woman."

"Manuel is the son you think I am corrupting?" Chloe almost snorted with laughter.

"It's not a laughing matter. You wouldn't believe what I found in his internet search history."

"Mother!"

"You check his internet search history?" said Chloe.

"Don't you dare question how I bring up my son."

"Bring him up? He's thirty-five years old. Is he not allowed any privacy?"

"He lives under my roof so he lives under my rules."

"Maybe he shouldn't live under your roof any more then."

"This is none of your business."

"You made it my business when you came into my shop shouting the odds. If Manuel's search history reflects something different to the very warped world view that you appear to give him then it can only be for the best. Now if you don't mind, I have a business to run and I'm going to have to ask you to leave."

"With pleasure. Manuel, come on, we're going home."

"Manuel hasn't finished his shift yet."

"Oh yes he has, he won't be working here again. Manuel, home now!"

But he was nowhere to be seen.

Barbara stormed out of the shop, very nearly taking the door off its hinges. A driver stamped on the brakes and blared his horn as she stepped out in front of him. She glared at him then carried on over the road. She got in the car and raced out of the car park.

"How dare she speak to me like that? Who does she think she is?"

Tears formed in her eyes, why did everyone have to be so horrible to her?

Manuel crouched in his safe place. He had created a space in amongst all the boxes where he could hide when he was upset. Nobody seemed to know about it or more likely, nobody seemed to notice when he was missing.

He pulled his knees to his chest and rocked himself gently.

Manuel was still cowering in the safe place, shaking. He held his ledger in his hand wondering what on earth to enter into the columns. The way his mother had talked to Chloe was a disgrace and needed a big entry in the debit column. On the other hand, he had never seen anybody stand up to his mother before and he had certainly never seen anybody stick up for him. Chloe had an even bigger entry for the credit column.

He was still shaking when Chloe came into the storeroom and closed the door behind her.

"Are you okay Manuel?"

He didn't know what the answer was.

"Where are you?"

He wanted to stay hidden but knew that Chloe wouldn't give up. Better to come out than for her to come looking and find his safe place.

"I'm here."

"What's that you have there?" said Chloe.

"Nothing." Manuel shoved the ledger back into his pocket.

"Is your mother always like that?"

"She's not always that nice."

"I caught her on a good day?"

"No such thing as a good day in her world, every day is a disappointment."

"Why don't you move out?"

"How would I survive? I can't cook, I don't know how to pay bills. I wouldn't last two minutes. That's why she controls my money."

"She controls your money?"

"She gives me pocket money."

"You're thirty-five Manuel. You shouldn't be getting pocket money. Why don't you pop round and have tea with me and Hannah one night? I'll teach you to cook."

"My mother wouldn't like it."

"I bet she wouldn't but this is about you not her. I'm sure you'll get on great with Hannah."

"I'll think about it."

"Okay, let me know," Chloe didn't want to put too much pressure on him, "but if you ever want to tell us what sites you were looking at on your laptop we'd love to know." She winked at Manuel and headed towards the door.

He blushed but didn't respond. As Chloe left the office he thought about what she had said.

"What if she is right? What if there is a life away from my mother?"

Manuel picked the pack of salmon from the refrigerated aisle. Chloe was heading back into the office as he shouted over "I'm just putting this through Chloe."

"Yeah, no problem."

He wasn't keen on her seeing what he was buying. He certainly wasn't keen on her seeing him when he picked up the rat traps from the storeroom and poured the poison into his carrier bag.

He put the carrier bag into his rucksack, shouted his goodbyes and headed for the bus.

As he passed Lynn's house, his admiration of the work he had done on the garden was distracted by the heated argument Lynn was having with the neighbours. They looked bewildered as she pointed her sausage like fingers in their faces.

He took out his ledger and looked at it again. She was deeply unpleasant woman, he didn't feel guilty about what he was about to do.

As he came through the door, Barbara was waiting. "Go and wash your hands, your tea is on the table."

He ran upstairs, threw his bag into his room and quickly washed his hands. He returned to the dining room where his tea was waiting. Poached haddock, new potatoes and green beans. The most boring tea of the week but he was expecting it so he ate it without complaint.

After a restless couple of hours where he pretended to read his book, Manuel said he was going for an early night. The confrontation earlier in the day wasn't mentioned.

He brushed his teeth and made for his room but lay wide awake until he heard his mother go to bed. When she did, he set the countdown timer on his digital watch to thirty minutes. When the thirty minutes were up he knew the eye mask and ear plugs will have done their job again and his mother would be fast asleep.

He sneaked back downstairs, out of the door and back towards Lynn's house and the scene of his garden clearance earlier in the week. He hoped that he wouldn't be around as long tonight but that was largely out of his hands.

The lights were off so Lynn must have been in bed. Perfect. He found a discarded pizza box in the garden, it hadn't taken long for the students to undo his good work. Removing the fish from his bag, he placed the opened packet on the pizza box and sprinkled it with the rat poison. He placed the box in the garden, hid in the corner out of the glare of the street lights. And waited.

Thankfully it didn't take long for the cat to wander out of the house and check him out; same as the other night. After getting bored of Manuel, Darcy went to search the rest of the garden and soon came across the discarded pizza box. Showing his owner's attitude to food, he was soon tucking into the fish. Manuel waited until the cat had eaten a few mouthfuls then took the box away as Darcy clawed at his legs.

"You still hungry?" He said and gave Darcy the rest of the fish. He devoured it all.

Manuel looked forward to Lynn's next visit to Shears when she could regale the staff about how her precious little cat was shitting and puking everywhere.

Manuel knew that he should feel sorry about the cruelty to the cat but he needed to balance the books. A little bit of sickness and diarrhoea wouldn't do him any harm, and he'd had a free fish out of it.

Normally when balancing the books, total strangers would be the recipient. This was one of the first times he had chosen someone twice but she had brought it on herself with her display in the store. Both her and his mother had been deeply unpleasant to Chloe. Someone had to pay the price.

Manuel dumped the pizza box and empty fish wrapper in the wheelie bin and updated his ledger.

The books were balanced, he could now go to bed happy.

CHAPTER TEN
Friday 27th May

The alarm sounded at 7:45, the volume turned up as loud as possible so that Lynn couldn't ignore it. She leant over with her eyes still closed and tried twice to locate the off button before bringing down her giant fist, sending it flying off the bedside cabinet.

She eased her feet over the side of the bed and searched for her slippers whilst she rubbed the sleep from her eyes. Her toes sought out the fur on her slipper but it had edged under the bed and she couldn't manoeuvre it onto her foot without bending down to pick it up; far too much effort.

With both hands, she pushed her hefty frame up and once on her feet, she padded off towards the bathroom, picking her phone up on the way.

Just before she got to the bedroom door she stepped in something wet.

"What the......DARCY!" She stumbled back onto the bed and looked at the cat poo that she had now squashed into the carpet. She lay back and reached for a tissue, struggling back into a sitting position. She then tried to lift her foot to remove the cat mess but, not having the most flexible of bodies, she struggled, stamped her poo covered foot onto the floor and fell back onto the bed again.

"Christ's sake, man." She tried again but still couldn't reach. She edged along to the corner of the bed and forced herself onto one foot, hoping to hop to the bathroom. Her weight soon sent her tumbling backwards. "I'm going to kill you, Darcy."

She reached out and managed to drag the chair along towards the bed. She shuffled from the bed to the chair and from there she could just about reach the door handle. Once out of the bedroom it was a couple of short hops to the bannister then she could ease herself towards the bathroom hoping that Darcy hadn't left her any more little presents.

Finally in the bathroom, she plonked herself onto the toilet and sat for five minutes to get her breath. It was then that the smell hit her. How could an animal so small create such a stink?

She turned on the tap and somehow managed to get her leg over the edge of the bath whilst still sitting on the toilet. She rinsed off her foot and watched the cat poo swirl round the plug hole before disappearing.

She'd put on a bit of a sweat with all her efforts and after composing herself, she went off to find out where Darcy was hiding. He knew that he would be in trouble so had probably tucked himself away in a corner somewhere.

As she reached the top of the stairs she noticed a pile of vomit. Then two stairs down there was another cat deposit.

"Darcy?" She started to panic. Lynn hurried down the stairs and hobbled into the kitchen avoiding more piles of vomit and poo on the floor. "Darcy, where are you, love?" She was no longer angry, just worried. She checked in the sitting room but still no sign. She got to the front door and fumbled with the lock. She raced into the garden, not caring that she was in her pyjamas.

She looked around the garden until she saw Darcy curled up next to the fence. She plodded across the lawn. "Darcy love, don't worry Mammy's here." The cat didn't look up. *"Probably in the huff,"* she thought.

"Sorry for shouting, I didn't know you had a poorly tummy." She leaned on the fence then eased herself into a crouching position to try and stroke Darcy. She couldn't quite reach so sunk onto her knees and went to pick up the cat.

No response.

"Darcy? What's wrong?" She picked him up but there was no movement at all, he was cold. "Come on let's get you inside and put the fire on."

103

It was then she realised and dropped the cat in shock.

"No, Darcy, no, no, no." Tears streamed down her face.

Manuel shook. He didn't know whether it was nerves or excitement. He knew that he should feel guilty about making the cat sick but he had to balance his ledger and Lynn hadn't done herself any favours.

The bus pulled up to the traffic lights outside of Lynn's house and stopped. He had deliberately sat on the left-hand side of the bus so he could see into Lynn's garden, even though it meant the numbers on either side of the bus weren't even. He hoped to see some evidence of the cat vomiting or shitting all over the place. What he didn't expect to see was Lynn in her pyjamas, slumped on the grass, crying with a dead cat in her hands.

This wasn't meant to happen, he was only meant to make the cat ill. As much as he disliked Lynn, he wasn't a killer.

"Jesus Christ."

The bus pulled away and he looked back out of the window. He was shaking with fear now.

He arrived at work and mumbled "Good Morning" to Chloe but headed straight for the office. He took the ledger out of his pocket, he could barely grip it, his hands were shaking so much. He took out a pen and looked to make an entry into the debit column. He'd killed. Did that make it a ten? It was only a cat. Maybe a seven? And it wasn't deliberate; a five.

A five was the highest he had ever entered for a single event in the ledger. He'd certainly never had a five for anything he had done himself.

"You alright Manuel love?" Chloe had walked in behind him.

"Err, yes, fine, just coming." He hid the ledger in his bag.

"Don't worry, I wasn't checking up on you, just exchanging pleasantries." Chloe went for the kettle. "You want a cuppa?"

"Yes, please." He needed one.

"What was that you had in your bag? Your little black book with phone numbers of your lady friends?"

"No." He wasn't going to expand.

"Ooh, you're in a one this morning. Your mother playing up again?"

"No more than usual."

"You should move out, get your own place. You can have friends back without your mother looking over your shoulder. It'll do you the world of good."

He knew she was right and he certainly wasn't in the mood to argue. "I will one day, I don't want to upset her at the moment."

"She doesn't seem to have a problem upsetting you. Come on, let's have a look at some flats." She had already logged onto the internet and got an estate agent's website up.

He feigned interest but all he could think about was the ledger. What if it didn't balance, what on earth was he going to do?

Meanwhile, back at Lynn's house, her neighbours cowered behind the curtains as a twenty stone pyjamaed woman brayed on the door whilst she brandished a dead cat at the window.

A crowd had now gathered outside of Lynn's neighbour's house. She wasn't afraid of causing a scene and she was more than happy for the world to know who had killed her precious Darcy.

The husband eventually answered the door, the wife still twitching behind the curtains.

"You've killed him, you evil bastards," said Lynn.

"Calm down love, killed who?" The words were out of his mouth before he spotted the dead cat in her arms.

Lynn shoved it in his face. "Darcy, you've killed my darling Darcy."

"Why on earth would we want to do that?"

"Because you hate him, you hate me, you're all against me."

"Now hold on, you can't go throwing accusations around like that."

"I'll throw them where I like," she turned around to the crowd, "are you enjoying this? Enjoy living amongst cat killers?"

"We haven't killed anyone, you daft bitch. If I was after killing something it would be you before your dumpy little cat."

"Are you listening? He's threatening to kill me."

"I'm not threatening anyone but I soon will be if you don't get your big fat arse off my doorstep." He put his hand up to put some distance between them.

"Don't touch me, that is sexual assault, I'm calling the police."

"Sexual assault? You should be so lucky. In fact, here you go, use my phone. If your big fat fingers can manage to press the keys you can call the police. I'd love to see what they'd make of this."

She was now on the back foot, it wasn't the reaction she had expected but she couldn't back down now. She snatched the phone off him and dialled 999.

"I've been sexually assaulted and my precious pussy is now dead." There were sniggers from the crowd. "Yes, the assaulter is still here."

The neighbour shook his head in disbelief. The crowd wondered whether there would be any more excitement and whether it would be worth being late for work. Their mind was made up when the sirens sounded.

A police car pulled up and a PC and WPC got out, moved through the crowd and down the garden path.

"Hello, can I ask what's happening here please?" said PC Sugden.

"They've killed my Darcy." Lynn pushed the dead cat into his hands. Shocked he stepped back and dropped it onto the path. WPC Cummins shook her head at him.

"Darcy!" Lynn bent to pick him up and her face was bright red when she straightened up.

"Can I have a word please? Is it Miss or Mrs Sherman?" said WPC Cummins.

"What do you think?" said the neighbour, tutting as he was led indoors by PC Sugden.

"Okay Miss Sherman, should we go indoors and you can tell me what happened?" she turned to the crowd, "Don't go anywhere, I might be wanting statements from you." That was enough for most of the crowd to disperse with only the diehard nosey neighbours hanging around.

She led Lynn indoors and sat her down to get her version of events. Not the way she'd anticipated starting the day. Dead pets rarely led to rational conversations.

"Okay, could you tell me in your own words exactly what happened and please try and stick to the facts?"

Lynn realised that there were very few facts other than she was sat in her pyjamas holding a dead cat and she had very little left in her life.

"Why do you think your neighbours killed your cat?" WPC Cummins was trying to keep an open mind but had already taken a dislike to Lynn.

"They hated him. They hate me," said Lynn.

"And why is that?"

"They said Darcy used their garden as a toilet?"

"And did he?"

"He's a cat, he goes to the toilet wherever he needs to."

"Did you ever try and do anything to stop him, take some responsibility for your pet?"

"You don't own a cat; the cat owns you."

"You didn't do anything to stop it?"

"Like what? Cat's need to go to the toilet, how could I stop him?"

"Getting a litter tray perhaps?"

"I'm not having a cat shit in my kitchen that's disgusting."

"That's probably what your neighbours think when he craps all over their lawn."

"I'm not the criminal here, they've killed Darcy." She thrust the dead cat towards WPC Cummins.

"Err, do you not want to put that somewhere? I'm not sure it's hygienic having a dead cat in the house."

"Maybe you should speak to my neighbours about that."

"Okay. We've established that your neighbours don't like your cat, it's a big leap to assume that they are cat killers."

"Who else could it be? Who else would want to murder my lovely Darcy?"

"We haven't established that he was murdered, it could have been natural causes."

"He was murdered and I'm sure that will show up in the post mortem." Lynn stroked Darcy's head.

"Post mortem?" said WPC Cummins.

"It's a suspicious death. I watch a lot of detective shows, they always carry out post-mortems."

"It's a cat."

"He's my baby."

"Let's stick to the facts. Your cat was unwell and died during the night. The neighbours whilst not necessarily cat lovers, don't strike me as murderers. Could it have been something he had eaten? What did you feed him last night?"

"Just the usual, Whiskas."

"He hasn't eaten anything unusual recently?"

"Are we nearly done here?" PC Sugden wandered into the sitting room. "I've had a good chat with your neighbours. They were at a works party last night and didn't get back until the early hours. They are animal lovers themselves but don't have a pet because they are at work all day and think it would be cruel. I've had a good chat with them and I don't think they are responsible for your pussy passing away."

Lynn sat back in her chair, she had been convinced that it was the neighbours. "If it wasn't them, who was it? Who would want to harm my Darcy?"

"Like I said, it could have been natural causes," said WPC Cummins.

"I don't believe that." Lynn was still angry, she had to point the finger at someone.

"I'm sorry that you think that way but I think you may owe your neighbours an apology."

Lynn was in no mood for apologies and she needed someone to blame. "Hold on, you asked if he'd eaten anything unusual." She stormed out into the garden and to the wheelie bin. The police looked on confused expecting her to dump the cat in there but instead she took out a food carton and handed it to them.

"This is the fish he had the other night. Do some forensics and I'm sure you'll be able to find out that this is what killed him."

"I'm sorry, we won't be doing any forensics on fish cartons."

"You had better do something about it or I will."

WPC Cummins weighed up the obese woman in her pyjamas brandishing a dead cat and a fish carton.

"I'm not making any promises but I'll see what I can do." She took the carton from her and headed for the door.

"What are you doing?" said PC Sugden as they got back in the car.

"Getting out of the mad woman's house. Let's get out of here then we can have a think about how we are going to placate her."

Jeff did a quick head count, there was one missing. Whilst he was generally happy for Lynn not to be in giving him grief, he didn't accept lateness. This wasn't the first time, she was on a final warning. Maybe this was his chance to finally get rid of her.

He gave it fifteen minutes then rang her.

"Hello?"

"Hello Lynn, it's Jeff, how are you?" He checked his watch, she was either very late or she wasn't coming in at all. Either way worked for him, they had strict rules about sickness and she'd abused it one too many times by not phoning in.

"Not good," said Lynn.

"Not good? What's up Lynn?" He thought she might have been crying.

"He's dead, they've killed him."

"Who's dead? Who's killed who?" He wasn't the best when people phoned in sick, he was totally out of his comfort zone when someone had died.

"Darcy, they've killed Darcy." She was now hysterical.

"Who the fuck is Darcy?" thought Jeff. *"Her Dad? Surely not a boyfriend?"*

"Darcy, Lynn, who is Darcy?"

"My cat, those evil bastards have killed my cat."

"Your cat?" He was relieved. "And who killed him?"

"That evil little lesbian at Shears."

It wasn't the answer he expected and tried to change the subject. "Okay Lynn. Do you realise that your shift started fifteen minutes ago?"

"Are you not listening? They've killed Darcy."

"Err yes, you said. I'm assuming that you aren't coming in then?"

"Of course I'm not bloody coming in, how can you even ask me?"

"You do realise that you have a responsibility to phone in an hour before your shift if you need emergency leave?"

"Emergency leave? Who said anything about emergency leave?" She was shouting now.

"Calm down Lynn, I'm not sure what you are asking."

"Do you not know how to do your job? It's a bereavement, it's compassionate leave."

"I'm sorry Lynn, I'm not sure it qualifies."

"Qualifies? You let Tracey have the day off last week."

"That was for her Dad's funeral, it's slightly different." He shook his head as he spoke.

"How?"

"One's an immediate family member and the other is, well the other one is a pet."

"Darcy is the closest family I've got."

"Lynn, we have strict rules about this sort of thing. I can see that you are upset so I'll try and bend the rules and get the emergency leave authorised."

"That's not good enough."

"I'm afraid it's not up for negotiation."

"I'll go to the union."

"You're not in the union."

"I'll join one."

"I'm not sure that's how it works. I'll expect to see you in tomorrow."

"You heartless bastard."

"There's no need for language like that Lynn. Do I need to remind you that you are on your final warning?"

"Stick your job up your hoop, you pointless little cretin."

He thought better of asking her to put that resignation in writing.

"Your boyfriend still work at Environmental Health?" said PC Sugden.

"He's not my boyfriend," replied WPC Cummins.

"Brainy friend with benefits then. Does he still work there?"

"Yes, why?"

"Can you get him to have a look at that fish as a favour?"

"Do I have to?"

"You do if you want that mad cat woman off your case. She's not going to go away."

"I guess so, I'll give him a ring."

She made the call and her friend was only too happy to help.

"We're a bit busy but we should have some results in a couple of days. If there's anything dodgy we'll pay them a visit," he said.

"Thanks, I owe you one."

"Drink tonight?"

"Can I take a rain check? My day started with a mad woman brandishing a dead cat in my face. I think it's going to be a long one."

"No problem, speak to you soon."

She got back in the car.

"All sorted?" said PC Sugden.

"He's going to have a look, hopefully we can put this to bed."

"We've been on this bus for hours," said Tony.

"Will you stop your whinging? I've already told you, we can't do this close to home, people might recognise us," said Oliver.

"Why couldn't we take the car?"

"Because we don't have one."

"I could have got us one."

"I'm sure you could but the last thing we want is the attention of the Police."

The old woman opposite briefly looked up at the mention of the police but then returned to attempting to understand how her mobile phone worked.

"I'm bored," said Tony.

"You're like a child. Just give me some peace and quiet until we get there."

Oliver looked out of the window. He wasn't sure where they were exactly, they'd left Washington. Probably some part of Gateshead.

They had to pick their targets well. A well to do neighbourhood might give the impression of rich pickings but they were naturally suspicious, especially when someone the state of Tony turned up on their doorstep. The poorer estates might be keen on making some easy money but they didn't have as much spare cash to lose. It was a gamble either way.

He'd chosen one of the new build estates. Whilst most of the owners would be in debt up to their eyeballs, they would also be keen to save money even if it was a little bit morally dubious.

They knocked on the first door. A woman in her early thirties answered, covered in flour and carrying a baby's bottle. A baby was squalling in the background. She took one look at Tony and shut the door.

They tried next door, no answer. Next door again; nothing.

They'd tried half a dozen houses before anybody even answered the door. Oliver was smartly dressed in a full suit, shirt and tie. Tony was his usual dishevelled self. It was a risk but it was all part of the scam.

"I'm really sorry to bother you madam, I'm wondering if you could do me a huge favour." He used all the charm he'd learnt from his time in the bank.

"I'm not sure, what is it?"

"I was on my way to an important meeting and this lad stepped out in front of the car. He's lucky I didn't run straight over him but the new top of the range BMWs have excellent brakes. I started giving him a piece of my mind but it turns out that he's one of those, what do they call them, mentally subnormal. He doesn't really know what he is doing."

"The poor thing."

"Now I feel totally guilty for shouting at him. I couldn't get much out of him but it appears that he is really lost and has no idea why he is here. I checked his pockets and he had some ID, he lives in Durham."

"He really is lost," said the woman as a small child clung to her leg.

"Problem is that I would like to give him a lift home but I have that important meeting to get to, could be worth hundreds of thousands and he's already made me late."

"I could give him a lift but I've got the little one here and I have to pick her brother up from nursery soon."

"Oh no, I wouldn't dream of putting you out like that. I want to put him in a taxi but I've foolishly left my wallet in the office and only have a few pounds in change. Now I know this is an incredibly cheeky thing to ask but could you possibly loan me twenty pounds until tomorrow so that I can get him home safely?"

"I don't know."

"I fully understand if you don't want to. I didn't become rich by giving money away to strangers knocking on my door." He produced a business card from his pocket. "Look here's my card. If you loan me the twenty pounds I will give you fifty tomorrow. If the business deal comes off there might even be a bottle of champagne in it for you."

"I'm not sure."

"That's understandable, I don't think I'm going to be able to concentrate in this meeting if I leave the poor lad stranded. I'd feel too guilty."

"Okay. Fifty pounds you say?"

"Yes, first thing tomorrow morning. You'll be an absolute lifesaver."

"Just a second, I'll get my purse."

Oliver winked at Tony. Tony glared back.

"Here you go," said the woman. "Would you like to come in and wait for your taxi?"

"No, we've wasted far too much of your time. We'll flag one down from the main road. You are a saint. It's rare to find people like you." It was becoming rarer each day to find someone who would fall for such a scam.

"No problem. Glad I could help. Good luck with your meeting."

"Meeting? Oh, yes, fingers crossed. Thanks again, see you tomorrow."

Oliver headed down the path and put his arm around Tony. "Wave to the nice woman."

Tony was ready to explode but waved and smiled through gritted teeth. When they got to the end of the street he pushed Oliver away. "Why do I have to be the simpleton?"

"Do you have to ask? Look at the clip of you. This is the only way it will work."

"You always have to be superior, don't you?"

"It worked, didn't it?"

"Twenty quid? All that for twenty poxy quid?"

"You have to keep the figures believable. If we'd asked for fifty quid she would have shut the door in our face. A few more houses and we'll have made a hundred quid in a couple hours."

"Come on then, let's knock on some more doors," said Tony.

"We have to at least get a few doors away so there's no risk of her seeing us."

"You always have to have the answers."

"I'm the brains of the operation, all you have to do is stand there looking simple."

"Very funny, you wouldn't be getting very far if I hadn't supplied the business cards." They struck lucky when they were cards for an internet company. Fitted perfectly with their cover story.

"Well done on your petty thievery. Come on, let's find some new victims. Try not to drool on yourself too much."

Lynn needed someone to talk to. She had alienated all her family, the few friends she'd had over the years had long since disappeared. Her colleagues had no time for her so her online friends were her only hope.

Her online persona was no more popular than her real life one however being a cat owner gave her a certain amount of leeway.

Help me find the murderers who poisoned my Darcy.

She posted one of her most recent photos of Darcy, she decided against posting the one of the dead cat as the moderators on the North-East Cat Owners Facebook Page could be quite strict.

My dear Darcy was poisoned last night, please share and help find the bastards who did this.

The comments came in thick and fast.

Beautiful cat.xxx

Evil bastards xxxxxxx

DEATH PENALTY FOR ANIMAL CRUELTY. I WOULD HAPPILY TIGHTEN THE NOOSE MYSELF.xx

Hw cn ppl b so cruel. I would happily chop of there hedz nd shit in the hole.xxxxxxxxxxx

Will be chinkys or muzzies send them backxxxxxxx

U OK Hun?xxxxxxxx

Let's get a thousand likes for poor Darcy.

Lynn named Shears as the prime suspects but her comment was immediately removed. She added another comment.

Police involved, they have chief suspects. Updates to follow when arrests made.

The notifications kept on coming as fellow cat lovers shared her status. Rumours of the culprits were as varied as they were wrong and the moderators had to work fast to delete anything potentially libellous. This led to accusations of the moderators being part of a cat killing conspiracy and the Facebook page was just a front so they could get details of cats in the region.

It was all getting out of hand but Lynn was liking the attention. Nobody took notice of her in the past, at best they were cruel about her appearance. Online she was nearly anonymous. Her profile picture was Darcy and the rest of the photos on her account were either the cat or motivational style posters such as a picture of Marilyn Monroe with the slogan **Real women have curves. Like and share if you agree.** And **Keep calm and eat cake.**

She took some comfort from the messages of support but she also found it addictive to see how many shares she got.

Then a message came through that could change everything.

Hi, I'm a reporter from the Echo and have picked up on the terrible tale of your cat. Would you be interested in doing an interview with us?

This could be her chance of fame. Her chance of getting some attention. Maybe people would treat her differently if she was in the paper. Who knew, maybe there may be some possible suitors who saw her photo in the paper and would get in touch.

Maybe Darcy dying was an opportunity.

To call Callum's warehouse an Aladdin's cave would be doing it a disservice. It had everything you could possibly want, all at rock bottom prices. Admittedly not all of it was brand new. Not all of it, in fact none of it, was strictly legit but it was cheap.

If you mixed in the right circles you knew where to come whether you were buying or selling. Callum made it his business to know everybody else's business and didn't deal with anyone he didn't know.

At six foot five and with years of gym work behind him, he was an intimidating sight. Few people messed with him.

On first entering the warehouse you would see rows and rows of boxes on shelves. Boxes with Chinese labels storing everything from Christmas decorations to mobile phone chargers. It was behind the first row of shelves were the real bounty was. TVs, games consoles, laptops, iPhones, if it could be stolen, Callum would stock it.

His motto? **Sell cheap, buy even cheaper.**

The people who sold to him were usually desperate junkies. They may be able to get a better price if they hawked their ill-gotten gains elsewhere but with Callum they knew there was no bartering, he gave them a price and gave them the cash there and then. No messing about, they got the money and went and bought their next fix. Easy.

He also had a pub in town. An absolute dive of a place but it was a cash business so a good front. He also had his 'office' there in case anybody he didn't know wanted to visit. He didn't want them snooping around in here.

He was bench pressing when he heard a knock on the shutters. "Go and see who that is." He said to his mate who was spotting him.

Two painfully thin teenage lads, tracksuit bottoms tucked into socks, obligatory Nike Airs and matching baseball caps. They didn't go out of their way to look like respectable members of society.

"Alright, Callum?"

"Alright lads, what you got?"

"iPhone, couple of credit cards, some lipstick and a box of Tampax," said one of them as he emptied a handbag.

"I'm good for make-up and fanny pads thanks. Give me a look at the phone. Where did it come from?"

"Outside the crem, some woman left it on top of her car whilst she was blaring on to another bird about her Dad or something."

Callum shook his head. "Why didn't you dump the handbag?"

"Thought you might want it, it's designer."

"It's Luis Vittom, that's designed for Jacky White's Market. I'll give you fifty quid for the lot."

"Fifty quid?" They looked disappointed but didn't argue when Callum started peeling notes off the roll.

"Now fuck off and keep yourselves out of trouble."

His mate shook his head and picked up the bag. Callum went to make a phone call about the credit cards. He should be able to shift them quickly before they got cancelled. Whilst he didn't approve of robbing people at funerals, he knew that the emotion of such an event meant that people didn't behave rationally and phoning the credit card companies might not be the highest thing on their agenda.

He'd rather not be dealing with little scrotes like that but every penny counts. He was the most respected fencer in the city. The toerags liked him because he always paid, the public liked him because everyone likes a bargain without any questions asked and the bigger crooks liked him because he always did them a good deal on big ticket items and he kept his mouth shut. It was always wise to keep them onside.

You wanted something, Callum was your man. He would know where to source it and how to source it quickly. New MacBook, no problem. State of the art TV, consider it done. Tablet for the bairn's Christmas present, what type and how many do you need? Nothing was ever a problem for Callum.

And then there were the guns.

"Fifty quid, all that for fifty quid," thought Oliver.

He looked at the notes in his hand. In theory, it had been a productive day. The same scam pulled five times, twenty quid each time although they'd been knocked back more times than they'd been successful. One hundred pounds for telling a few lies, not a bad day's work but when you factored in giving fifty percent to Tony and the fact there were now five new victims that would happily put him back in prison, he didn't feel too great.

"Is that for me?" The door burst open, there really was no point in locking it.

"Hi Dale, err yes, I was just about to drop it off."

"I've saved you the bother then," he snatched it from his hand, "should charge you extra for providing such a service."

Oliver had no idea if he was joking. "Did you want something, Dale?"

"Yes, that work you agreed to do."

"I didn't agree to anything, I'm going to pay Josh's debt off as soon as I can."

"Here it is." He stepped aside as Brett carried in a safe.

"Where do you want it boss?"

"Stick it in the corner there."

He kicked the chair out of the way and put it down.

"What's in there?" said Oliver.

"Don't worry, nothing bad. Just my books, wouldn't want them falling into the wrong hands."

"And what do you want me to do with them?"

"I want you to tell me how to make the contents disappear. Not literally, I just want my hard-earned cash to stay hidden from prying eyes."

"I'm not an accountant and I've been out of the finance game for a number of years as you know."

"Yes, but you are the best we've got. I heard good things about you from my friends inside."

"I'm not sure I can help."

"You can." It wasn't up for debate.

"I'm not sure you want to be leaving confidential information in here, it's not exactly the most secure of places."

"I know that you choose to surround yourself with criminals and low lives but it will be secure. It's in a safe after all."

"What's to stop someone picking it up and walking off with it?"

"Are you mad? It weighs a ton. Who's going to be able to pick it up and walk off with it?"

"He just did." Oliver pointed to Brett.

"There's few who can lift what he can. Stop worrying. We're putting a better lock on your door." He pointed to the joiner who had already started work. "The contents are your responsibility now."

"But…" Oliver realised that there was no point in arguing.

"There's a laptop in there," said Dale, "so you can do all your calculations. Don't think of using it for anything else. Keep it off the internet, I don't want you on gambling sites or dodgy porn. If that laptop gets hacked we're in all sorts of bother. Right, I'll leave it in your capable hands. We'll speak in a couple of days."

Dale walked out and the joiner threw a new key onto Oliver's bed and closed the door behind him.

Oliver walked over to the safe. There was a Post It note with the combination on it and a warning.

Do not fuck this up.

The doorbell rang and Lynn checked her hair in the mirror before answering. She'd been getting herself ready since the Echo contacted her.

"Hello, I'm Amy and this is Mike our photographer. Actually, he's just on a placement from the university, we can't afford our own these days but he's very good."

"Come in, would you like a cuppa?" said Lynn.

"No thanks, we won't be here long."

"It's no trouble, I've got some cake in." She was already halfway to the kitchen and Amy raised her eyebrows at Mike. He shrugged.

Lynn returned with mugs of tea laden with sugar. She hadn't bothered to ask how they drank it. Both grimaced as they sipped it. Lynn also produced a Victoria Sponge.

"I'm being good so I shouldn't but as I've got guests." She then cut herself a quarter of the cake and offered the plate to Amy.

"No thanks, I'm training for the Great North Run."

"I've always thought about doing that," said Lynn.

Mike turned away and looked out of the window so she couldn't see his grin. He pretended that he was checking light levels.

"Lynn, do you want to tell us about your cat? Darcy, was it?"

"Yes, he was murdered by those evil bastards."

"Err, it's a family newspaper Lynn, I'd appreciate it if you could keep the language to a minimum."

"Yeah, sorry, I'm just so angry."

"That's understandable, could you tell us what happened?"

"I went and bought him some fish in the local Shears, can I say the store's name?"

"We'd rather you didn't. Our readers will be able to work it out."

"The staff in there are always up themselves. Think they are something special. For God's sake, they only work in a shop, they should get a proper job."

"What is it you do Lynn?"

"I work in a call centre."

"Okay, thank you. Carry on."

"I'd been telling them about how the gypsies had tidied my garden."

"Gypsies?"

"It was probably gypsies, you know what they are like. She was rude about my garden, as I said she was up herself. I told her so, put her right in her place. She must have taken offence and swapped the fish."

"Swapped it for what?"

"Another fish but this one was laced with poison."

"You think she had a fish ready, laced with poison just on the off chance somebody with a cat upset her."

"When you put it like that it does sound a little silly but do you have a better explanation?"

"I'm not sure I do. What about the gypsies you mentioned, where do they fit in?"

"The more I think about it, the more it couldn't have been gypsies. They are filthy buggers. Even if they had tidied my garden they would probably have had a big shit in the middle of it."

"Okay, right, back to the cat."

"Yes, I had a light tea and fed Darcy the salmon, he always eats better than me."

Mike checked the light levels again.

"And when did you notice that he was unwell?" said Amy.

"Yesterday morning, when he'd shat all over the stairs."

"How long did that last?"

121

"I don't know, I found him outside in a pile of shit and puke, he was already dead."

"I'm sorry to hear that. What happened next?"

"I went to see the neighbours, to see if they knew anything about it."

"And then?"

"And then the police came."

"The police? Do they normally attend pet deaths?"

"They do when it's murder. They are doing forensics to find the poison." Lynn took another bite out of her cake, dropping crumbs down her front.

"And do they have any suspects?"

"Yes, they do, they know it's them stuck up bitches at Shears. They are just gathering evidence."

"We're going there next to get their side of the story."

"Why do you want their side, they are evil murdering bastards?"

"We are a responsible newspaper, we need to check the story from all angles. I think we have enough here, I'll get Mike to take some quick snaps and we'll get out of your hair."

"I hope you get my best side," said Lynn.

"How could I miss it?" Mike once again checked his light levels and stifled his grin. "Right can we have you in the armchair next to the window please?"

Lynn shuffled across and sat with a big grin on her face.

"You look beautiful Lynn but this is a sad news story, we'll need you to look a bit glum," said Mike.

"Really, I've gone to loads of trouble with my hair and make-up."

"I can tell but your cat has just died, you're not going to get much sympathy from our readers if you are grinning like a Cheshire...well you know what I mean."

He took a couple of photos, then Lynn produced a framed photo of Darcy from behind the settee.

"Would it be better if I held this?"

"That would be perfect." He finished off his photos and packed up his things. "You know, if you are thinking of doing the Great North Run, there are still places left if you run for a charity. Maybe you could do it for the cat protection league."

Amy glared at him.

"Maybe I will," said Lynn, "do you fancy being my training partner?"

"Can't, err old knee injury." He suddenly gained a limp and hobbled outside where Amy smacked him on the arm.

"You're going to get us into trouble one of these days."

"Did you believe a word she said? I bet the fat bugger's eaten the bloody cat," said Mike.

"Didn't believe it but it only matters if our readers do and as they are mainly a bit dense, I'm sure they will."

"Hi, I'm Amy and this is Mike. Are you okay to talk?" She stuck out her hand.

"Yeah, no problem, come through to the office. Would you like a cuppa?" said Chloe.

"Is it safe, you're not going to poison me, are you?"

Chloe raised her eyebrows.

"Sorry, that was in poor taste. I'd love one thanks."

"Mike?"

"Yes, please."

They all gathered around Chloe's desk.

"Right Chloe, I'm sure you know what this is about. If you don't mind, I'm going to ask you a few questions and get your side of the story."

No problem," said Chloe, "but there isn't really a 'my side' to the story, there's just the facts."

"And what are the facts as you see them?"

"Quite simple really; Lynn is an occasional customer of ours and she has a cat that unfortunately became poorly and died."

"And Lynn claims that the cat died because of contaminated fish she bought from this shop."

"It's not possible. The fish is vacuum packed. Our refrigeration systems are checked regularly, we always receive top marks for hygiene. Environmental Health are coming out but I have no concerns."

"Environmental Health are coming out?"

"It's standard when someone makes a complaint. Like I say, we're not concerned." She produced a folder with all their hygiene certificates.

"It does appear that you have a good record."

"We do and we are very proud of it. I have a good team here."

"And what about Lynn?"

"What about her?"

"What do you think of Lynn as a customer?"

"All our customers are very valuable to us."

"I bet she's more valuable than most when she enters the bloody cake aisle," said Mike.

They both stared at him.

"Sorry, just thinking aloud."

"I know that all your customers are valuable," said Amy, "but what about Lynn in particular. Have you ever had any disputes with her?"

"Amy, I know you have a job to do but I only agreed to speak to you to show that we have nothing to hide. All press requests are meant to go through Head Office. If you think I am going to slag off my customers then you are speaking to the wrong person."

"I'm sorry, I had to ask. She does seem a little confrontational."

"She's just lost her cat, I'm sure she's a bit upset."

"Would you mind if we got a photo of you outside of the store?"

"I'm sorry. Like I said, this interview was only done as a favour. I'm not one for publicity myself."

"No worries. Do you mind if we take a photo of the store from outside?"

"It's a free country. Fire away."

Chloe led them to the door and shook their hands as they left. They went to the other side of the road so Mike could line up his shot.

"She hates the fat bitch, doesn't she?" said Mike.

"Oh yes, there's far more to this story than meets the eye."

Mike took his photos and briefly checked his viewfinder not noticing Manuel staring back at them from behind the shelving.

CHAPTER ELEVEN
Monday 30th May

Manuel got off the bus and walked towards Shears. He noticed the crowd but didn't think much about it until he got closer. The crowd was ninety percent female and some of them had banners. It was a protest. What it was about he couldn't think until he read some of the banners.

CAT KILLERS!

BOYCOTT MOGGY MURDERERS!!!

He felt sick and his legs started to wobble. He put his hand against the wall to steady himself.

"What have I done?" he thought.

He straightened up and marched into the store, not stopping or listening to the shouts from the crowd. He didn't have to wear a uniform so they didn't realise that he worked there. They must have mistaken him for a customer and whilst some abuse was hurled in his direction, it was half hearted. After all, it was still early in the morning.

Once he got through the door, Stacey and Alex weren't far behind him.

"Did you get through okay?" asked Chloe.

"Yes, they shouted some insults but I get worse from my mother before I leave the house."

"I'm glad you're okay. Let's grab a cuppa and decide what we're going to do."

"I don't understand what they are protesting about," said Stacey.

"It's that daft fat bitch," said Alex, "stirring things up on Facebook."

"Let's not sink to their level Alex. She's upset and she's lashing out," said Chloe.

"She's accusing us of murder. I'm not having that."

"Accusing who?" said Manuel.

"All of us, she's saying we killed her cat deliberately."

"It wasn't deliberate," said Manuel.

"Never mind deliberate, it wasn't us."

"That's what I meant." Manuel had gone bright red and was sweating.

"Look Manuel, you don't need to be here today, you can do the stocktaking later. I don't want you to get caught up in all this," said Chloe.

"I don't mind, I'm here now." He didn't want to walk out through the crowd again and despite not owning up, he still felt responsible.

"He's one of us, aren't you Manuel?" Stacey put her arm around his shoulder.

"Yes." He felt a fraud.

"Okay, there's not much we can do about them outside. Let's not antagonise them and as long as they stay outside of the store we'll ignore them as best we can."

"I'm still not happy, why should she get away with slander?" said Alex.

"She won't get away with it. Let's bide our time until this blows over. We've done nothing wrong, it will still go away."

An egg smashed off the window.

"I'm going to have to clean that off," said Stacey.

"Not now."

"The longer I leave it the harder it will be to remove. And it will stink."

"At least we know it wasn't that lardarse who threw it. That would be far too much like exercise," said Alex.

"Alex, what have I told you about stooping to their level. Now go and reduce the price on the cat food. Let's see how long their protests last when there is a bargain to be had."

As the team went about reducing the price of cat food and generally ignoring the protest outside, Chloe went into the office and logged into her laptop. She had a mountain of paperwork to catch up on and the protest had been a distraction.

Before she got started on the work of the day, she logged onto Facebook to see what had caused the outrage. It didn't take long for her to find out. By clicking on the North-East Cat Owner's page not only did she see a photo of Shears with the protestors outside, she also saw a picture of herself, taken from the company website, with the slogan **CAT KILLER** emblazoned underneath.

She knew that she had done nothing wrong and suspected that the campaign would die off soon enough. It was frustrating that she was being implicated but there wasn't a great deal she could do about it.

She was about to click out of Facebook when she noticed the comments under her photo.

Wouldn't be surprised if she sacrificed it in some voodoo ritual.

Fucking Dyke. Bet it's not the first pussy she has ruined.

Shud b snt bck to Africa where she cums frm.

Chloe was shocked. She'd encountered casual racism throughout her life, even homophobia but this was brutal. She felt a little sick and fought back the tears. She could just about put up with a few angry cat lovers but when the racist groups tagged onto the campaign, she knew she was in trouble. She knew she should close it down but each one of the comments had well over forty 'likes' so it wasn't a one-off, they were being encouraged. She clicked on the list of 'likes' and the first name that appeared was Lynn Sherman.

Chloe had been willing to give her the benefit of the doubt, after all she had just lost her cat. But this was unacceptable. She closed her laptop and only then did she realise that Manuel had been stood behind her.

"Did you read that?" she asked.

"Yes, don't let it upset you, it's only words on a computer screen."

"It's more than that Manuel, much more. But you're right, I shouldn't let it get to me. I'm better than that."

"Do you want a cuppa?" asked Manuel.

"Yes, please," said Chloe. Hiding her surprise that it was the first time that Manuel had ever offered. "Don't tell the others, it'll only wind them up."

"No problem." Manuel knew that he was responsible and didn't want to make things worse. He put on the kettle.

Meanwhile, with the lack of customers, Stacey was browsing Facebook on her phone. She noticed that someone that she had previously classed as a friend had liked the campaign to boycott Shears.

"She'll be getting deleted," she thought. She clicked on the link to Chloe's photo and then the comments beneath it.

"The evil fucking bastards! This is war."

Grace went through her usual morning routine before leaving for the shops. She read the Echo story again about the dead cat. She had a great deal of sympathy with the owner, especially as she seemed to be a lonely type.

On the other hand, she refused to believe that Chloe and the store had anything to do with it. Shears wasn't named but it didn't take Miss Marple to work it out. She was going to show a bit of solidarity.

She was a little shocked to see the size of crowd outside of Shears and even more surprised to see the size of some of the people in it.

There were a couple of banners but whatever was on them didn't interest her much and she tried to push through to get to the door.

"Excuse me, please." She was either not heard or ignored. She tried again. "Excuse me."

Lynn turned to face her, "Where do you think you are going?"

"In there if you would be so kind as to let me past."

"Do you not know that they are cat killers?"

"Who are?"

"Those in the shop, killed my Darcy," said Lynn.

129

"Don't be ridiculous, that bunch wouldn't hurt a fly."

"They would and they did. We're going to get the place closed down."

"And where would you expect me to shop then?" said Grace.

"I don't care, get a bus into town. You get a free bus pass, don't you?"

"I've asked politely, more than once. I won't ask again. Now get out of the way." For an old woman of such a tiny frame, Grace had quite a serious glare.

Lynn stood her ground and used her size to try and intimidate Grace. "Go and shop elsewhere, you silly old woman."

A few in the crowd were shocked and distanced themselves from Lynn.

"I might be old and frail," said Grace, "but I'm not scared of you. I've got my walking stick in this trolley and I still have some moves. If you want to be humiliated by a little old lady, that's your choice."

Lynn moved aside. "It'll be your cat next."

Grace pushed her way through the door and was greeted by Chloe. "Hi Grace, sorry you had to put up with that outside. It's all a bit of a misunderstanding. You could have phoned and I would have brought your shopping round."

"Nonsense, I've dealt with bigger rabbles than that. What's it all about?"

"The ringleader's cat died the other night. She somehow thinks we are responsible."

"Is that the big one, blocking the light out?"

"Ha ha. Grace, you are very cruel."

"She's all fart and no shite that one. I wouldn't let her bother you."

"If you put it like that Grace. Do you fancy a cuppa before you go back out there?"

"No thanks love, I'll just get my bits and pieces."

"We can let you out the back way so you don't have to go through that again."

"Don't be daft pet, I quite enjoy winding up people like that. Wait until I tell her that cat food is on special. You should put the cream buns on half price, she'd soon break her boycott then."

"You're wicked at times Grace."

"I don't like bullies. Especially bullies who pick on my friends. You get any trouble off them, let me know and I'll sort them out."

"Very kind of you Grace but I think I can handle them."

Manuel stood in the corner examining his ledger.

"Morning Manuel, still got your head in that little book I see?" said Grace.

"Morning, Mrs Peebles." He tried to hide the book behind his back.

"What have you got in there, your girlfriend's phone numbers?"

"He'll never tell us, Grace, I've been trying to get it out of him for weeks," said Chloe.

"It's good for us to have secrets sometimes."

"I guess you're right Grace," said Chloe.

"Okay, now I know you've got the cat food on special but I think my Ruby deserves a little treat. I think a nice piece of fish might be in order."

"Have you seen this, Chloe?" said Alex.

"What's that?" Chloe had calmed down since reading the comments on Facebook and the chat with Grace had boosted her mood.

"Alex ,man." Stacey glared at him. "It's nothing, Chloe."

"If you're talking about Facebook, yes I've seen it. People get very precious about their animals, best to ignore it."

"Is that it? Ignore them?" Alex was fuming. "Have you seen what they have said? It's disgusting. People like that shouldn't be allowed to own animals." He kicked the lottery stand. In his rage, he kicked it a lot harder than he intended and it knocked over a display of washing powder. "Sorry."

"It's okay, Alex. I'm angry but we shouldn't let them get to us. It's me they are having a go at, you shouldn't get upset."

"If they attack you, they attack all of us," said Stacey. "She might be twenty stone but I fancy going out there and smashing that fat face of hers. Might do her some good if she can't eat for a few weeks."

"I appreciate the concern but they really aren't worth it. We'll only escalate things if we react."

"But what if they don't stop the protest?" said Alex. "We've barely had any customers in. Anyone who comes near the door gets abused and they keep on walking."

"We could lose our jobs if we don't get any customers," said Stacey.

"It won't come to that," said Chloe.

"It will. If we don't get any customers, we don't get any money and the bosses at HQ won't keep us on."

"It won't come to that because I won't let it. If it looked like anyone was losing their job, and it won't, they'll want a sacrificial lamb and I'll give them one."

"What do you mean?" asked Stacey.

Manuel loitered in the background, nervously shifting his weight from foot to foot. He thought that Chloe suspected him but didn't think she would give him up so easily.

"I'll resign," said Chloe.

"Why would you do that? You've done nothing wrong," said Alex.

"It doesn't matter who has done what and who hasn't. What's important is that things get back to normal as quickly as possible."

"If you resign, I will too," said Stacey.

"Me as well," said Alex. "Wouldn't be the same here without you."

"Me too," said Manuel. He was a surprised as everyone else that he had said it.

"There's no need for that. We'll sort something out." Chloe was immediately worried that the others would follow her lead if she walked. Whilst she was confident that Stacey and Alex could get another job, she was equally confident that Manuel wouldn't.

Alex was already taking matters into his own hands. He was busily typing a reply to the comments on Facebook.

If the cat's owner didn't have a sponge cake constantly in front of her nose she might have seen that her cat wasn't well and she could have done something about it.

After speaking to Alex and Stacey and following them back into the store to check everything was okay, Chloe headed back into the office and shut the door behind her not noticing Manuel working quietly in the corner. She jumped.

"Jesus Manuel, how do you do that?"

"Do what?"

"Manage to frighten people without actually doing anything. I hope you're not on Facebook abusing people as well."

"No, my Mam doesn't let me on Facebook."

"Why is that not a surprise? What's her problem?"

"She says it is dangerous and full of perverts and show offs."

"Has she ever been on it?"

"I doubt it but she reads about it in the Daily Mail."

"That figures. Why doesn't she let you find out for yourself?"

"She said it was pointless as I had no friends so I would have nobody to add."

"Wow, she's charming. What about Stacey and Alex? You could add me."

"Best not, you're not exactly her favourite person at the minute."

"I don't think I'm anybody's favourite person at the minute. How am I going to get out of this mess, Manuel?"

"I'm not an expert on how to make people happy but maybe we should back off Lynn a bit. She's upset and people do strange things when they are upset."

"I've already told Alex and Stacey to pack it in with the Facebook comments, they aren't helping anyone. We need to find a way of getting Lynn to stop her campaign."

"Maybe it's not all her fault."

"Do you know something, Manuel?"

"No, just saying. If we could make her happy, she would leave us alone."

"I doubt that she's ever been happy. I've tried to tell the guys to back off her but they are angry. She's been vicious in her attacks on me."

"We have to try."

"We have to try something Manuel. If we don't find a way out of this we'll all be out of a job."

"I thought you said nobody would be losing their job?"

"Do you trust me to look out for you?"

"Yes, sorry."

"No need to apologise. I stand by what I said, nobody will lose their job, I will sort it. I just haven't figured out how yet."

"Maybe I could help?"

"Best thing you can do Manuel is keep on being you. I think we need at least one level head around here."

"Level head?"

"You're reliable, reliable people are what I need right now. You do the same thing day in day out and never cause me any problems. Don't ever change, Manuel."

Manuel wasn't used to praise, he blushed. He wanted nothing more at this moment in time than to sort out the mess he had created for Chloe.

He retrieved his ledger from his pocket and looked at the debit and credit columns. Maybe he had a plan to balance them.

Oliver reached for the pack of Rennies and shoved a handful in his mouth. Gaviscon was more effective but he couldn't afford them. The acid was burning away his stomach from the inside and it was now at his throat.

He'd cut out the spicy food, he rarely drank but he couldn't avoid the stressful situations. They came to him.

Like the safe anchored to the corner of his bedroom. He didn't want to open it; once he did he was incriminated.

Whilst Dale had told him that it was only books in there, he was hardly a man you could trust. It could be drugs, guns, God knows what could be lurking inside.

But he had no choice.

He rinsed out his mug then gulped down a mug full of water; delaying the inevitable.

He walked over to the safe and took the Post It note from his pocket. He entered the combination, the safe whirred then the door opened with a reassuring pop.

He took out the laptop first and fired it up. It was basic and came with Excel. Some decent accounting software would have been nice but he didn't expect it.

He took out the three ledgers. The top one seemed to be all Dale's legitimate businesses. He had quite the portfolio. Car washes, nail bars, sunbed shops and various other enterprises. All cash ventures, all very convenient.

His security work was also in that ledger, a legitimate front but anyone with the vaguest knowledge of pubs knew the truth.

When Oliver had gone to prison, Dale was just a bouncer with a side-line in money lending. He'd done well for himself.

The second book wasn't a ledger but a list of people, or at least their assumed names, how much they owed him and how much interest they were being charged. Oliver knew from personal experience that Dale's interest rates put the Payday loan companies to shame.

The third book was the interesting one, the one that Oliver was scared to look into. It contained Dale's real businesses. There was a code but Oliver was sure that a five-year-old could crack it given ten minutes. Tobacco, alcohol and as he feared, drugs.

His stomach gurgled away. His brain pounded as if it was trying to leave his skull. He felt faint and perched on the edge of the bed.

There were other entries that he couldn't quite work out. He would worry about them later.

Right now, he had to somehow get everything from books two and three to go through book one and hide enough of it so a real accountant wouldn't be overly suspicious; impossible.

Standard money laundering rationale was that criminals were willing to lose about thirty percent to make their money clean. He was confident that Dale didn't think like that. He was going to have to put up a convincing argument.

The lack of internet was going to be a pain as it would have been useful to do some research on how much an average car wash made. He had no idea and if he put too much through there it would set alarm bells ringing.

He wasn't the man for the job. He knew that but there was no arguing with Dale.

Oliver made his mind up. He was going to have to think of a plan to get some money, big money, and escape all this.

Easier said than done.

With barely a customer through the door all day, Alex and Stacey took to Facebook. They hadn't personally been targeted yet but they were unhappy at the abuse Shears was getting and Chloe in particular.

Are you sure the cat's dead? Maybe it's just stunned after seeing its owner get out of the shower.

Did it starve to death after the owner kept eating his tea?

It wasn't long before somebody in Head Office picked up on it and Chloe received a phone call.

"Hello Chloe, it's Patrick from Head Office."

"Hi Patrick, how are you?"

"I haven't phoned for a chat. Have you seen what is being said on Facebook?"

"Yes, Lynn is just angry because she has lost her cat. She is venting and we are an easy target."

"I didn't mean that fat mess, I meant your staff."

"My staff?"

"Alex and Stacey. They are aware of the company's social media policy?"

"Yes, they've both read the handbook." Chloe couldn't remember the policy herself but she was sure there was something in there somewhere.

"Have you any idea why they are blatantly contravening it then, especially when they are meant to be working?"

"We haven't had many people in today, we've been quiet," said Chloe, frantically trying to log onto Facebook again to see what they had said.

"I'm not surprised if that's the way they speak to our customers."

Chloe saw what had been posted.

And the responses that followed.

That's evil. The poor girl has lost her cat and all you can do is mock her size. I was going to give you the benefit of the doubt but I'm definitely boycotting Shears now.

Reel gurls hav curvs.xxx

Hope someone starves you to death.

"I'll sort it." Chloe hung up without discussing it further with Patrick. "Alex, Stacey, office now."

They had never seen Chloe angry before and hurried into the office.

"What the hell are you two playing at?"

"What do you mean?" said Stacey.

"This." Chloe turned the laptop screen towards them and showed the number of comments coming through. "We were in enough trouble before, it's now a hundred times worse."

"We were only trying to help, she was saying some horrible things about you."

Chloe sat down. "Look, I know you are trying to protect me but I'm a big girl, I can look after myself. I'm meant to be protecting you. I thought I knew you both. You're not nasty people, why have you resorted to her tactics?"

"She's an evil fat bitch," said Alex, "I'm not bothered if I get sacked, I'm not letting her say things like that about you?"

"Me too, Chloe," said Stacey, "sack me if you have to but I'm not letting racists win."

"Look," said Chloe, "I love you like you were my brother and sister and I appreciate your support but it has to stop."

"It's not fair," said Alex.

"Life's not fair," said Chloe. "Do you trust me?"

"What do you mean?"

"Do you trust me?"

"Of course." They both nodded.

"Then leave me to sort it my way and keep yourself out of trouble. Nobody is getting sacked, not even me. I will sort this."

They headed back into the store. Chloe had no idea how she was going to sort it but she had to give them the impression that she knew what she was doing.

Manuel had listened to the whole conversation from outside of the office. He should step up and say something. Take the blame, let Chloe know it was all his fault.

But his feet remained firmly planted on the floor.

"We've got the results back," said the environmental health officer.

"Anything?" WPC Cummins wasn't hopeful.

"Rat poison."

"What?"

"The fish was contaminated with rat poison."

"Deliberate?"

"No idea but we're going to pay the shop a visit. I'll let you know how we get on."

"It sounds like the fat bugger may have been right after all. Maybe I owe her an apology."

"About that drink…"

"I'll get back to you, I've got to speak to the chubby cat woman. God knows how she will take it."

She was soon to find out.

Lynn had returned from the protests when interest dwindled and people got hungry. She was in the sitting room with the curtains closed. She was surrounded by fast food cartons. Apart from the protests she hadn't left the house or changed out of her pyjamas since Darcy had died.

She had nothing left, nothing at all. Darcy was dead, she had no friends and she was fairly sure that she was unemployed. The takeaways had been paid for on her credit cards that were almost at their limits. She needed some good news from somewhere.

The phone rang.

"Hello Miss Sherman, it's WPC Cummins from the other day. We've had Environmental Health run some tests and they have found some unusual results."

"What do you mean unusual?"

"There were traces of rat poison. At this moment, we don't know where they have come from. They are doing some more investigations."

"I knew it. It'll be that silly black dyke in Shears, I'll kill her."

"Miss Sherman, can I remind you that you need to stay away from the store and let the Environmental Health carry out their investigations?"

"She killed Darcy."

"We don't know that, we've yet to establish where the poison came from. Please do not do anything that would jeopardise that."

Lynn wasn't to be dissuaded. She knocked over the chair as she stood and left it there. She hung up on WPC Cummins and barged into her bedroom to get ready.

That stuck up bitch is going to get what is coming to her."

The Environmental Health officers showed their ID and asked who was in charge.

"That will be me," said Chloe.

"Is there somewhere we can speak in private?"

"Yes, come into to the office." She led them through, "Manuel, could you give us a few minutes please?"

"No problem." He straightened up his paperwork and headed for the door. As he was leaving he noticed the Health Officer take the fish wrapper out of his briefcase. It was in an evidence bag. He froze.

"Did you forget something, Manuel?" said Chloe.

"Err no, just going." He closed the door behind him, he was shaking.

"What's happening, Manuel?" said Stacey.

"I'm not sure, Environmental Health, they know about the poisoned fish."

"The poisoned fish, what are you talking about?"

"Err nothing." He wandered into the shop and started straightening items on the shelves.

———

139

Alex joined Stacey, "What's up? They looked official."

"Something about the fish according to Manuel. I thought the fat lass was making it all up, I didn't think it was anything to do with us. You're in charge of the fresh produce, what do you think it is?"

"How would I know?" said Alex.

"I'm just asking, I don't have anything to do with the fridges."

"As long as you're okay then?"

"That's not what I meant. They can't close us down can they, I need the money."

"I'm responsible for you losing your job now as well?"

Glass shattered behind them. Manuel stood there with a broken pickle jar at his feet.

"Manuel, what the hell are you doing? You better get that cleared up, what if Environmental Health see it?"

"Sorry." He still didn't move.

"If you want a job doing…" Stacey grabbed a cloth and shoved Manuel out of the way.

"Can I get you a cup of tea?" said Chloe.

"No thanks, comes with the job I'm afraid. You learn to not touch anything if you don't have to."

Chloe tried to smile. "Don't blame you. What can I do to help?"

"Was this fish bought here?" He showed her the evidence bag.

"It certainly looks like one of ours."

"We also have this receipt showing that it was bought here."

"Well done, Columbo." Chloe didn't mean to be sarcastic, it just slipped out.

He raised his eyebrows. "We've done tests on the fish and the wrapper and we believe that it has been contaminated with rat poison."

"They are sealed packets, I'm not sure how that could have happened."

"That's what we are trying to establish. Do you have a problem with rats?"

"Personally?"

"In the store?"

"No, we have a contract with a firm who looks after it for us. I can show you the paperwork."

"I'd rather you showed us the traps you use."

"There's one right behind you." Chloe pointed to the one next to the fridge.

The colleague who had remained quiet up until this point went over with his rubber gloves on, collected some of the poison with his tweezers and put it into an evidence bag. He returned to his seat without speaking.

"We're going to take that away for tests but I'll give you a little heads up as I'm a nice sort of guy. The poison we found on the fish is the standard poison used by your pest control company. The tests are going to come back positive. It wouldn't take Columbo to work out where the contamination came from."

"They are the biggest pest control company in the business, it could have come from anywhere."

"You really believe that."

"Yes, I really do." She ran a tight ship, there is no way this could happen.

"I admire your confidence. I'm afraid that we're going to have to do a full inspection of the store. You are going to have to close for the night."

Chloe knew that there was no point in arguing and went to give everyone the news. "There's nothing to worry about, it's just a standard inspection. Don't worry, you'll still get paid."

Stacey and Alex didn't need a second excuse and grabbed their coats. Manuel stayed where he was. "Go on, Manuel. I can manage here, see you tomorrow."

He walked out, still shaking. How did they know? What had he done? He was only trying to balance the books.

The crowd had largely dispersed when Manuel left work. They'd made it known that they'd be returning the next day but apart from the odd insult hurled his way, he was ignored.

The crowd didn't bother him but having to leave early had hampered his plans. He loitered about hoping not to be noticed and hoping that it was worth the wait. When he passed the newsagent on the other side of the road, he knew that it was. Grace was just leaving with her copy of the Echo. He hoped that she didn't see him and he kept his distance, surprised at how slowly old people walked. He sat on the wall as he could see all the way along the road and he was confident that he could catch her up as she turned the corner.

Manuel sprang off the wall and ran down the road, he got to the end of the road slightly out of breath. He wasn't much of a sportsman and the road was longer than he thought. Fortunately, he could still see Grace as she went through the garden gate and entered the house. He made a note of the address and caught the bus home. His mother would be wondering where he was.

Chloe watched as the Environmental Health Officers went to work. They may not have wanted a cuppa but she did. Once she convinced them that she wasn't destroying evidence by making a cup of tea she sat and waited.

She provided whatever paperwork they needed when they needed it. They donned full body overalls and masks and poked into every nook and cranny with their torches and rubber gloves. The thought did cross Chloe's mind with what she would do to them with rubber gloves and a torch.

After two hours, they were finished.

"Right that's us done, you'll be hearing from us shortly."

"Was everything okay?"

"We'll be in touch shortly."

"Can I open tomorrow?"

"I don't see why not," he seemed disappointed, "but you are far from out of the woods." His silent colleague waved the evidence bag with the rat poison. "If we find that you were responsible for poisoning that cat, there will be prosecutions and possibly prison."

Chloe knew the place had been spotless, there was no way Shears could be responsible for the poisoning. Nobody was going to prison and this bloke was just flexing his muscles.

As she led them to the door she heard a banging on the shutters. They inched open as she turned the key to reveal the large intimidating figure of Lynn Sherman.

"You bitch, you killed Darcy."

Luckily, the door was still locked so she could only shout through the glass as Chloe and the Environmental Health Officers watched on.

"What's that?" said one.

"That is Lynn Sherman; former owner of a dead cat and an altogether unpleasant woman. I think we'll give it a couple of minutes until she calms down."

"Is there a back way out of here?"

"Surely you aren't that scared? Do you not need to talk to her anyway, find out where that poison really came from?"

"I think she's made up her mind."

"You could be right but she's not going anywhere. If we try to go around the back she will only come around and catch us there."

"New Year will get there quicker than her."

"Your car's parked over the road, you're going to have to pass her at some point," said Chloe.

"I think it's you she wants to kill, I'll take my chances."

Lynn banged on the glass.

"Lynn, I'm going to let you in but you are going to have to calm down. If you don't, I'm going to have to call the police."

"Calm down? You killed my Darcy." Tears had formed in her eyes.

"I'm opening the door now Lynn, we can talk this through rationally."

The Health Officer held his mobile in his hand, ready to dial 999 at the first sign of trouble.

Chloe unlocked the door and Lynn barged through before it was fully opened.

"Who the hell are you?" she said.

The Health Officer held up his ID as some sort of protection "Environmental Health."

"It's true? You've come to close them down because they killed Darcy."

"It's not as simple as that," he said.

"They've done a full inspection, we're spotless," said Chloe.

"It's not as simple as that."

"Which one is it then, did she kill Darcy or not?"

"It will all be in our report." He tried to squeeze past her but she used her ample weight to bounce him back the way he came.

"If you aren't prepared to shut them down, I will." She took a swipe at one of the shelves but couldn't reach and her momentum sent her into the silent officer, sending him flying. He lay with his back against the counter. Lynn was on all fours.

"I'm dialling 999," said the other officer.

"You should, get her arrested for murder." Lynn pointed at Chloe.

"Don't be ridiculous," said Chloe, "do you really think I would want to harm your cat?"

"Yes, to get at me. You're jealous of me."

"Mental," said the officer lying on the floor. Everyone glared at him.

"I'm warning you," said the other officer, "I'm going to dial 999."

"Don't bother, I'm going. You haven't heard the last of this you jumped up little tramp." Lynn scrambled to her feet and grabbed at the handle of the door.

Chloe didn't bother replying and looked on bemused. She didn't know what Lynn had in mind but she didn't think it would be good. She only prayed that it wasn't a dirty protest.

Manuel nipped back to the shop and picked up the cardboard box he'd hidden outside the backdoor before he left work. He already had the fish he'd bought earlier. It was a risk buying it in the store again but nobody seemed to question it.

He returned to Grace's house and waited until all the lights went out. He wasn't sure that his plan would work. He wasn't sure that he had much of a plan at all.

He placed a little bit of fish in the garden and crouched behind the wall. It was a quiet street without the procession of students that bothered him at Lynn's house.

After nearly two hours, success, Ruby stuck her nose out of the cat flap. Eventually, after taking in her surroundings and deciding that she was safe, she went for the small piece of salmon fillet on the grass.

Manuel was tempted to make his move and grab the cat but he'd waited for two hours, he could wait a bit longer. After what seemed like an age, Ruby headed in his direction. In the direction of the remaining fillet. In the direction of the cardboard box which was soon to become her transport.

She arched her back as she approached Manuel and he tentatively stroked her. She ate a little bit of the fish from his hand then climbed onto his lap. This was easier than he could have imagined. Put the cat in the box and head off, job done.

Except nothing was quite that straightforward in Manuel's life. As soon as Ruby noticed the box she sensed something was up and darted from Manuel's arms. He dived across the garden and just managed to grab the cat's tail. Yanking it back he almost launched it like a hammer throw. He managed to keep his grip but only succeeded in spinning around with the momentum. Ruby looking for some purchase, extended her claws and dug them into his face. He did all he could not to scream. He dragged the cat from his face as she clung on, drawing blood. Wrestling her to the ground he lay on top of her trying to work out his next move. Dragging the box towards him with his right leg he swung around and dumped Ruby in it without letting go. She dug her claws into his jacket and tore it. How was he going to explain this to his mother?

He ripped his right arm from the clutches of the cat and managed to close one half of the lid. A paw attempted an escape from the top of the box but he now had control and shoved it back in whilst closing the other half of the lid. Ruby had begun to make some very strange noises along with the bell on her neck ringing away and he hoped it didn't wake Grace or attract the attention of the neighbours.

He was glad that he had come prepared and taped the lid of the box down. He'd already punched several holes in the box so Ruby could breathe and if she stopped struggling she would notice that he had left some more fish in the box. He'd also considered leaving some water but couldn't work out a practical way of carrying the box without spilling it so he hadn't bothered. A cat could survive one night without water.

He waited for a couple of minutes hoping that the cat would calm down but there was little sign of that happening.

He grabbed the box and ran out onto the pavement, picked up the pace as he headed towards Lynn's house.

This wasn't going to plan for Manuel. Whilst the cat was in the box, it wasn't going quietly. He was out of Grace's street and therefore out of immediate danger but the cat was now wailing and he had gained the attention of a few onlookers.

"Going to the vets," he said as he raced down the road.

He regretted leaving the water out for Ruby as it seeped through the bottom of the box onto his hand. Then he remembered, he hadn't left any water out. He sniffed his hand and it stunk of ammonia. He didn't understand what people saw in cats.

He was now sweating and stopped for a rest. Ruby stuck a paw out of the box in an attempt to escape but he slapped it back in. He took the parcel tape from his pocket and sealed the top of the box again. He'd put enough air holes in the box for the cat to breathe but he added a couple more. He didn't want another dead cat on his hands.

The cat seemed to calm down so he set off again. He hadn't gone far when the smell hit his nostrils. Not ammonia this time.

"You filthy beast."

He speeded up knowing that the increasingly soggy box wouldn't hold out for long and he didn't want to be covered in whatever Ruby had just deposited.

He made it into Lynn's street without any further mishaps. It was thankfully quiet with most of the students still in the pub. There were still lights on in Lynn's house but this didn't concern him. He walked up the path and placed the box on the doorstep. He taped the envelope to the top of the box, rang the doorbell and ran.

His calculations had been correct. It would take Lynn a lot longer to ease herself out of the armchair and waddle to the front door than it would for him to race down the path and around the corner. He still managed to be out of breath as he leaned on the wall and waited for the door to open.

It edged open and Lynn stood on the doorstep in her dressing gown. She looked up and down the street to see who had rang the bell at that time of night. Manuel hid behind the wall.

He wasn't sure whether it was the noise or the smell that forced her to look down but Lynn eventually noticed the box on her doorstep.

She ripped the envelope from the box but didn't open it and instead opened the box and Ruby leapt out covered in her own filth.

Lynn went to pick her up but noticed the mess.

"You smelly little bastard."

The cat ignored her insult and started rubbing against her leg.

"You're getting shit all over my PJs. Let's get you inside and get you cleaned up."

She headed indoors, "Are you coming or what?" Ruby hesitated for a moment then followed her and they happily went into the house together.

Manuel, satisfied that his mission was complete, returned home thinking about how he would explain to his mother how he was four hours late and stinking of cat piss.

CHAPTER TWELVE
Tuesday 31st May

Grace woke at her usual time, her body had its own internal alarm clock. She got out of bed, slipped her dressing gown over her nightie and went into the bathroom.

As she came out she thought something wasn't right but couldn't put her finger on it. Then she realised, Ruby wasn't there rubbing against her leg wanting to be fed.

"She must still be downstairs," she thought.

As she walked into the kitchen there was still no sign. She filled Ruby's food and water bowls and went into the sitting room. She wasn't in there.

"Ruby, come and get your breakfast." Grace would expect to hear the cat racing through to the kitchen from wherever she had been hiding with the bell on her neck jingling but there was nothing.

She opened the front door and looked out into the garden. Ruby would quite often venture out at night but was always back before the sun rose. This was very unusual.

Grace poured herself a bowl of bran flakes and made a pot of tea but she couldn't enjoy her breakfast without the familiarity of Ruby by her side.

Once she'd finished her cereal she went into the garden again and shook a bag of kitty treats.

"Ruby, where are you, love? Breakfast is ready."

A passer-by on his way to the bus stop gave her a funny look. She went back inside and poured herself another cup of tea. She didn't bother to read the Echo, she couldn't settle. She'd been up for over half an hour now and there was still no sign of Ruby. This had never happened before.

She ventured to the end of the path but the cat was nowhere to be seen. "Ruby! Stop being silly and get yourself home."

Next door's curtains twitched.

Grace went out into the street and walked to the end of the road. She then walked the full length the other way hoping to find Ruby. No luck.

"Have you seen this, love?" said the neighbour whilst peering through a gap in the curtains. "Grace from next door is out in her dressing gown. Poor love has finally lost it."

"What's that?" said his wife.

"Grace has gone doodlelally."

"What are you talking about?" The wife walked into the sitting room.

"Look," he pointed through the gap and Grace caught them staring. "Shit, she's seen us."

"And you're just letting her wander the streets in her nightie. Go and get her."

"I'm in my pyjamas. What if she's gone mad, she could be dangerous."

"She's in her eighties for Christ's sake. She's been our neighbour for over ten years and not been a spot of bother but you're worried about being seen in your pyjamas?"

"It's not our problem."

"It never is." His wife grabbed her coat and headed out of the door. "Grace, are you alright, love."

Grace looked lost and confused. "She's gone, I can't find her."

The neighbour wondered who she could be speaking about. "Who's gone Grace?" It looked like she had finally lost it.

"Ruby, she hasn't come home," said Grace.

"Ruby?" Then it registered. "your cat?"

"Yes, my cat, who did you think I was talking about?"

"Nobody, come on inside and get in the warm."

"I'm not coming in until she comes home."

"We'll find her, don't you worry about that. I'll send my husband out." She put the coat around Grace's shoulders and guided her inside.

"Grace has lost her cat; can you go out and have a look for her please?"

"I wouldn't know where to start, it could be anywhere. Could be under a bus by now."

His wife glared at him. "Is there any need?"

"I have to get to work, I have a meeting. Anyway, the police will probably help."

"The police?"

"I called them when you were outside, we're not trained to deal with old people who have lost their minds."

"She hasn't lost her mind, she's lost her bloody cat."

"How was I meant to know that?"

As they argued, Grace sneaked out of the door unnoticed. Back into the street. Back in search of Ruby.

Grace wandered off in search of Ruby with no luck. She took out a box of dried kitty treats and was shaking it frantically to no avail. She didn't realise how far she had walked until the police car appeared alongside her.

"Mrs Peebles, are you okay?"

"Of course I'm okay, what do you mean?"

"The dressing gown and the slippers, we thought you might be a bit, you know, confused?"

"You're the ones who are confused, I'm looking for Ruby."

"Why don't you hop in the car and we'll take you home and have a nice cup of tea. We can have a chat about Ruby and where she might be."

"I don't want to talk about bloody Ruby, I want to find her."

"And so do we, but we'll not find her like this. Come on get in the car." PC Sugden got out of the car and opened the rear door.

Grace realised that it was futile to argue with them, they weren't going away. She reluctantly climbed into the back of the car and fought back the tears.

As the police car pulled up at Grace's, PC Sugden indicated for WPC Cummins to take Grace indoors whilst he waited in the car; the implication being that he was going to phone Social Services.

———

WPC Cummins led Grace indoors and they headed for the kitchen where she put the kettle on. "Tell me about Ruby, were you close?"

"Of course we were close, she was my cat."

"Your cat?"

"Yes, my bloody cat. Did you think I was out searching for my long-lost sister with a box of kitty treats?"

"I'm sorry, it's just when we spoke to your neighbour and they said that you were a bit confused, we just assumed, you know with your age and everything."

"You thought I'd gone mental? Looks like I'm the only sane one around here."

PC Sugden entered the kitchen. "Social Services are on their way, they might be a little while."

"Err, think you'd better cancel the call. Seems that there may have been a little misunderstanding." WPC Cummins was bright red. "It seems that Grace was out looking for her missing cat, she hadn't gone … well anyway, cancel the call."

Grace had finished making the tea but hoped to get them out of the house as quickly as possible. Ruby had gone and she wasn't going to find her by sitting chatting to the Keystone Cops.

"Look I'm sorry that we made some assumptions, Grace," said WPC Cummins "We'd love to stop and help you find Ruby but strictly speaking we shouldn't be looking for lost cats. If you give us a photo we will keep an eye out for her."

"That's very kind, thank you."

"Do you think it might be related to the cat poisoning the other night, you know at the big unit's house?" PC Sugden realised that he shouldn't have spoken as WPC Cummins stared at him.

"I'm not sure what you are talking about," said WPC Cummins unconvincingly.

"Don't worry, I already know about it," said Grace. "That mad fat lass isn't wired up right. I'm sure Ruby will be okay, she'll just have wandered off somewhere. She is old, she's probably just a bit confused."

PC Sugden and WPC took the hint, finished off their tea and left. "We'll let you know if we see or hear anything, Grace. Thanks for being so understanding."

Grace shut the door behind them and decided to return to what she knew. She got out the Echo and started reading through it. If she returned to her routine, maybe Ruby would return to hers.

After finishing reading the Echo, she got ready, the mad cat woman look wasn't doing her any favours. She would do her rounds as usual. Maybe a catch up with young Chloe would do her good.

She closed the door behind her and shuffled down the garden path ignoring the twitching curtains next door. She was dressed as she was any other day with one slight adjustment. A pocket full of kitty treats.

Lynn had cleaned the cat, fed it and put it into Darcy's basket. She blocked the cat flap in the door to stop her getting out and hoped that it was trained enough to use the litter tray. She'd trained Darcy to go outside as she hated cleaning the litter tray but she kept one for emergencies.

The cat seemed happy to pose for photos that she instantly placed on Facebook to the delight of her cat loving friends. There was also great admiration for the cat lover who had given up their beloved puss to make up for her loss.

She went to bed happy with her new arrival. Darcy was gone but she had a new friend.

Lynn rose from bed he next morning and edged down the stairs. They still stunk of the bleach she had used to scrub Darcy's sick and shit from the stair carpet.

She went into the kitchen eager to see the new arrival. The smell got to her before she saw the cat. She was sitting in her basket purring. Lynn couldn't see where the smell was coming from. She checked the basket then the litter tray and looked all over the kitchen floor; nothing.

Then she looked in the kitchen sink. In amongst all the dirty dishes that Lynn had been too lazy to wash was a big cat turd. "Ooh you filthy little get." She wasn't quite as keen on her new cat as she thought she was.

She looked down at the cat purring at her feet and picked her up. "You might be a shitty arsed little bastard but I guess I'm stuck with you." She then noticed the name tag on her collar. "Ruby eh? Strange name for a cat but I suppose that you didn't choose it."

She turned the taps on full and hoped the worst of it would be washed away. As she looked from the cat to the sink she noticed the envelope that had come with the box the previous night. She hadn't bothered reading it. Maybe it was a warning from the previous owner about the cat's filthy habits. She opened it.

There was no mention of who had left it. Just a message that they hoped that she enjoyed the new cat and it made up for her loss. Then the line that caught her attention.

Don't be too harsh on the people in Shears, maybe they aren't to blame.

It was a red rag to a bull. Had the shop replaced her cat to try and placate her? Shut her up? Or, had they replaced her beloved Darcy with a shitting substitute deliberately to annoy her?

The cat started rubbing against her bare calves but she shoved it away with a slippered foot then headed to the sitting room and powered up the laptop.

She was furious. She went onto the cat lovers Facebook page and ignored the hundred likes she had received for the photo of her new cat and immediately went into attack mode.

That evil black dyke has gone too far now. If she thinks that dumping a stinking shitting cat in a box on my doorstep is going to stop me suing them she has another thing coming.

She closed her laptop and felt a little faint. Maybe her blood sugar levels were dropping, she grabbed a doughnut. Devouring it in two bites. She put the kettle on and got another doughnut out for her breakfast. She did her best to ignore the cat who was hovering by the fridge waiting to be fed.

It was war before. Now she was going to destroy Shears. She had been nice for far too long. She was going to annihilate them. She opened her laptop again and fired off an email to the Echo telling them of Chloe's latest crime.

She then phoned work. There was no way she could go in now; the whole episode had made her physically ill. She conveniently forgot that she had told Jeff to stick his job the other day. Jeff made a note in his diary for a disciplinary meeting if she ever returned.

She tipped a packet of cat food into the bowl and kicked it towards Ruby. "Try not to shit that out all over my kitchen."

She grabbed another doughnut in the hope of fighting off her sickness.

The crowd outside the shop seemed bigger than yesterday. Regardless, Chloe pushed through them ignoring the abuse. Some of it was personal, mainly from the ringleader but the majority was generic cat related insults. She thought that maybe she should have done her Master's thesis on pet owners, they were a strange lot. Some would apparently rather see her dead than see a cat harmed.

She let herself in and after switching off the alarm she headed straight for the kettle in the office. Manuel wasn't far behind her. "Cuppa Manuel?"

"Yes, please." He rummaged about in his bag and produced his ledger.

"You ever going to show me what's in that book of yours?"

"It's nothing." He shoved it back in his bag.

"I'll find out one day." The shocked look on his face made her reassure him. "Don't worry, we've all got secrets, you don't have to tell me if you don't want to."

"It's nothing." He zipped the bag and put it in his locker.

"Okay, here's your tea. Any idea why that group of cat freaks outside has got bigger this morning? I would have thought they would have got bored yesterday."

"I know nothing about it, why do you automatically think it is something to do with me?"

"Whoa. Who said it was anything to do with you? I was just asking."

"I'm just saying. It wasn't me."

"What wasn't you? Manuel, what have you done?"

"Why do I always get the blame?"

"Manuel, I'm your friend. When have I ever blamed you for anything? If you've done something daft, tell me and we can put it right."

"I haven't done anything. Leave me alone. You are just like my Mam."

"Okay, okay. No need for insults. Forget I mentioned it. Come on, let's see what that daft bugger outside is complaining about on Facebook now."

Manuel shuffled in his seat. He hadn't touched his tea. "I've got work to do."

"Your shift doesn't start for another twenty minutes. We've got to see what we are up against. I need your help, I can't fight them on my own."

Manuel knew what was coming. He'd already checked the page before he'd left the house. Despite his mother's ban on Facebook, he had joined to keep an eye on the situation. He would deal with the fallout from his mother later.

Chloe clicked onto the North-East Cat Lovers Facebook page, it was now in her favourites.

"She's got a new cat? She didn't hang about."

Manuel said nothing.

"Somebody left it on her doorstep? Who would leave her a cat in a box. Surely if a fellow cat lover wanted to donate their cat they would knock on the door. All a bit weird if you ask me but I guess that's cat owners for you," said Chloe.

Manuel still didn't reply but sat not looking Chloe in the eye and gripping the base of his chair tightly.

"She isn't half giving me some abuse, just because somebody left her a cat. Why would she think it was anything to do with me?"

155

"I don't know."

"Hold on, somebody left a note saying not to blame Shears and she somehow thinks it was us. Why would anyone do that? I don't get it."

"She's mad, maybe she's making it up," said Manuel.

"Hold on. You've been acting weird since you came through the door. More weird than usual. Manuel, what have you done?"

"Nothing, I haven't done anything." Manuel looked at the floor.

"Manuel, tell me now. Tell me where you got the cat from whilst we still have a chance to do something about it."

"I can't. I was only trying to help." He'd let go of the chair now and his right hand was grabbing his left elbow. He looked terrified.

"Manuel?"

"It's not my fault, I was only trying to balance the books."

Manuel and Chloe had barely spoken since the accusation in the office. They both went about their work for the rest of the morning without their paths crossing. As Manuel was naturally quiet, nobody else realised that there was a problem but Chloe knew that she was going to have to break the ice before it became an issue.

Chloe was considering how she was going to broach the subject again when the door to the shop opened. The crowd outside was still keeping the shoppers away and it was only a hard-core of regulars who could be bothered with the hassle.

Chloe was pleased to see that it was Grace. "Morning Grace love, hope that rabble outside didn't bother you too much."

"What? No. Where's the cat food?"

Chloe noticed that Grace's blouse wasn't buttoned correctly, a couple hair grips were missing so her hair slipped out over her face and her tights were crumpled. "Are you okay, Grace?"

"Yes." She didn't look at Chloe and filled her basket with cat food.

"Are you sure? Have you got time for a cuppa?"

"No, I've got to get back for Ruby, she didn't come home last night." She put the basket on the counter and Chloe begun to ring them through.

Manuel stood in the doorway of the office listening. He was rubbing his elbow, his hands clammy and he was shaking. Chloe didn't seem to have made the connection but when she did it would be all over.

He breathed a sigh of relief when Grace headed for the door without any more conversation.

"Look after yourself Grace," said Chloe "we're always here if you fancy a cuppa and a cake."

"Okay," said Grace as she left the shop and pushed her way back through the crowd.

"Watch the till Alex," said Chloe "I've got something urgent I need to sort in the office."

Manuel didn't fancy the awkward silence so decided to do some shelf stacking.

"No you don't." Chloe pushed her hand in his chest and forced him back into the office and kicked the door shut behind her. "Sit!"

He did as he was told and tried to speak "What's this ..."

"Don't even try and speak Manuel." Chloe was shaking with rage, he had never seen her like this. "Open Facebook."

"Why?"

"Don't question me just do as you are told."

He clicked on the favourite bar and opened Facebook. She raised her eyebrows, he knew which page she wanted to look at. He clicked on the North-East Cat Lovers link.

The main photo was of Lynn's new cat. "Click on that," said Chloe. "Scroll through the comments."

"What are you looking for?" He didn't need to ask, he already knew.

"There, that comment right there. Can you see it?" She pointed at the screen whilst staring at Manuel. "Don't look at me Manuel, look at the screen."

"I don't need to, I know what it says." He stopped looking at Chloe and looked at the floor.

"Of course you know what it says. Ruby. It bloody says Ruby. Her new sodding cat is called Ruby. Have you any idea what you have done?"

"I was only trying to help."

"Trying to help? Did you see the state of Grace when she came in? She's all over the place. You've caused that, Manuel. Do you never think about what repercussions your actions have?"

"All the time." He headed for his locker.

"Sit down. All the time? It looks to me like you never give it a second thought."

"I'm sorry."

"You don't have to say sorry to me, it's Grace who needs your apology. And I'm guessing Lynn as well?"

He nodded "It was an accident."

Chloe shook her head. "Manuel, I can help you but you have to tell me the whole story and don't leave anything out."

"I can't, you wouldn't understand."

"You could go to prison. You have to let me help you."

"I can't." He wasn't sure why he couldn't tell her about the ledger, he just couldn't.

Chloe grabbed her hair and stifled a scream. "Right we'll come back to the why later. For now, we have to work out what to do next. We have to think of a way of getting Ruby back to Grace without her ever finding out it was us who stole her."

"Us?"

"I'm an accomplice after the fact. If she sees these photos it's all over."

"She won't see them, she's an old woman. She won't be on Facebook."

"Thank Christ for small mercies." Chloe scrolled through the comments on the page as she tried to formulate a plan. Then one post caught her eye. "Oh shit. We are finished."

"What?"

"The silly bitch has gone to the Echo again. The story is going to be in on Thursday. With photos of her and the cat."

Manuel didn't speak. He walked to his locker, removed his bag and walked out of the door.

"Manuel, where are you going? I'm not finished with you yet."

He headed out of the shop and pushed through the jostling crowd whilst raking about in his bag looking for his ledger.

Manuel came home later than expected, dishevelled and distressed from his day. What he didn't need was an inquisition from his mother but knew that he couldn't avoid an onslaught from her.

"Where have you been?" said Barbara.

"Work." Manuel dropped his bag and hung his coat over the bannister.

"On the coat hooks please, you don't live in a zoo."

"The zoo? Do monkeys hang their coats up?"

"Don't cheek me Manuel, you're in enough trouble as it is. I do know that monkeys throw their muck at each other and it appears that you have been doing the same. What is that on your coat?"

"Nothing." He grabbed it off the bannister, picked up his bag and headed upstairs.

"Where do you think you are going Manuel Frost? I didn't give you permission to leave."

"I'm not one of your pupils that you can shout at. I'm a grown adult with a job. When are you going to start treating me like one?"

"When you start acting like one. I've counted the biscuits in the biscuit tin. You've been eating more than you are allowed. You know that you're only allowed one with your cup of tea."

"Is that really all you have to worry about?" Manuel was nearly at the top of the stairs.

"It barely scratches the surface young man. I haven't finished with you yet."

"Well, I'm finished with you." Manuel went into his bedroom and booted the door shut. He slumped on the bed and took out his ledger. He fought back the tears as he looked at the mess he had created.

He heard the footsteps coming up the stairs and hid the ledger under his pillow. He dried his eyes just as Barbara came barging in without knocking.

"How dare you speak to me like that?"

"You started it."

"You started it? I thought you wanted to be treated like an adult and now you behave like a five-year-old."

"I'm sick of you picking on me. Why can't you just let me live my life the way I want to?"

"Because you're doing such a good job of that," said Barbara.

"You can talk."

"Don't you dare. Look at the state of you. Lying on your bed crying like a spoilt teenager. You've got no friends apart from that, that, I can't even bring myself to say the word."

"Lesbian?"

"Don't use that filthy word in my house."

"It's a perfectly normal word, Chloe is a perfectly normal person."

"Is it any wonder you don't have a girlfriend with an attitude like that. Why would any girl want to be friends with you?"

"Chloe's my friend, she's a girl."

"I meant a real girl, not whatever it is she thinks she is."

"She is a real girl."

"You know fine well what I mean Manuel Frost, don't try and twist my words."

"Your words are twisted enough without my help," said Manuel.

"You are treading a very fine line. If you don't watch your mouth you will be out of this house. Then what will you do? Find yourself a nice wife who will let you eat as many biscuits as you like? I'm telling you now, it won't happen. Nobody will have you."

"Are you still on about the biscuits?"

"No, I'm not on about the biscuits. You are a pathetic mess Manuel Frost. You always have been and if it wasn't for me you'd be living on the streets with the druggies and the lesbians. You'd probably enjoy that."

"Lesbians don't live on the streets."

"They should, they bloody well should!" With that Barbara left the room and slammed the bedroom door behind her.

Manuel wasn't sure what he had witnessed but he was sure it was nearing the end of his relationship with his mother. He needed to get out of this house and away from her; for good. He would ask Chloe for help if he ever got out of the mess he was in. He took out his ledger and added up the columns. He was in a lot of debt and he wasn't sure how he was going to balance things out.

Would telling Chloe the truth about the ledger be enough or would he still have to do something big? Speaking to Chloe would be the first step. She would know what to do.

He realised that he was starving but there was no chance of getting his tea now. He was going to have to wait until his mother went to bed and raid the biscuit tin.

"Put these through the till for me please Stacey." Chloe handed her a basket of shopping.

Stacey started putting them through. Shepherd's Pie, veg, cream cakes, tea bags and a bottle of sherry. "Planning a cosy night in with Hannah?" She raised her eyebrows.

"Got a little errand to run first."

"Grace?"

"You noticed as well?"

"She looked a bit of a mess earlier, very unlike her. I hope she's okay."

"She's an old woman, it comes to us all."

"It's upsetting when you see someone as strong as her looking so weak though."

"I know," said Chloe, "Let's hope I can cheer her up a bit."

"Give her my love, if there's anything she wants let her know she just has to ask. I can always pop around after work or on my way in on a morning."

"I'm sure she'll appreciate the thought. You get yourself off home now, I'll lock up here."

Chloe cashed up, set the alarms and brought down the shutters before heading off to Grace's. She'd be in trouble for shutting the shop early but she wanted to catch Grace before she turned in for the night. They hadn't made much money the last few days so an extra couple of hours wasn't going to make a difference.

The protestors had already gone home or gone to the pub over the road for their tea. Their anger and sense of injustice didn't stretch to missing a meal. It was still light as she passed Indy's store and gave him a wave.

She knocked on Grace's door and noticed next door's curtains twitch almost immediately. Grace had mentioned about her nosey neighbours. Well-meaning busy bodies. God knows what they'd make of the black, pink haired, pierced young girl standing on Grace's doorstep.

Chloe heard movement inside the house and waited until Grace reached the door. She opened it. "Come in Chloe love. What brings you here?"

"You should get a chain on the door Grace, you don't know who might be on the other side."

"Don't be daft, I knew it was you." She shuffled towards the sitting room in her dressing gown and slippers.

"How did you know it would be me?" Chloe worried that Grace might be claiming to have some sort of pensioner's sixth sense.

"CCTV," she pointed at the television, "Just because I'm an old woman doesn't mean I can't use technology."

"CCTV?" said Chloe with a little bit too much fear in her voice. "Is it all around the house?"

"Yes, but to be honest it's the one at the front door I use the most, just to check who is there. Saves me getting out of the armchair if it is just a salesperson, a charity collector or the neighbourhood watch from next door."

"Yeah, I noticed them as I came up the path. Who needs CCTV when you have them on permanent watch?"

"They mean well but I prefer the CCTV, at least it is silent."

"Does it record?"

"No, just live pictures unfortunately," said Grace. "Shame as I would like to be able to see where Ruby got to last night."

"Ruby?" Chloe felt like a fraud pretending that she didn't know that Ruby was missing.

"She never came home last night, poor love. I'm worried sick."

"I'm sure she'll come back in her own time."

"Nice of you to say so Chloe but I'm not so sure. She's getting on a bit and has never been missing for so long before."

"And the CCTV doesn't give any clues."

"No, it doesn't record and the twitchers next door didn't see anything."

"That is a shame," said Chloe. She hoped the relief she felt didn't show. Despite Manuel not admitting it one hundred per cent, he was obviously the culprit and Chloe wouldn't like to have to explain it to Grace.

"I'm forgetting my manners pet. Would you like a cuppa?"

"Don't worry I'll put the kettle on. Now have you had your tea yet?"

"I had a biscuit earlier, I haven't got the appetite."

"I'm not going to lecture you Grace, you're far too long in the tooth to listen to advice from the likes of me but don't you think you should try and eat something?"

"I can't be fussed. A biscuit will do."

"If you don't eat Grace, I'm going to worry and I can't be here all the time to keep an eye on you. I'll have to get the neighbours to pop in and check on you."

Grace laughed for the first time that day. "If you put it like that, maybe I do feel a little peckish."

"Thought you might."

"Can't believe that you would resort to blackmail, you always seemed like such a nice young girl."

"You'd be surprised what I'm capable of when I'm worried about people I care about."

"That's lovely of you but you don't have to worry about me, I'm fine."

"I'm sure you are but it gives me an excuse to share a shepherd's pie with my favourite octogenarian."

"I hope that Hannah knows what a good one she has in you."

"I'll make sure to tell her if I ever see her."

"You two okay?"

"We're fine but the shifts are killing us, we're rarely in the house together for more than five minutes."

"You get the veg on. I'll make us a cuppa and you can tell me all your problems," said Grace. "It's good to talk."

Chloe hoped she was hiding her grin. Her psychology training was finally paying off, getting Grace to talk about something else so she was comfortable. They had plenty of time to discuss Grace's problems.

Grace was pleased that she had turned the conversation around. She didn't want Chloe to know how upset she was about Ruby. She was a lovely girl but the last things she wanted right now was pity.

CHAPTER THIRTEEN
Wednesday 1st June

"What am I looking at?" said Tony.

"People," said Oliver.

"I get that smart arse. Why?"

"We're going to get rich Tony."

"By watching housewives popping into the Paki shop?"

"He's not a Paki he's a … never mind, not by watching, it's all to do with what they do when they go in to the paper shop."

"Buy papers?"

"Not papers, Euromillions Tickets."

"Your plan to get rich is to win Euromillions? And I'm meant to be the thick one."

"Not win it, rob it."

"Rob Euromillions, what the hell are you on about? Have you been at my stash?"

"Look at how many people are going in. Nearly every one has bought tickets and most people have bought more than one. For some reason, there's a protest outside of Shears and nobody is going in. It'll get even busier by Friday. He'll be taking thousands, possibly tens of thousands. Old bloke on his own, he's an easy target."

"We're just going to walk in and ask him for the money?"

"Baseball bats."

"What about them?"

"Can you get hold of some?"

"Of course I can, I can't imagine you going in swinging though," said Tony.

"I don't have to, we just have to have the threat."

"I can get us guns."

"Jesus Christ, Tony. I've just got out of prison, I'm not planning on going back in."

"We'll not get caught."

"We will if we go in with guns. Let's keep it simple. Get us a couple of bats and I'll get us some masks."

"Batman and Robin? Can I be Batman?"

"I'll see what I can get hold of."

"You sure you don't want a gun?"

"I'm sure. This is an easy job, just do as you're told and we'll be rich."

"Who put you in charge?" Tony hated Oliver talking down to him.

"I did, we haven't got time to discuss it. We need to do this before Friday." Oliver didn't want a discussion because he knew that he would talk himself out of it the more he thought about it.

"Keep it simple, don't let Tony fuck it up and it'll be fine."

"Okay, keep your hair on Godfather," said Tony.

"Let me know when you have the bats. Come on, let's get away from here before someone notices us."

"How are we going to get away?"

"Walk, you only live five minutes away. I'm sure you'll get home before it rains."

"Not now man, when we do the robbery. Think we are just going to walk out of the shop and stroll down the street with our masks and baseball bats and a swag bag over our shoulders?"

"Shit, I hadn't thought of that."

"Not the criminal mastermind you thought you were, are you? Don't worry, I'm here. I'll get us a car."

"Where from?"

"Don't you worry your pretty little head about that, I'll sort us out."

"I'll see you later so we can do a bit reconnaissance." Oliver walked out already regretting how much he relied on his hapless sidekick.

The Echo had got back to Lynn quickly. Pet stories were always good for public interest and this one had two mysterious cat incidents. They were coming around this morning and whilst Lynn couldn't be bothered she decided to have a shower and tidy herself up. You never knew who would be reading the story and looking at her photo. *"That photographer was quite cute as well, he was definitely flirting with me last time."*

It was the same reporter as last time but no photographer. Lynn was disappointed.

"He only comes on certain jobs, he has his university work to do," explained Amy. "Don't worry I've got my camera so we can get a photo of you and the cat." Amy stroked Ruby as she sat on the settee next to her.

"She seems to like you," said Lynn.

"Has she got a name yet?"

"Ruby, it's on her collar."

"She had a collar?"

"Yes, why do you ask?"

"Must have been somebody's pet," said Amy.

"I guess so. They left her on my doorstep with a note, they mustn't want her anymore." Lynn kept her arms folded.

"Can I have a look at the note please?"

"There," Lynn slapped it on the arm of the settee. "They wanted me to have her."

"Do you mind if I take a photo of the letter?"

"Why?"

"It adds to the story. Plus, we might be able to track down the owner from the handwriting."

"Track down the owner? Why would you want to do that? They didn't want her."

"Nobody's saying they did. It's just a good human interest story. Someone doing a good deed for somebody they don't know. The story could run for a while, keep you in the headlines for a bit."

"Oh, I see."

That seemed to have placated her.

"We don't often get stories like this. A bit of mystery and intrigue. You never know, it might be a secret admirer."

"A secret admirer?" Lynn blushed.

"You never know, it takes all sorts."

"What do you mean?"

"Nothing, let's get a photo of you and Ruby together. Do you still have the box she came in?"

"No I threw it out straight away."

"That's a shame, would have made a better photo."

"It was covered in shit."

"I'm sorry?"

"The box. Ruby has a bit of a leaky rear end. I'm trying to train her to go in the neighbour's garden instead of in the house."

"Right, I see. Never mind, let's get the two of you together."

"Is here good?" Lynn picked up Ruby and stood in the middle of the room.

"Maybe take a few steps back so I can get you both in." Amy stepped back so she was right up against the settee. She wasn't much of a photographer but she knew that she was going to need a wide angled lens to fit someone the size of Lynn in the frame. She pretended to take a couple of photos. "Maybe we'll try for a close up now."

"Can I see them?"

"Best to wait until our photographer has had a look at them. He can work wonders with Photoshop."

"What do you mean?"

"Nothing. Was there anything else you wanted to add to the story? What would you say to Ruby's previous owner if we want to find them."

"Thank you I guess. I don't know, what if it was the shop? Trying to buy me off?"

"You think that is likely?"

"Why would the note mention not blaming them?"

"Maybe they aren't to blame."

"So you're another one of these PC do-gooders?"

"PC do-gooder?"

"Taking her side because she's a black lezza."

168

"A what?"

"Chloe from Shears; stuck up cow."

"I've met her once. She seems to be a lovely girl."

"That's the face she shows to the public. She's evil. I hope you are going to print that she's to blame."

"I'd rather just deal with the facts if it's all the same to you. Let's try and find the mystery cat donor and take it from there." She started to pack up and was eager to get out of the house.

"What if I don't want to find the previous owner?"

"Then we don't have much of a story. Woman gets new cat isn't going to sell papers. It should be in tomorrow night. I'll be in touch." With that she headed out of the house and shut the door behind her not giving Lynn the chance to follow her.

Lynn cradled Ruby in her arms. "Nobody is going to take you away from me Ruby. You're all mine now, I don't give a shiny shite what anybody else says. She can stick her Echo story up her hoop."

"We can't fuck this up," said Oliver.

"I know man, I'm not planning to fuck it up," said Tony.

"There's a lot at stake here. We need to get Dale off our back and I need to get some way of getting back in the good books with this lot." Oliver pointed to the photo pinned to his wall.

"You're not the only one with family you know?"

"That scruffy mutt doesn't count as family."

Tony covered Rizla's ears. "I'm not talking about him man, I'm talking about proper family."

"Your mother disowned you years ago when you burgled her house."

"It wasn't burglary, she owed me. I never got pocket money when I was a kid."

"And that's justification for breaking into her house?"

"Course it is. Anyway, I'm not talking about her, she's a grass, I want nothing to do with grasses."

"Who are you on about then?"

"My daughter."

"Your daughter?"

"Aye, man. What are you smirking at? Think you're the only bloke in the world ever to produce kids?"

"No but you've never mentioned her before. Where've you dreamt this daughter up from?"

"I haven't dreamt it, she's real."

"Who would be desperate enough to have a child with you?"

"It wasn't planned."

"You don't say?"

"Don't be like that, her Mam's a stunner."

"You got a stunning woman pregnant?"

"Aye, why's that so hard to believe?"

"Have you looked in the mirror?"

"That's not fair. This was over eight years ago, I was a bit of a looker myself back in the day."

"I'm sure you were. And where did you meet this stunner, Fantasy Island?"

"In town, she was on a night out with her schoolmates."

"Woah, hold it there Tony. She was a schoolgirl?"

"Nowt like that, sixth form. She was seventeen; I'm not a nonce."

"Not far off it, taking advantage of schoolgirls."

"It wasn't like that, she approached me. Asked me to buy her a drink."

"You buying a drink? That's a first."

"Like I said, she was a stunner."

"And how long did this romance last?"

"About ten minutes, took her in the back lane near the bins and did the business. She was then sick on my new trainers so I headed home on my own."

"And who said romance was dead?"

"I'm not staying with a lass who can't hold her drink."

"This family you are talking about is a daughter you've never met who is the result of a drunken knee trembler with a schoolgirl?"

"She's still my daughter."

"How do you know she's even yours. The mother doesn't seem to be the most virtuous character?"

"I saw her a few months later," said Tony, "when she was heavily pregnant. I recognised her and went to say hello."

"And she spoke to you?"

"Not as such, I asked if it was mine and she didn't say anything. If it wasn't, she would have said so."

"That's hardly conclusive proof."

"Maybe but I followed her home, found out where she lived. Told her I was going to go for access and DNA tests, the lot. Her Dad gave me five hundred quid and told me to fuck off and never bother them again. If she wasn't mine why would he pay me?"

"You sold access to your daughter for five hundred notes?"

"I was skint. Could have gone the other way, she could have taken me to the CSA and demanded money from me."

"What a charming tale. And now you want to be involved in her life?"

"If this thing comes off, I'll have the money. Her mother's with some rich bloke now; fancy car, big house the lot. Doubt I'll ever win her back but I should be able to get access to my daughter."

"Win her back? You shagged her in a back lane and dumped her."

"You know what I mean. I don't care about her, I just want to be able to see my daughter without having to hide in the bushes outside of the dance school."

"Do you realise how bad that sounds?"

"I'm well aware, Oliver. Despite what you think of me I'm not a total idiot. I've regretted taking the money ever since but I've also known that if I did get to meet her I would screw up her life. I'm a drunk, a pot head and a thief. I'm skint and I'm in and out of prison. Nobody wants a dad like that but if this robbery comes off I'll have money. I'll be able to get my own place, a car. Take her out for weekends."

"You'll be getting named Father of the year next."

"Don't take the piss Olly, you're not the only one who can dream of having a happy family." Tony grabbed Rizla's lead. "Come on Rizla, let's go somewhere where we are appreciated."

Tony returned to the bedsit with a skip in his step. For once Oliver had formulated a decent plan. This was better than shaking a bucket or pretending to be simple to earn a few quid. They were going to be rich.

First thing he would do would be to move out of here. Get a nice flat for him and Rizla, one that his daughter could visit maybe.

He browsed for estate agents on his phone. He wouldn't be greedy, he didn't need something on the seafront. Just a nice housing estate, like the one they scammed the other day, that would do. Somewhere he could be respected.

He patted the bed and Rizla jumped up beside him. "This time next week mate, we're going to be rich. Might even buy you a new collar. What do you reckon?"

He lay back on his bed, dreaming of the luxury lifestyle he was finally going to get.

A nice car would be good, he'd be able to take his daughter to dancing lessons and not be intimidated by the prick who chinned him. With money behind him he could employ some fancy solicitors to get him access to her. Not the type of solicitors he'd been used to dealing with, they were useless.

Maybe a caravan at Haggerston Castle, his daughter would love that. He went there once as a child, the only holiday he'd ever had. He hated it. None of the other children would play with him, said he stunk but his daughter wouldn't have that problem, the other kids would be queuing to play with her.

She'd like Oliver as well. He was posh, or at least he was posh compared to Tony. Things were looking up for Tony. He wasn't a bad man, he'd just been unlucky. Other people had been given things on a plate, he had to work for it.

About time he got what he was due, he was going to make sure that they couldn't fail.

He struck up a joint. "This is our time Rizla, time we got what we deserve."

"What is that smell?" said Callum.

Tony approached the table. "Hello mate, how you doing?"

"What do you want Tony?"

"What do you mean what do I want?"

"You'll be on the scrounge for something, you always are."

"I'm not, I mean I do want something but I've got money. I've been waiting for you for hours."

Tony didn't have quite as much money as he came in with but they wouldn't let him sit around waiting without buying a drink. And if you buy one drink, you might as well buy another. He was swaying a little bit.

"You with money? That's a first."

"It'll not be the last of it," said Tony, "I'm going up in the world."

"Of course you are Tony, of course you are. Now did you want something, I'm a busy man?"

"Yeah, I wondered if you could do a bit of business."

"With you?"

"Yes, with me, who else?"

"What are you selling?"

"I'm not selling," said Tony, "I'm buying."

"You're buying? You are seriously telling me that you are buying something?" A large grin set across Callum's face.

"Is my money not good enough?"

"I still don't believe that you've got any."

"I have, here." Tony went for his pocket.

"Not here, you fucking idiot." Callum's giant hand grabbed Tony by the wrist and squeezed. "You better not be fucking me about."

"I'm not, honest."

"You haven't said an honest word in your life. Go to the toilet but head upstairs, I'll be up in five."

Tony almost skipped to the back door with excitement and ran up the stairs where he ran into the bulking frame of one of Callum's doorman colleagues.

"Going somewhere?"

"Callum told me to wait for him up here, we're doing a little business."

"And he told you to tell me that, did he?"

"Not exactly, just said to wait for him."

"Then do what he says and keep your mouth shut." The doorman shook his head. "Go in there and sit down."

Tony went into the office, if you could call it that. One desk, two chairs. Paint peeling off the walls and a bare light bulb dangling from the ceiling. He sat. He could feel the damp from the walls creeping into his bones, it was freezing.

Ten minutes later Callum arrived. "Strip off."

"What?"

"Strip off, I won't tell you again."

"I'm not stripping off for you? Do you make everybody else do this?"

"No, just you Tony, we have to take precautions."

"What's that meant to mean?"

"You never have two pennies to rub together and now you want to do some business with me. I smell a rat. In fact, I smell a lot of things with you. Strip off so we know you aren't wearing a wire."

"Fucks sake man, I've worked hard for this money."

"Course you have. I haven't got all day."

Tony started stripping whilst still mumbling under his breath. He got down to his boxers. "Happy?"

"What the fuck are they?" Callum stared at Tony's shredded Superman boxers, half in amusement, half in disgust. "Never seen air conditioned boxers before. They've got more holes than a golf course. Get them off."

"Really?"

"Off."

Tony dropped his boxers to the floor and his hands went straight to cover his private parts. The cold wasn't showing them in a favourable light. He shivered.

"Lift your hands up and turn around," said Callum.

"Fucks sake." Tony did what he was told.

Callum laughed. "What a fucking state." He clipped Tony on the back of the head and pointed to the CCTV cameras that Tony hadn't noticed.

"Is there any need?" Tony had begun to blush, at least it warmed him slightly.

"Right, what can I do for you Tony?"

CHAPTER FOURTEEN
Thursday 2nd June

Manuel sat in his safe place in the storeroom, he was holding the Echo. The sweat from his palms had already soaked the edges of the paper. He could barely bring himself to read it. His hands shook as he turned the pages, the paper rattling.

Nothing on the first couple of pages, someone blaming the council for something, a few charity stories, one about somebody unhappy with the street lighting. Then there it was, as he feared. The story of Lynn was prominent on page seven and he knew that there was no chance that Grace would miss it.

Proudly holding her new cat, who was named in the story as Ruby, Lynn was the very definition of unmissable.

He dropped the paper onto the box below and brought his knees closer to his chest. This hadn't gone as planned, not that there ever was much of a plan.

He had a limited window of opportunity as he knew that Grace got the Echo each day at 6.30pm. He had to act but had no idea what he had to do. He should ask Chloe, she had offered to help after all but he didn't want to put this on her. This was his fault and he had to work out what to do next.

He wiped his hands on his trousers and took out his ledger. His head throbbed as he looked at how unbalanced the books were. They had to be balanced but this was an emergency, the books may have to get worse before they got better.

He'd been a waste of space all day at work and knew it was time to leave. He slid off the box, put on his jacket, pulled his hood up and headed to Indy's newsagents.

Lynn read her story in the Echo again as Ruby lay on the windowsill watching the passers-by. She'd returned home early as the protest petered out due to waning interest. She'd felt the tide of support slowly turning against her. She'd got a new cat and now had a second story in the Echo, some thought she was milking the attention.

Her rant against Chloe had also backfired, yes, she couldn't prove Chloe was responsible but who else could it be?

Lynn wasn't racist or homophobic, why were people saying she was? Chloe was black and a lesbian, why was she being criticised for pointing that out? This wasn't going as planned.

She scooped another handful of Quavers into her mouth and closed the Echo. She opened her laptop and checked the North-East Cat Lovers page to see if anybody had anything new to say.

They did, and none of it was very good.

The customers were streaming in and out of the newsagent all day. Indy was doing a roaring trade in lottery tickets and there was also the knock-on effect of people buying chocolate and other bits and pieces whilst they were in the shop.

Oliver and Tony had been in the car for over an hour waiting for an opportunity but it hadn't slowed down. Oliver was fighting the urge to look at the Bookies across the road. The roulette machine blinking away each time someone opened the door.

"What are we waiting for?" said Tony.

"Waiting for it to quieten down a bit, we don't want any witnesses."

"If you'd got the masks like you'd said it wouldn't matter about witnesses."

"We didn't have time and it's too risky. If I'd got the masks like I'd said they'd be able to trace them back to the shop I got them from. More witnesses. Keep it simple, you have a hood and a scarf, easy enough to hide your face."

"Why don't we do it now?"

"Less customers, less risk, is that too hard to understand?" said Oliver.

"If we wait any longer we'll have to do it tomorrow."

"I've told you, if it's like this tomorrow, it'll be a nightmare. It will be mental being the day of the draw," said Oliver.

"At least there'll be more money in the tills," said Tony.

"If there's not a gap in the customers, it doesn't matter how much is in the till, we're not going to get our hands on it."

"We'll just have to take some customers out whilst we're in there."

"We're not taking anyone out Tony. We just need to scare them."

Tony sighed. He was a coward and would flinch at the sign of a fight but he had a baseball bat and it stood to reason that the customers would be scared. He wanted to take advantage of the situation and get out his frustrations with a few meaty swings at a have-a-go hero.

"Let's give it another ten minutes and see how it goes. If there's no change we're just going to have to go for it," said Oliver. "I'd rather take the risk of being identified by a customer than spending another hour in the car with you."

Tony stroked his baseball bat in anticipation. He looked in the wing mirror at the person hurriedly walking down the street.

"Look at this queer fucker," said Tony.

"Who?" said Oliver.

"This weird paedo looking bloke."

"You're calling somebody else weird? Have you seen the clip of yourself?"

"Leave it out man, I was just saying," said Tony.

"Keep your mind on the job. Are you ready?"

"Aye man, I've been ready for ages. Let's go and do the Paki bastard."

"Cut out the racist shit man. Try and stay professional."

"Professional? We're robbing the corner shop, not Barclays."

"And that's the sort of attitude that will get us locked up," said Oliver.

"At least I'm keeping my eye on the job. That weird bloke has just gone in the paper shop. We'll have to wait."

"For fucks sake. We can't wait until the place is completely empty, there's going to be people coming and going all night. We might as well do it now."

Oliver got out of the car. "Button your coat so nobody can see the bat. If we do this properly we'll not need to use them, just need to show him the handle and let him know what's on offer. You understand me?"

Tony sulked as he got out of the passenger side.

"I'm going to smash his face in," said Tony.

"Nobody is smashing anybody's face in. Get in, scare the shit out of him and leave with the money. Let's keep it simple."

"I know, I know. I was just saying."

Indy had just hosed the front of the store again. He hadn't had a chance this morning and it was beginning to smell. The students didn't mind where they pissed on the way home from the pub.

Despite the steady stream of customers, Indy had managed to make himself a cuppa and was having a flick through the Echo. He liked to know what was going on locally so he could chat to the customers.

The newsagents had been hectic the last couple of days due to the huge Euromillions jackpot and the boycott of Shears up the road. It wasn't so much that people were boycotting it rather they couldn't be bothered pushing through the crowds. He also benefited from a lot of the protestors being overweight females who loved their chocolate and fizzy pop.

He quite liked Chloe and the rest of the staff at Shears but was happy to profit from their misfortune, you have to take it where you can get it.

It had been a long day, almost non-stop customers and possibly one of his record days in the way of takings.

He picked up the phone and dialled home. "Hello love, forget about making tea tonight. Get the family ready and we'll pop out for something to eat. It's been a good week, I think we should celebrate."

He detected the surprise in her reply. "I do spend my money occasionally," he said.

As soon as he'd cashed up and put the takings in the safe, he would head straight to the restaurant to meet them.

He went past the stories on the front page of people blaming the council for their business closing due to potholes in the road. People always wanted someone to blame.

On page seven there was a story about the cat woman who was protesting outside Chloe's store. She was a scary looking creature. "*I wouldn't know whether to fuck her or fight her.*" He thought then laughed to himself, one of the phrases he had learned from his customers.

"Hi Manuel," he said, "didn't notice you come in."

It took Manuel a few seconds before he reacted. "Hello." Putting his hood up hadn't been much of a disguise.

"You're not boycotting your own shop, are you?"

"No." Manuel walked off behind the shelving and started looking at the papers.

Indy skimmed through the copy of the Echo that he was reading, threw it onto the pile and headed out the back with his empty mug. "Back in a couple of minutes, just going to wash my mug."

Manuel stared at the pile of papers, there were far too many for him to grab and run out of the newsagents with. He needed inspiration and looked around the shop. He saw just what he needed.

Matches.

Manuel checked that Indy wasn't coming back and nipped behind the counter grabbing a box of matches. If he just burnt the Echos it wouldn't be too bad surely, a three at most in the ledger.

His hands lingered above the papers willing himself to strike the match and solve his problems. This was crazy, what if something else caught fire? What if he ruined the shop? He would need a whole new ledger for the damage he had caused.

He peered over his shoulder, worried that Indy would return and catch him in the act. He had to make a decision and make it quickly.

Then he noticed the hose.

Shoving the matches in the pocket of the jacket, Manuel dragged the hose from behind the counter and turned the tap on full. A jet of water sprayed out straight onto the pile of Echos. *"Perfect,"* he thought.

Manuel left the newsagents without buying anything.

Oliver and Tony leaned against the car opposite the shop. "Paedo Pete is on the move again, where's he off to? He's one weird little fucker," said Tony.

"Who cares about him? Keep an eye on the newsagent and what's going on. We need be in and out of there as quickly as possible," said Oliver. "Come on let's go and get a closer look."

They walked across the road and into the store, stepping over the hose without glancing at it.

Indy walked back in from the back of the shop and didn't notice the hose at first, just the two suspicious looking blokes with their hoods up. He watched them out of the corner of his eye and kept glancing at the CCTV screen. He hadn't seen them steal anything but they didn't appear to be in a hurry to purchase anything either.

He decided to approach them. He stepped out from behind the counter, watching them all the time. With his eyes on Oliver and Tony, he didn't notice the hose until he felt the dampness in his shoe. He glanced at the stream of water and it took a moment to register what was happening.

He raced to turn off the tap but it was too late to save the newspapers and he went out the back to grab a mop.

As Indy was gone, the pool of water spread under the shelving, the flood inevitably connecting with the exposed electrics.

A fizz, then a bang, the result was catastrophic. The sparks caught on with the unsold copies of The Sun and within seconds the whole shelf was alight.

"Shit, what's that?" said Oliver.

"The bloody place is on fire, let's get out of here," said Tony as he hurried to the door.

"The owner's still in there. We're going to have to help."

"That Paki isn't our problem. Let's get out of here."

"Shut it, you racist shit, the bloke could die."

"Not our problem. What's the police going to say when you say you just happened to be loitering in the shop with another well-known criminal?"

Oliver went for the door that Indy had gone through but Tony grabbed his arm. "Look he'll be fine, Paedo Pete is on the case. Put your toe down and get us out of here before the police arrive."

Tony was right for once, they couldn't hang around.

Manuel had been resting on the wall near their car filling in his ledger. Trying to decide how big of a bad deed the flooding was. He thought it was quite high before. Now it was off the scale. He shoved the book in his pocket and ran across the road.

Despite the need to get away, Oliver hesitated. They were here for a reason.

"Grab the money," said Oliver.

Tony jumped over the counter and started pressing buttons on the till. Nothing happened. "It's stuck."

"What do you mean, it's stuck?"

"It won't open, it's locked."

"Take the whole bloody thing, we'll smash it open at home."

Tony tried to get hold of the till but it was partly enclosed in a custom-built compartment in the counter. "I can't get hold of it."

"You're fucking useless, can you not do anything right?" Oliver pushed Tony out of the way and tried to drag the till out himself but he couldn't get a grip. "Sod it, let's go." He bashed his fist on the buttons and dragged Tony out of the door.

As Oliver got to the door he heard the till ping open, he turned towards it but Indy was racing in from the back of the store.

Oliver cut his losses and ran to the car, Tony trailed behind him passing Manuel on the way.

Indy had just come into the shop and spotted the flames. He ran for the hose but Manuel manhandled him away from it. Using strength he didn't realise he possessed. "Leave it, it's too big. You'll not stop it with the hose."

"I have to. It's my shop, my family's shop. It's all I have."

"You can't, you need to get out." Even in the extreme circumstances Manuel felt for the ledger in his pocket. He needed to fill it in.

"I have to save the shop."

The enormity of what Manuel had done hit him. He started to hyperventilate. He crouched by the counter and started to cry with his head in his hands. How was he going to get the books to balance now?

Indy stood with one hand on the hose and looked at Manuel. It was one thing to risk his own life for the Newsagents but he couldn't risk anybody else. He grabbed Manuel by the arm. "You win. Let's get out of here." He dragged Manuel out of the store and dialled 999 from his mobile. They sat on the wall waiting for the fire brigade.

Indy looked at his former shop then up the street where the crowd of protestors had been earlier in the day. "Guess the fatties are going to have to break their boycott as all my chocolate will be melted now." The tears running down his cheeks betrayed the brave face he was trying to put on.

Manuel sat on his hands, desperately trying to stop himself from taking out the ledger.

"What the hell happened there?" said Oliver as he flung the car around the corner.

"I don't know, the place just went up in flames."

"What did you do?"

"Nothing, why does it always have to be my fault?"

"Well, something happened and it wasn't me."

"Why would I start a fire, we were just about to rob the Paki twat?"

"Because of your stupid racist nonsense. Who knows what you are capable of?"

"It wasn't me." Tony stared out the window. Sirens could be heard in the distance, fire or police, it didn't matter they were out of the way now.

"Whoever it was, we've left empty handed. We need to find another way of making some money and we need to find it fast." Oliver smacked his hand on the steering wheel.

"We'll think of something, we always do," said Tony.

"We always do? When have you ever come up with an idea? You're nothing but a liability."

"And you're nothing but a posh gobshite who can't properly plan to rob someone from a Third World country."

Oliver slammed on the brakes and pulled up to the kerb. "Get out."

"What do you mean get out?"

"I've had enough of you, get out."

"Ha'way man, can you not drop me at the door? We're miles away."

"We're in a stolen car you simpleton, do you really want to be seen getting out of it outside your front door?"

"Why do you get to decide, it's not your car."

"It's not yours either. Get out and shut up, I need time to think. I'll call you tomorrow."

Tony got out, slamming the door behind him. "Dickhead."

The door was barely shut before Oliver had sped off down the road.

"Tell us what you saw, from the beginning." WPC Cummins had her notebook out and was on the wall alongside Manuel.

"I didn't see a great deal, I just popped into the shop. Spoke to Indy briefly. Next thing I knew the place was on fire and Indy was dragging me out."

"Was there anybody else in the shop when you were there?"

"Anybody else?"

"Any other customers?"

"Err, yeah a couple of people."

"Can you describe them?"

"Not really, no."

"Male? Female?"

"Male, both of them."

"White? Black? Asian?"

"White, or at least I think so. They had hoods up."

"Okay, tall or short? Fat or thin?"

"One of each."

"What do you mean, there were only two of them."

"Sorry, one tall, one short. Short one was skinny, tall one was just sort of normal." Manuel wasn't very good at lying. He knew this and decided to tell the truth about the two blokes he had seen earlier. At least he might then sound convincing. He was confident that they hadn't seen him with the hose.

"That's good, Manuel. Is there anything else you can tell us? Did they say anything?"

"Say anything? I'm not sure, I wasn't watching them, I was just looking at the magazines."

"Which ones?"

"Which what?"

"Magazines, which magazines were you looking at?"

"I can't remember."

"Top shelf eh? Don't worry, your secret is safe with me."

Manuel had been caught in a lie but seemed to have got away with it. He blushed as he mumbled. "Don't know."

"Don't worry, it's not important," said WPC Cummins. "You work in Shears up the road, don't you?"

"Yes."

185

"You've been having a bit trouble with protestors recently. What do you know about that?"

"Nothing."

"Nothing? They've been outside the shop for two days; did you not ask what it's about?"

"I mean not much. It's something to do with a cat."

"Do you think they could have had anything to do with it?"

"To do with what?"

"The fire?"

"Oh, that? I don't know, I'm not sure what they are unhappy about. They just seem to shout and eat a lot. It's mainly women, big ones. I don't think I'd have missed them if they'd been in the newsagent."

"Ha ha. Okay. Seems a bit strange having the protests and a fire within a few hundred yards of each other. We'll need to look into it further."

"I'm sure they aren't connected," said Manuel.

"Thanks for the tip but you can leave the detective work to us."

"Sorry."

"Don't worry about it. Was there anything else you wanted to tell us?"

"What do you mean?"

"About the fire?"

"I don't know. I don't know what happened."

"Do you know Indy well?"

"He's friendly. He always says hello. I don't know him well. I don't think I know anybody well."

"Do you think it could have been a racist attack?"

"Racist? I'm not racist."

"No, I'm not saying you are. The two men you saw, was there anything distinctive about them? There's a lot of unpleasant people around here who dislike Muslims. Maybe that was why they attacked the shop."

Manuel should have stayed quiet but couldn't help himself. "EDL."

"EDL?"

"The small skinny one, he was wearing an English Defence League hoody under his denim jacket." He had now perfectly described two men who just happened to be in the shop earlier. Two men who were now in the frame for a fire he caused.

"That's really useful, Manuel. See you did see more than you thought." She called PC Sugden over. "Looks like it could be a racist attack. We've got a good description thanks to Manuel here."

PC Sugden patted him on the back. "Thanks Manuel. Could be vital as there's no way the CCTV survived that inferno. I hate these racist bastards. Don't worry, we'll get them, they are usually too stupid to stay quiet for long. Probably bragging about it on Facebook as we speak."

"You think?" Manuel was too far into the lie now and just had to play along.

"We'll catch them. Don't get upset about. The sort of person who would do something like this isn't wired up right. They always trip themselves up eventually."

Manuel slid off the wall and returned home with PC Sugden's words going around and around in his head. *They will always trip themselves up eventually.*

Grace turned the corner and saw the blue flashing lights of the fire engines.

"Indy!"

Grace was shocked when she saw the state of Indy's shop. It was cordoned off and she couldn't get close enough to see but it looked totally burnt out.

Indy had just finished talking to the police and spotted Grace at the cordon. He went over to speak to her.

"What happened? Are you okay?" said Grace.

"Never mind the store, how are you Grace? I heard about your cat. Any news?"

"Nothing yet, Indy. She was getting on, a bit like me. She's probably just crawled somewhere quiet to die."

"Don't say that love, I'm sure she'll turn up."

"Nice of you to be optimistic Indy but it looks like you have your own problems."

"Nothing a full rebuild won't sort out. At least nobody was hurt."

"As long as you're alright."

"I'm fine. Sorry it looks like you're going to have to do without an Echo tonight. I asked Chloe to keep one back for you but they'd already sold out."

"My routine's all to pot anyway. I'm sure I'll cope but it was lovely of you to think of me in the middle of all this."

"You're my most loyal customer Grace, I'll need to win you back once the shop is rebuilt." He winked at her.

"Look after yourself, Indy." She took his hand in hers and squeezed it. "Don't let the bastards grind you down." She winked back.

Grace headed for home, her routine well and truly disrupted. Without an Echo, she would have to revert to reading one of her Agatha Christie books.

Tony hadn't stayed at home long and was back at Oliver's bedsit.

"That was an unmitigated fucking disaster." Oliver sat on his bed, his back against the headboard.

"What does unmitigated mean?" said Tony.

"It means we're fucked." Oliver's head was in his hands. "Shit, shit, shit." He stared at the safe in the corner.

"We just need another plan," said Tony who was sat on the floor.

"Another plan? We just managed to stumble across this one. What do you think our chances of finding another opportunity like this at short notice? That's it, we're dead men walking."

"Maybe we can reason with Dale. Get an extension on the loan."

"Is that the best you can come up with?"

"You never know, if we tell them we have a plan."

"But we don't. And even if we did, we wouldn't want them fuckers knowing anything about it. If we'd told them about the newsagent they would have done it themselves or at least taken fifty percent of what we made."

"Which was nothing."

"I'm well aware of that, idiot." Oliver threw a pillow at Tony, wishing he had something heavier to hand.

Tony picked up the pillow and sat on it. "Thanks."

"Give me that back."

"Aw man, I'll get piles sitting here."

"I don't give a shit, I don't even know what you are doing here."

"We're thinking of a new plan."

"And you're doing a great job of that, aren't you?"

"Says you, the criminal mastermind."

"Don't start Tony or you'll go out of that bloody window."

"You're a hard man now, are you? You're not the boss of me."

"Somebody needs to be because you can't look after yourself. Look at the clip of you."

"What's the matter with me, man? These are my best jeans."

"And they haven't seen the inside of a washing machine since you stole them from Asda."

"I'm wearing them in."

"You stink like that scruffy mongrel of yours."

"That's another thing, why won't you let him in here. He's one of the gang."

"The gang? Is that what you think this is?"

"We need a name. Most good gangs have names."

"We're not a gang," said Oliver.

"We would be if we had a name."

"For Christ's sake, do you have any idea how much trouble we are in?"

"I'm trying not to think about it."

"One of us has to. Those gangsters aren't going to leave us alone. We need a plan."

"I need a beer."

"Is that all you can think about at a time like this?"

189

"I think better when I've had a couple of cans," said Tony.

"And where do you think the money for cans is coming from?"

"We could nick some."

"Is this what we have come to? From an armed robbery that was going to set us up for life to nicking a few cans?"

"Have you got any better ideas?"

Oliver shook his head. "Go and nick some cans if you want, it'll give me some peace and quiet and some time to think."

"Where should I go?"

"What?"

"To get the cans."

"Do I have to think of everything for you? Does it matter?"

"Dunno, depends on what cans you want."

"I don't care, I just want you and your smell out of here."

"I was only asking, there's no need to be rude."

"Tony sooner or later you are going to have to take the hint. People don't like you, you smell, you're pissed or stoned most of the time. You're thick as pig shit and you haven't said an interesting word since the day I met you."

"And I'm the only friend you've got, what does that say about you?" Tony threw the pillow at Oliver. "I'll be at Shears if you need me."

Oliver pushed the pillow into his face, trying to hide his tears. He heard the door slam downstairs as Tony set off on his shoplifting mission.

He looked at the picture of his family on the sideboard and resigned himself to the fact that he was never going to see them again.

"Shears!"

He leapt off the bed and grabbed his jacket. He ran down the stairs and out of the door. "Tony, hold on, I've got an idea."

Oliver was out of breath when he caught up with Tony. "Hold on mate, I've got a new plan."

"I've got a plan as well, I'm going to get some cans. And I'm not your mate." He tugged at Rizla's lead and sped up.

"That's it, the cans, Shears," said Oliver.

"That's your new masterplan? Steal some cans? And I thought my plans were shit." Tony didn't slow down and didn't look Oliver in the face.

"No, wait Tony. Just listen to me for five minutes." He grabbed him by the arm.

Tony tried to shrug him off. "I'm not interested."

"You will be if you listen to me. Are you that desperate for a drink that you can't listen for five minutes. I can tell you as we're walking along."

"Guess I've got no choice."

"We'll rob Shears instead."

"That's it? Have you forgotten that it's been boycotted for the last two days? They'll have no money."

"They were boycotted but now the newsagents has burnt down, where are people going to go? Their turnover is going to double overnight and they also sell lottery tickets. This is going to be even bigger than we thought."

Tony stopped walking. "You reckon?"

"Think about it. The newsagent was doing a roaring trade but is now shut. Everyone who has avoided Shears will be going back to stock up."

"I guess I've heard worse plans."

"It's perfect. Why don't we test the security by nicking some cans then we can stake the place out and do it tomorrow?"

"No harm in giving it a look I suppose," said Tony.

"Told you I'd come up with something good."

"You think it will work?"

"I know it will."

Buoyed by their new plan, Oliver and Tony headed to Shears. "What do you want?" said Tony.

"Stella, whatever. Remember we're just testing the security."

"I have done this before."

"I'm sure you have but don't do anything stupid, we don't want to ruin our plans."

"I'm an old hand at this."

"And how many times have you been inside?"

"Okay man, this is just nicking a few beers. You go in first and distract them." Tony tied the dog to the fence as Oliver went into Shears.

He needn't have worried about distracting the staff as there was already a massive queue at the tills. All the tills were busy and the only other member of staff was the weird bloke they'd seen earlier who seemed to be stocking the shelves. A good sign. He picked up a basket and walked up and down the aisles.

A couple of security cameras were pointing towards the aisles but importantly none seemed to be pointing towards the office at the back. The door was ajar and there didn't appear to be anybody in. He was tempted to go for a look around but didn't want to push his luck.

He joined the queue for the tills and saw Tony come through the door. He tried not to make eye contact. As he got to the front of the queue there was a young girl on the till.

"You're busy today," said Oliver.

"Yeah, it's gone mental since the newsagents burnt down earlier."

"Burnt down?"

"Yeah, real shame, Indy is a lovely bloke."

"But good for you I suppose, the extra business?" He realised that he was talking too much and shut up.

"Just means more work, probably have to work double shifts. It's extra money I guess."

Oliver handed over the money for a Mars Bar. "I'll not keep you then, the queue is building. See you later."

"Bye."

He left the shop and waited on the wall on the other side of the road. Tony followed later with eight cans of Stella.

"How did you manage that?" said Oliver.

"They were too busy, nobody was watching so I just walked out with them."

"What if you'd been caught?"

"But I wasn't. I guess you won't be wanting to drink one then?"

"Give me one here." Oliver took a can from Tony and cracked it open. "There's one or two cameras in there but nothing for us to worry about."

"Absolutely zero security. Just the paedo bloke stacking shelves, a young lad and two lasses. Don't know why we didn't think of doing this place first," said Tony.

Oliver took a long swig from his can. "This could be it Tony."

Oliver and Tony drank their way through the cans whilst sat on the wall watching the customers coming and going.

Traffic ebbed and flowed, there was a steady stream of people going about their daily business. Nobody took any notice of them, they might as well have been invisible.

"How much do you reckon we will make?" said Tony.

"Enough. This is going to be the easiest job you've ever done."

The closed sign went up in the shop and the last customers filed out. The girl and the young lad from the tills left leaving just the weirdo and the girl with the pink hair.

Half an hour later they left as well.

"Interesting," said Oliver.

"What is?"

"No money bags, they're not depositing the takings at the bank. Must be keeping it in a safe."

"Would have been easier to rob them on the street."

"Yeah but more chance of witnesses and have-a-go heroes. If we do it in the shop there will just be us and them. Easy money."

"I'm going to give that paedo a kicking as well."

"We're not giving anyone a kicking. Get in, get the money, get out. Keep it simple. Come on, we've seen enough." Oliver stood up and realised that he had a bit of a wobble on after four cans of Stella. He also realised that he needed the toilet quite desperately. "Keep an eye out, I need to go for a piss in the back lane."

"I need one as well."

"You'll have to wait. You can go when I'm finished, just make sure that nobody is coming."

Oliver jogged around to the back lane and hid behind a wheelie bin as he relieved himself. The relief was immense. He stared at the sky as he enjoyed the moment. He then sensed somebody beside him.

"Tony, what the fuck are you doing? You were meant to be keeping an eye out."

"I was busting man, I couldn't wait." He started pissing up the wall, splashing everywhere.

"Could you not have gone downstream?"

"I didn't want to get your piss on my shoes."

"And I want yours on mine?"

As they were arguing neither of them saw the police car pull up at the end of the lane.

"Ah shit." Oliver noticed. "You fucking idiot."

A policeman got out of the car and started heading up the lane towards them.

"They weren't there when I came around."

"Obviously. Just zip yourself up and leave the talking to me. I'll say we have a medical problem."

"Both of us?"

"We'll say we've just come from the hospital, I'll think of something." Oliver fastened his trousers.

"I can't stop pissing."

"You're going to have to."

"It's not something I can do on command."

"Tie a knot in it then."

Oliver faced the officer. Just then his radio came to life. The police officer spoke into it and he turned back to Oliver. "Next time you two, I never forget a face." He then ran back to the car and jumped in. The lights were flashing and the siren was blaring before he'd closed the door.

"It's shit like this that will get us into trouble. Why can't you follow a simple instruction and do as you are told?"

"If you could hold your beer you wouldn't be pissing in a back lane."

"Just go home Tony. Stay off the beer tomorrow, we need to be at our best."

194

"Not even a couple to calm the nerves?"

"No, and none of your whacky baccy either. This is our one big chance, we cannot fuck it up."

Chloe got home and put the kettle on. It had been a tough day. For once her and Hannah's shifts had aligned and it wasn't long before Hannah came through the door.

"Hi, love," said Hannah.

"Hi, do you want a cuppa?"

"Love one." Hannah came into the kitchen, slipped her arms around Chloe's waist and kissed her on the neck. "Good day?"

"Not really."

"You want to talk about it?"

"Not really." She didn't mean to be short with Hannah but she was tired, pissed off with Lynn and her gang of cat cretins, upset about Indy and his store and suspicious about whatever the hell it was Manuel was up to. When she thought about it like that, it had been quite the day. She handed the cuppa to Hannah. "Sorry, it's been one of those days. How about you?"

"Death and destruction, the usual for a day in A&E."

Chloe didn't know if Hannah was having a dig. She knew her job was more stressful. People dying on you every day can't be nice but this week had been a bad one for Chloe by anyone's standards.

"Are we still going out for something to eat like we planned?" said Hannah.

"No sorry, do you mind if I take a rain check? I don't feel up to it after the day I've had."

"Okay. You fancy just getting a takeaway and a bottle of wine and relaxing in front of the telly for a change?"

"No, I've got work to do. I'll throw a pizza in the oven."

"It's okay to take a night off from your studies once in a while you know."

"It's not. I need to get this right or I'll be working in that bloody store for the rest of my life."

"I thought you liked Shears?"

195

"I do but sometimes it just gets under my skin. The customers, the staff, they don't know what I have to go through to keep them in a job."

"I'm sure they appreciate you," said Hannah.

"It certainly doesn't feel like it today." Chloe walked past Hannah and took a pizza from the freezer. "Spinach and ricotta?"

"Yeah, whatever." Hannah grabbed a bottle of wine and wandered off into the sitting room.

Chloe put the pizza in the oven, got her text books out and sat at the kitchen table.

CHAPTER FIFTEEN
Friday 3rd June

Manuel followed his usual routine getting ready for work. He dressed the same, his breakfast was the same, his interaction with his mother was the same but today was different. Today he didn't feel well. The fire made him feel sick. It was an accident but nobody would believe him.

"Why does it always happen to me?"

He forced his breakfast down and cleared away his dishes as normal.

He got on the bus and took his seat. He had an urge to take his ledger out of his bag but it would make him feel ill. He knew what was in it, every word in every column. It didn't make for pleasant reading.

The bus passed Lynn's house and her relatively neat garden. It seemed like a lifetime since he poisoned the cat. Was it really less than a week ago?

He got off the bus and walked to work trying not to look at the destroyed newsagents. He stared at the cracks in the pavement instead and quickened his pace.

"Manuel?"

He looked up, it was Indy.

"Hello Indy, how are you?"

"Apart from my business being ruined and my life being in tatters, pretty well. How about you?"

The colour had drained from Manuel's face. "Err, um, I'm sorry."

"Don't be sorry son, it's not your fault. Life goes on and I'm insured. We'll get this place back up and running in no time."

"Got to go, I'm late for work."

"Maybe I'll pop in and see you later."

"Pop in and see me?"

"Think I could do with buying one of those Euromillions tickets everybody is getting excited about."

"Oh I see."

"Don't think I've even said thanks for yesterday Manuel; remember there'll always be a job for you here if you ever decide to jump ship."

Manuel felt the sick rising in his throat and swallowed it back down. His mother had always blamed him for everything but now he had something to feel guilty about. He didn't like it. He wasn't sure how he would get through the day.

Chloe was already hard at work when he got the store. "Morning, Manuel. We've got a busy day ahead of us." She barely looked up from the laptop screen.

"Morning." He walked straight through to the storeroom and put his coat and bag in the locker.

"You making a cuppa Manuel? You couldn't make me one please? I haven't had a chance yet."

"Yes." He went through the motions of making the drinks without even thinking. He took Chloe's mug out to her.

"Thanks, you're a lifesaver. Err, have you forgotten something?" She handed the mug back to Manuel.

He looked at the mug and back to her. "What?"

"Milk? Don't worry I'll get it myself."

"No sorry, I'll get it." He made a grab for the mug but only succeeded in spilling the tea all over the desk.

"You're not with it today, are you?" said Chloe.

"Sorry, I'll clean it up." He headed back to the storeroom to get some paper towels. He realised that his hands were shaking. He took some deep breaths and went back into the office.

He left his cuppa and after cleaning the mess he started stacking the shelves. He hadn't even noticed the shop had opened until he tripped up a customer whilst he was knelt stacking the bottom shelf with bags of rice.

"Sorry," said Manuel as he blushed.

"Don't worry son, no harm done. Maybe you should be wearing one of these." The builder pointed to his Hi-Viz jacket.

"Manuel, bread delivery at the back door," shouted Chloe.

He went out the back where the truck driver was waiting. "Morning, son. Looks like you have a busy day ahead with Indy's place burning down. Decent bloke is Indy."

Manuel didn't answer and grabbed hold of the first crate of bread dumping it on the floor of the storeroom. He dealt with the other crates quickly and threw the empty crates from yesterday on the back of the truck.

"You're like a machine today Manuel." The driver gave him a delivery note to sign, jumped back in the truck and drove off. Another delivery truck arrived.

Manuel helped unload that with the same efficiency.

"Hold on, we've forgotten one," said the driver. He handed Manuel a tray of Baked Beans and without thinking he dumped it on top of the bread.

"Err, do you think that's wise Manuel?"

"Christ." He picked up the tray but the bread was already flattened.

"Good luck explaining that one to Chloe."

Manuel signed the delivery note then went about stacking the shelves again.

"What's happened to the bread?" It hadn't taken long for Chloe to notice. "Did you sign for it in this state?"

He considered lying but realised that it wouldn't help. "It was okay when it turned up. It was my fault."

"You're a mess today Manuel. The fire must have affected you more than I thought. Get yourself away home until you get your head right."

"I'm okay, we're really busy."

"It's my fault Manuel, I should have noticed. The important thing is that you look after yourself. The shop will survive without you for a day."

"I don't mind, honest."

"I'm not asking you Manuel, I'm telling you. We can't have you making mistakes all over the place. Go home and don't come back until you feel better."

He trudged into the storeroom and collected his coat and bag. He left without saying goodbye to anyone. He wasn't sure where he was going but he wasn't going home. His Mam would know and he couldn't be bothered with the questioning.

He walked around to the park and sat on a bench, removing his ledger from his bag. His mistakes today didn't even warrant noting.

Yesterday's did; it was staring back at him in red. Just one word, in capitals. FIRE.

Lynn read her story in the Echo again, then the comments on Facebook. Her fifteen minutes of fame were nearly up and she'd almost made herself more unpopular than she was before the whole saga started.

She knew that she had to return to work. Being on the sick and appearing in the Echo weren't compatible and she was on her last warning. She had told Jeff to stick his job but she seemed to have got away with it. As much as she hated it, she needed the job. She said goodbye to Ruby and squeezed into the car.

A couple of days without using the car and the battery was flat yet again. *Christ's sake.* She headed for the bus.

She was in luck when the bus pulled in as there was a double seat spare. She knew that she would get the seat to herself for the rest of the journey. The odd brave soul would perch themselves on the end but most of the time nobody wanted to squeeze on next to the fat lass.

There was the occasional dilemma where an aisle seat was free but she struggled to get any more than one cheek on with the window passenger squashed against it in horror.

Then there was the nightmare scenario of having to stand and running the risk of someone offering their seat assuming that she must be heavily pregnant.

She hated public transport.

She put her headphones in and listened to Take That whilst reading the latest in the Fifty Shades series.

Bus trip over she took the five-minute walk to work, silently cursing the runners and cyclists who sped past her on the way to the office.

Without waiting to be asked Frank opened the wheelchair access gate to save her the embarrassment of trying to squeeze through the turnstile. She waited for the lift to take her up the one flight then wandered towards her desk.

Lynn's team barely acknowledged her as she came in, all of them discussing a night out she hadn't been invited to. The cans of Red Bull and bacon sandwiches indicated that it must have been a good one.

On arriving at her desk, she noticed various photocopies of her Echo story pinned up. Each one Photoshopped to show the cat replaced with various items. A Greggs bag, a cake, a pie and worst of all, a giant dildo.

She tore them down, ignoring the muffled sniggers from her team.

They were nothing but a bunch of bitches, she decided not to care anymore about what they thought, if she ever did in the first place.

She caught up on some emails including one from Jeff asking to discuss her absence record. She knew that she was coming to the end of her career and logged into the phones to speak to customers who hated her almost as much as her team did.

The smell of the Red Bull and bacon was making her feel nauseous.

"Why are we here so early?" Tony sat in the passenger seat and fidgeted with the glove box.

"Leave that." Oliver slapped his hand. "We're doing some early recon so there won't be any slip ups later."

"Why would there be any slip ups?"

"You can't remember as far back as yesterday then?"

"That wasn't our fault," said Tony.

"Our fault or not, we can't take any chances. Keep your eye out for anything unusual."

"I'm hungry."

"Are you five-years old? You've just had your breakfast."

"It was only toast."

"And we're only going to be here an hour. Pipe down and do as you're told."

Tony slumped in his seat and stared out of the window.

They'd been there nearly forty-five minutes when they saw the first thing of note.

"Look," said Tony, "There's that funny paedo bloke again."

"Where's he off to?"

"Looks like he's heading home for the day."

"He's barely been in an hour."

"Look at the state of him, he's white as a sheet. Doesn't look well at all."

"All the better for us," said Oliver, "one less person to worry about."

"I was looking forward to giving him a clip."

"The only person getting a clip will be you. I told you there was a good reason for arriving early. Its shit like this that we need to know."

"Now that we've seen it, any chance I go home and get some bait. I want to get some kip before we rob the place."

"Have you got nothing better to do with your time other than eat and sleep."

"You've told me I can't drink or smoke, what else is there?"

Oliver didn't bother arguing, started the car and dropped Tony off at home.

He arrived back at the bedsit and stared at the picture of his family again.

"This time I'll get it right and I'll win them back."

He set his alarm and lay back on his bed. Might as well get some sleep as well, what else was there to do?

Barbara was writing on the whiteboard as there was a splat just above her right shoulder. She looked up just as something whizzed past her left ear. Paper pellets covered in saliva and fired from the barrel of a biro. Kids had been doing this since she was at school, would they not think of anything new?

"Who was that?"

The whole class kept their heads down trying to stifle their laughs.

"I'm not going to ask again."

Another pellet shot by and hit the board behind her.

"I saw that, it was you, wasn't it?" She wasn't sure where it had come from but she picked on the most likely suspect.

He held his hands up with a big smile on his face, "Wasn't me, Miss."

Yet another pellet hit the board.

"Who was that?" She darted over the other side of the class. Everyone was laughing now. She could feel her blood pressure rising. "Was it you?" Another likely culprit.

"Was what me? Dunno what you're talking about."

Out of the corner of the eye she noticed one of the girls filming on her phone. "Give me that." She snatched at it but the girl was too quick. Barbara wasn't to be beaten and she attempted to wrestle it from the girl's grip.

A chair went over, the girl did too. Barbara found herself lying on the floor with the phone in her hand. She stood up and threw it off the wall just as the Headmaster entered the room.

"Miss Frost, could I have a word please?"

The class cheered but were silenced by a stare from the Headmaster.

She waited in the office. She knew what was coming.

"Barbara, you've had a long and distinguished career at this school. I know we haven't always seen eye to eye but I do respect you."

"Can you get to the point?"

"Yes. Certainly. I think we can both agree that things have possibly been getting a little too much for you recently."

"What do you mean?"

"The incident in the classroom just then being a perfect example."

"Mobile phones aren't allowed in class."

"Understood, however we have a duty to act more professionally than our pupils. Wrestling a teenage girl and smashing her property falls well below the standards I would expect, wouldn't you agree?"

"They were firing pellets."

"Nobody disputes that is a difficult job, Barbara."

"Miss Frost."

"Pardon."

"My name is Miss Frost."

"As you please. Miss Frost, your behaviour today and indeed for the past few months is not what myself nor the governors expect from our senior teachers. I've had several complaints and I don't want to take the disciplinary route."

"Get to the point."

"Have you ever considered early retirement?"

"Have you?"

"Every day Bar … sorry Miss Frost, every day."

"Well I haven't, no."

"It was more of a rhetorical question. I am asking you to retire with a bit of dignity. You can leave with your head held high and your pension intact."

"And keep your school out of the headlines?"

"That as well, it's for the best."

"For you maybe."

"For everyone concerned."

Barbara headed for the door. "I guess there's nothing more to discuss then."

Barbara was relieved to close the door of her Ford Fiesta and close herself off from the rest of the world. Teachers, pupils, Headmaster, she hated them all. The feeling was mutual.

She knew her time was up. Retirement was around the corner, then what? Manuel no longer respected her, if he ever had and she had no friends to speak of.

She had the church but she wasn't convinced that Father Russell took her as seriously as he should.

A slap on the back window woke her from her thoughts. A group of pupils wandered off laughing. She could get out of the car. Shout at them, demand to know who it was but she knew there was no point. She would just look foolish.

She started the car and left the car park for the last time.

Barbara drove around aimlessly, she didn't want to go home straight away, she had to clear her head. She was angry, she was hurt, she was humiliated. How was she going to tell Manuel that she had lost her job? He was the irresponsible one. How was this setting a good example?

Instead of driving straight home she took a detour and pulled into the church car park. The large wooden door creaked open and she wondered about the security of the church's open door policy. You never knew what type of people would come through the door, stealing, defecating and performing God knows what other ungodly acts under the eyes of the Lord.

As it happened the church was quiet. One woman lighting a candle, two other elderly women kneeling in prayer. *"Have they nothing better to do with their time?"* she thought.

She dipped her fingers in the holy water and did the sign of the cross then headed down the centre aisle before genuflecting and sliding onto the bench three from the front.

She stared at the giant crucifix looking for inspiration.

Nothing.

She knelt, joining her hands in prayer and closed her eyes. The events of today, the last few weeks, her whole life went through her mind. She tried to summon up a prayer, something that would help her make sense of what was happening.

"This is nonsense."

She marched down the aisle, not genuflecting as she left, her heels clacking on the stone floor whilst the other three women in the church glared at her. She ignored the font of holy water and yanked the door shut on the way out.

She went around the side of the church, through the tidy garden and up to the door of the rectory. She rang the doorbell and knocked heavily until it was answered.

The housekeeper knocked gently on the bedroom door, not wanting to open it. "Barbara Frost is at the door."

"Again," said Father Russell, "what does she want now?"

"She wouldn't say. Just that she wanted to see you and she wasn't leaving until she did."

Father Russell was having his 'afternoon nap' and the housekeeper knew not to disturb him unless it was urgent. The thought of Barbara Frost had put him off the task in hand anyway and he closed his laptop screen. Hopefully she'd managed to get those websites that Manuel had been visiting.

"I'll be down in a minute. Don't offer her a cup of tea, I don't want her hanging around for ever."

He got dressed, put on his dog collar, the priestly one, not the one he wore in his own time, made a mental note to clean up the used tissues before the housekeeper saw them and headed downstairs.

"Afternoon Babs, what can I do for you?"

"Babs?" She glared at him.

"Sorry, Miss Frost, not sure where that came from, still a little drowsy from my nap." He knew exactly where it came from, the film Babs Massive Wabs that he had just been watching. He thought it best not to share.

"I need to talk to you, Father."

"I'm here Miss Frost, what is troubling you?"

"I think I am losing my faith."

Father Russell paused. This statement was one of the first ones they learned to deal with in priest training college. He'd dealt with it many times over the years. God moves in mysterious ways. Get your reward in heaven, all that nonsense. Anything to keep the person onside. If that wasn't working, go down the Doubting Thomas route, put some Catholic guilt on them. It always seemed to work.

Over the years, Father Russell had learned that not everyone was worth saving. The matriarch of a large family who attended every week and generously filled the collection plate, then you would pull out all the stops. Someone who was high maintenance and donated very little, then you may not try quite so hard.

Barbara Frost fell into the latter category. It wouldn't be the worst day in the church's history if she didn't return.

He still had to go through the motions. "And why do you think that is Barbara? You don't mind me calling you Barbara, do you?"

She did mind but decided not to challenge it. "It seems that everything in my life is going wrong Father. My son is a deviant, his father could be anywhere from Toulouse to Timbuktu, my family don't speak to me, I have no friends and as of today, I have no job."

"No job?" Thought Father Russell, no income means no money in the collection plate. He would try to jettison her if he could.

"Have you thought why this may be, Barbara?"

"What do you mean?"

"Why do you think Manuel has turned out the way he has? Why does your family not talk to you?"

"God is punishing me in some way."

"Our God is not a vengeful God, maybe there is a lesson to be learned."

"A lesson?"

"You're a teacher, were a teacher sorry, why did you teach?"

"Because it was my job."

"Yes, but it's more than that. You wanted the children to learn, to grow, to become better people."

"I just wanted them to do as they were told."

"Maybe that is the lesson that God would like you to learn."

"I'm sorry, I'm not following you Father."

"Do unto others as you would have them do to you. Luke 6:31." It was one of the few quotes he could remember from the Bible.

"But people need to be told."

"Yes, Barbara, occasionally they do however there's many ways of approaching it."

"I'm not sure I like the tone of your voice."

"Exactly, Barbara, exactly."

"What? I have no idea what you are talking about."

"Have you ever considered that whilst you may be delivering the right message, the method of delivery may not be as, how can I put this, as appropriate as it should be?"

Barbara's face reddened. "Are you suggesting that I don't know how to speak to people?" Her volume raised slightly.

"I'm not suggesting that you don't know how to deal with people Barbara. Just that sometimes, maybe in the heat of the moment, you may come across as a little abrupt."

"Nonsense."

"Barbara, you came to me looking for guidance and I am trying to help. Whilst I can provide advice and guidance from the Lord, I believe the answer lies deep inside of you. Only you can change things. Only you can change yourself."

"I'm too old to change, I don't want to change. Why won't people just do as they are told?"

"Barbara, if you want your life to change for the better, you need to stop looking to the Lord and start looking to yourself."

"Stop looking to the Lord? I thought that it was your job to get people to look to the Lord."

"And it was your job to teach children. Sometimes things don't follow the path you expect."

"I'm not listening to this rubbish anymore." She grabbed her handbag and stood up. "Myself and Manuel will not be returning to this church."

"Manuel will still be coming to see me with those websites?"

"He won't be setting foot in this place again."

He really wanted those websites but it was a small price to pay to get rid of Barbara Frost. "I'm sorry you feel like that Barbara, if you ever wish to return you know where we are. The Lord will always welcome you back."

She shook her head.

"The housekeeper will see you out," said Father Russell.

"I will see myself out and," she pointed at his foot, "you have a tissue stuck to your shoe."

Barbara reversed out of the church car park straight into the oncoming traffic. She wasn't fazed by the screeching brakes and beeping horns and continued on her way home.

By anybody's standards today hadn't been a good day. The priest had been the final straw, she was finished with work, finished with the church and all she had left was Manuel. She was pretty much finished with him as well.

As she got into the house Barbara headed straight into the dining room. She pulled out a seat, and with her head in her hands, she sobbed.

Barbara took a tissue from her pocket and wiped her eyes. She had no time for tears. She crumpled the tissue and threw it in the bin. Events were spiralling out of control but she knew that she still had one thing that was within her power.

Manuel.

She took the stairs two at a time and swept his bedroom door open. Time for a thorough inspection.

She started with the laptop. Internet history, hidden folders, trash, she looked in all corners of the laptop but couldn't find anything too incriminating. He had joined Facebook against her explicit instructions but as far as she could see he had only looked at one page. North-East Cat Lovers. Bizarre.

He was becoming more devious these days, maybe he was better at hiding things. *"No matter how clever he thinks he is, he's not clever enough to fool his mother. I know he is up to something."*

Next was his bed. She stripped it completely, looking in the pillow cases and quilt cover and then removed the mattress, still nothing. She upturned the base of the bed and checked the lining for any loose stitching. Was he smart enough to hide something then stitch it back up? She wasn't sure, she would come back and tear the lining off if she didn't find anything else.

209

She went to his chest of drawers and removed each one in turn, spilling the contents onto the floor. Socks, underpants, jumpers and the odd t shirt. She had never been keen on him wearing t shirts, far too casual.

She checked the back of the drawers to see if anything was taped to them. Still nothing.

Barbara then poured his pens out of the pen holder and inspected it. An Airfix model hung from the ceiling. A rare moment of weakness on her part when she'd allowed him to have what he wanted for his birthday. The glorification of war was not something she encouraged and she took a certain amount of pleasure in ripping it down. She snapped it in half and checked its insides but there was still nothing to be found.

She got on her hands and knees and went around the skirting boards looking for any loose carpet where he could have squirrelled something away. It was all firmly nailed down.

Nothing hidden behind the radiators, or in the hems of the curtains.

Fortunately, she did not allow Manuel to have posters on his wall. She'd had the misfortune to see the film Shawshank Redemption and knew what went on behind the poster. *"Disgusting film,"* she thought.

She had allowed him to have a world map on his wall. It was for educational purposes only, he was never going anywhere. She tore it down.

The only place left to look was his wardrobe, this was where he was hiding his dirty little secrets. She yanked open the doors.

Manuel didn't own a lot of clothes. She removed two shoe boxes from the bottom of the wardrobe. The first one was empty, it was for the shoes he was wearing today. The second contained a perfectly polished pair of shoes. She checked inside the shoes. Nothing.

A pair of old training shoes sat in the bottom of the wardrobe. She allowed him to wear them for PE when he was at school but they were never to be worn elsewhere. She wondered why she hadn't made him throw them out. She picked them up and inspected them but drew a blank.

She looked behind the wardrobe and under it but the search was fruitless.

"I know he is hiding something."

She screamed in frustration and started tearing his shirts from the coat hangers and throwing them to the ground.

She grabbed his old school blazer and went to throw it but the weight of it knocked her off balance. Why was it so heavy?

"Got him!"

She placed the blazer on the upturned bed and started going through the pockets. It wasn't long before she struck pay dirt.

Matches.

The filthy little animal was a smoker. He was in so much trouble now. She placed them in her pocket and headed for the door. Then stopped. A box of matches weighed next to nothing. There was something more in there.

She went through the remaining pockets and found nothing but then she noticed a tear in the lining. A tear big enough to house a notebook. She pulled out the notebook, then another, and another. They were all named Ledger with the corresponding year. There must be at least twenty notebooks in total.

Shaking with rage she opened the first one.

"I could do with a shit," thought the lorry driver as he waited in the queue to get off the ferry. He wasn't sure if it was nerves. He'd done plenty of tobacco runs in the past and it was always easy money but this was for a new client. He didn't have a name, just a phone number. Dale had insisted on that, he didn't want the driver knowing who he was.

He was choking for a cigarette but didn't want to light up until he was clear of customs, it would make him look shifty. As well as the tobacco for his client, he'd also brought a few boxes for himself. All the lads at the club knew he was doing a run and put their orders in. He'd be having a good drink on his takings tonight.

He edged further forward until it was his turn to disembark. *"Stay calm, don't make eye contact and everything will be fine."*

He fought back his grin as the thought of his first cold pint of Fosters came into his head. Couple more minutes and he would be on the open road. Half an hour after that he was to make the call to find out his drop off. That was when he would move his personal stash into the cabin.

"For fucks sake."

He was being waved into one of the bays.

"Good afternoon sir, can I see your papers please?"

He handed them over. Now was probably a good time to strike up that cigarette. "Here you go mate."

"Can you put that out please? Are you transporting anything in addition to what's on the paperwork?"

"Just personal use mate." He waved the cigarette at the customs officer. It was a feeble lie but the onus was on them to prove they weren't his cigarettes. "Forty a day man."

"Would you mind stepping out of the truck whilst we inspect the back?"

"No problem, sir." Now was probably a good time to be polite. He stepped down and went to open the back of the lorry. *"I really need that shit now."*

He opened the back of the truck, confident that he could convince the customs officers that the tobacco was his no matter how ridiculous that would sound. The door swung back and four pairs of eyes stared back at him from the darkness.

"Personal use you say?"

"Why the hell have you brought that thing along?" said Oliver.

"Rizla's okay man, he's just going to sit in the car whilst we're inside," said Tony.

"When have you ever heard of someone taking a dog on an armed robbery with them?"

"You never heard of a burglar's dog? He can alert us if the police are coming."

"And how are you going to hear him when we're inside Shears?"

"Have you heard how loud he gets when he goes off on one?"

"And he's trained to just bark at the Police and not at any passing cat or floating crisp packet?"

"He's not trained but he hates the coppers as much as I do."

"Unbelievable."

They waited in silence for a while. Whilst neither of them would admit it, they were both nervous.

Tony fidgeted inside his jacket.

"Keep that under wraps until we get inside."

"What?"

"The baseball bat, we don't want to draw any unnecessary attention."

"Right," said Tony. "I'm hungry."

"Is that all you ever think of?"

"No, just saying."

"You better not have the munchies. If you've been smoking before we came here I'm going to take this bat to your head."

"I haven't, I was just thinking. Maybe we could open a cafe."

"What, now?"

"No, when it's all over and things have calmed down. We could do with a decent bait place around here. Bacon sarnies, full English. Mince and dumplings on a dinner time. We'd make a killing."

"Two ex-cons without a penny to their name suddenly open a business in the same street where an armed robbery took place?"

"It was just an idea," said Tony, "I'm hungry."

"I'm going to get my old life back after this. Get back with the wife and kids. Sensible job, shake off my past."

"Oh."

"Oh what?"

"I just thought…"

"Thought what?"

"Me and you?"

"What about me and you? Are you wanting to marry me?"

"No, I just thought, you know, we make a good team. We could go into business together."

"Why would I want to go into business with you? Could you imagine anyone coming into a cafe run by you? You stink and so does your dog. Environmental Health would have a field day."

"But what am I going to do?"

"What do I care?" said Oliver.

"We're a partnership, the Dynamic Duo."

"Dynamic? We're an absolute shambles. Both of us are penniless, our biggest chance of getting out of it went up in smoke yesterday. We're in the last chance saloon. As soon as this is over that's me finished with the criminal life."

"Me too."

"And everything associated with it."

"We'll still be mates?"

"It's better if we keep our distance."

"I just thought...."

"You're doing a lot of thinking for someone who hasn't got much up top. The only thing you should be thinking about is how we get in and out of this store with our arms full of money."

"Don't be like that man."

"Someone needs to tell you. At least you'll have that smelly mutt of yours."

Tony stroked Rizla's head. "At least he's loyal."

As much as Grace loved Agatha Christie, she wasn't enjoying it today. Something was nagging at her. Maybe the break from routine had bothered her more than she thought.

After the Echo had sold out in Shears the previous day and there was likely to be more demand today, she decided to leave earlier than usual to get a copy.

"Hi Grace, just the Echo, is it?"

"Yes, please Chloe love. Feels a bit strange buying it from you."

"Terrible shame what happened to Indy but it's made us ridiculously busy. Don't worry, I'll keep a copy back for you each night, no need to break your routine."

"You're an angel, what would I do without you?"

"Just looking after my friends, I'd love to stop for a cuppa and a catch up but I haven't had a minute all day."

Grace looked around and saw the queue forming behind her. "I won't keep you, love. Don't work too hard."

Grace headed for home, looking forward to reading the Echo after missing out for a day.

She wanted to keep to her routine and only read the front page but as it was about Indy's store burning down she read the story on the inside pages as well.

The nagging feeling had returned. Something wasn't right.

She went and got the Echos from the last week and found the story about the obnoxious girl whose cat had died. There was something gnawing at Grace. One cat dead, allegedly poisoned by Shears, Ruby missing and Indy's store burnt down. Could they be connected? It was all a bit too close to home.

Maybe she had been reading too much Agatha Christie but she couldn't settle. Chloe was too busy to talk earlier but the shop would be closing soon. Maybe she would have time to chat about her suspicions. Not that she had any real suspicions, just a hunch that something wasn't quite right.

After her dealings with the police she had absolutely no faith in them to catch the criminals and there was no way on earth they would listen to her theories. They already thought she was mad, this was just the excuse they needed to put her in a home.

Maybe she was going mad but if her suspicions were correct and the incidents were connected then Chloe could be in danger. She needed to speak to her and it couldn't wait until the morning.

If she was quick she could catch Chloe before the shop closed. Grace put on her coat locked the door behind her and returned to Shears.

Manuel loitered in the park for as long as he could get away with without drawing attention to himself from the mothers with children on the swings. He then wandered the streets for a couple of hours, returning to the park with his head no clearer.

He took out his ledger again.

Eventually he made a decision.

He headed back to Shears. His safe place was somewhere he could think clearly. Hopefully he could think of a way of putting right the mess he had created.

He went to the delivery entrance and as expected nobody had noticed that the door wasn't locked. He slid it open slightly and squeezed inside. The store was still very busy and he snuck into the storeroom and hid behind the shelves in his little shelter that he had created. His safe place.

He wasn't sure why he was there or what he was going to do but he felt that he should be there.

He watched through the gap in the boxes as Chloe and the gang dealt with the customers. He felt guilty at leaving them short but they seemed to be coping.

These people were the closest thing he had to friends, in fact they were his friends. They genuinely cared about him. He cared about them. That's why he had to do what he was about to do.

First, he would confess to Chloe, then he would hand himself into the police. He knew that Chloe suspected him anyway and he couldn't bear lying to her anymore.

He hoped that they would forgive him for getting them into this situation but he had done it with good intentions.

Everything was a mess.

He'd noticed Grace come into the shop for her Echo. He wanted to run out and apologise there and then but he stayed hidden in his safe place. He owed it to Chloe to explain.

He took out the ledger once more. He knew that confessing wouldn't redress the balance but it would go some way to putting it right.

Customers came and went and eventually Alex and Stacey got to head home for the night. Chloe was left with just a couple of customers and Manuel watched as she skilfully guided them out of the store.

She changed the sign to closed and pulled down the shutter half way so everyone would realise that the shop was closed.

"What a day," said Chloe to herself.

She emptied the tills and went into the office to cash up.

Manuel almost stopped breathing, worried that she might hear him.

Chloe, oblivious to her secret spectator, got on with the job in hand.

Oliver and Tony had been sat in silence for some time. Oliver broke it.

"There's the last two leaving."

They gave it five minutes to make sure there were no surprises. "This is it Tony, are you ready?"

"Born ready, Olly."

"Come on let's go. And don't call me Olly." They pulled up their hoods and drew scarves across their faces.

They got out of the car and jogged across the road which was quiet for this time of the day. Good, fewer witnesses.

They ducked under the shutter and pushed the door, it opened. Oliver was secretly relieved as they hadn't planned for what would happen if it was locked.

The shop was empty, they headed towards the storeroom and the office. The change of light in the doorway startled Chloe.

"Sorry we're closed."

"We know."

"What?" Chloe then noticed Oliver and Tony removing the bats from under their jackets. "Oh."

"Oh indeed," said Oliver, "Let's not make this any more difficult than it needs to be. Open the safe and give us the takings. We'll be on our way and nobody needs to be hurt."

Chloe's heart raced. They had covered scenarios like this in training but nobody ever took it seriously, it was never going to happen to them.

She knew that she should just hand over the money, that was the training.

Meanwhile Manuel hid behind a pile of boxes, clutching his ledger and praying. *"Please just give them the money Chloe, don't do anything stupid."*

Chloe considered the two men in front of her with their baseball bats. Then she made a decision.

"What is that smell?"

"I know nothing about them, I don't know where they came from." It had been over half an hour since he was stopped, he should be making his call now. Instead he was in an interview room.

"Afghanistan, it would appear."

"They're nothing to do with me."

"And the tobacco is all for personal use?"

"Yes"

The customs officer raised his eyebrows. "You expect us to believe that? You do realise the sentence for people smuggling? You could be doing a fair whack of jail time for this."

He always knew he ran the risk of taking the rap for the tobacco, he understood that, but he had been stitched up here, he never agreed to illegal immigrants in the back of his truck. "Look, maybe we could do a deal?"

"I'm not sure that you are in a position to do deals but let us know who you are working for and I'll see what we can do."

"I don't know who I'm working for."

"But the tobacco isn't yours?"

"No." He wasn't going to take the rap for this any longer.

"None of it?"

"No."

"So, you are working for somebody else?"

"Yes."

"But you don't know who it is?"

"No."

"Can you see why that might be a problem for us?"

He knew he was in serious trouble. He didn't know who he was working for but that also meant that he owed them no loyalty. What did he have to lose? "I've got a phone number."

"Care to share it with us?"

He handed it over and one of the customs officers went away with it.

"Can I have a tab whilst we're waiting?"

"No."

"Come on man, I'm clamming."

"All your cigarettes have been confiscated."

"Even the ones from my pocket."

"You've just said none of it was yours."

"You're taking the piss now."

They waited in silence until the other customs officer returned. "It would appear that the mobile number you shared with us is a dead line. You're not very good with the truth, are you?"

He began to sweat. "That can't be right, that's the number I was given for the drop off."

"As you can't give us a name or a number for your contact, the only assumption we can make is that you are working independently."

"That's bullshit." He needed the toilet now; desperately.

Half an hour along the road another truck driver made a call on his hands free. "Alright mate, the decoy went like clockwork see you in a bit."

Dale placed his phone onto his desk. "Looks like we're on lads."

"Smell?" said Oliver.

"There's an awful stink in here and it's not me," said Chloe, "so it must be one of you two."

Oliver and Tony looked at each other. "It's him," said Oliver pointing at Tony, "stinks of his bloody dog and dope."

"Don't be telling her I've got a dog man," said Tony, "she'll be able to tell the police."

"If you had a wash occasionally we wouldn't be in this situation."

Chloe watched in wonder as they argued amongst themselves. She knew she was dealing with amateurs. What she didn't know was whether that was a good or a bad thing.

Oliver realised that he was getting distracted from the goal. They'd already been in there longer than intended. "Never mind about the smell love, just open the safe and we'll be on our way."

"Don't you love me, you sexist prick."

"I'm sorry, I didn't realise that we were dealing with Millie Tant. If you would be so kind as to open the safe we'll be out of your hair."

"I can't."

"Can't what?"

"Open the safe."

"Why not?"

"It's on a time lock." She realised as she said it that it was ridiculous but it seemed to work.

"A time lock?" Oliver was new to this sort of robbery, he had no idea how safes worked. He'd seen films where banks had safes on time locks, she could be telling the truth.

Tony eyed the pile of cash on the desk in front of Chloe. "Let's just take this and get out of here, there must be thousands."

"But it's not what we came for." Oliver knew that they needed to get out of there quickly but there wasn't enough on the desk to start a new life. "When does the time lock open?"

"What?" Chloe could only play for time now, "Here, do as your smelly mate says and just take this." She started bagging the money.

"He's not in charge here, I am," said Oliver.

"We're a partnership," said Tony.

"Shut it Ton…." Another slip up. "Just shut it and let me do the talking."

"Here." Chloe offered a bag where she had stuffed a few fivers and some coins. She'd also managed to elbow one of the bigger piles of twenties onto the floor unnoticed.

"Hold on," said Oliver, "do you think we are idiots?"

"All the evidence is pointing in that direction," said Chloe.

Manuel was still on his box. He was close to wetting himself. He knew he should do something to help Chloe but he was frozen to the spot. He was a coward. *"Why won't she just give them the money?"*

The notebooks were all filled with columns. Pages and pages of columns. Notebook after notebook all filled with the same.

It took Barbara some time to take it all in and work out what they were. She sat on the upturned bed as she read them.

Mother shouted at neighbour. 2 in the credit column.

Helped neighbour put bins out. 2 in the debit.

Mother rude to old lady at church. 3 in the credit column. (A star beside it denoted that it scored a three due to it being in church.)

Helped put hymn books away. 1 in the debit.

Helped old lady into car. 2 in the debit.

"How dare he disrespect me like this?"

She went through each one. It wasn't just her, there were things he witnessed on the bus, on the way to church, at work. She noticed that entries regarding her started dying off a few years ago to the point where there were virtually no entries for her in last year's. Had her behaviour improved or had he finally come to realise that her way was the correct way to behave and people needed to be told?

As she held last year's ledger in her hand she realised that there was one missing, this year's. Manuel must have it on him and she was going to find out what was in it.

As she grabbed her phone, she heard the matches rattle in her pocket. She had almost forgotten about them.

Manuel was in so much trouble he wouldn't know what had hit him.

"You really do think we are idiots," said Oliver. "Where were you going to put the money?"

"What money?" said Chloe.

"The money in front of you. Once you'd counted it, where were you going to put it?"

"Yeah bitch," said Tony.

Both Oliver and Chloe stared at him and he looked at the floor. "The bank."

"You were going to count tonight's takings and bank them but leave last night's in the safe. I'm not buying that. I'm not daft."

Chloe raised her eyebrows.

"You are beginning to piss me off," said Oliver, "get the safe open now."

Despite her training telling her to give up the money, all her instincts were telling her not to give in. She didn't care if the company lost the money. Shears was insured but she knew if they left with the money that would be the end of the place. Head Office wouldn't put up with all the drama after the Environmental Health fiasco. She owed it to her staff to save the money.

"I can't."

"Not this shit again. It's not on a time lock, just get the bloody thing open."

"I don't know the combination."

"Maybe we could crack it," said Tony.

Chloe snorted a laugh through her nose. "You couldn't crack your knuckles."

Tony lunged towards her with the bat but Oliver pulled him back. "No unnecessary violence, let's just get what we came for and get out of here."

"But she thinks she's cleverer than us."

Chloe tried her best to hide her smirk.

"As you can see, my friend here is a little agitated and I must admit, so am I," said Oliver. "I'm a reasonable man. I'm going to give you one last chance to open the safe or we're going to have no option."

"I don't know it. I'm not trying to be difficult but it needs two of us to operate the safe. I only know one half of the combination; my colleague Manuel knows the other half but I sent him home earlier because he was unwell."

Manuel gasped from behind the boxes, he hoped they hadn't heard him.

Whilst it sounded vaguely plausible, Oliver wasn't having it. "This is bullshit. Surely people go home sick all the time. You must have procedures in place."

"We do but it involves phoning Head Office and going through various security procedures, including remote checks on the CCTV feed." She was thinking on her feet but they seemed to be buying it. "It'll never work."

"Let's just smash it open," said Tony.

"Smash it open? It's a bloody safe," said Oliver.

"Okay then, blow it open."

"Blow it open with what? Did you bring the explosives?"

"Put a match to the noxious fumes coming off Mastermind there and you could blow the whole bloody shop up." Chloe knew she shouldn't have said it as soon as the bat came crashing down on the desk sending money flying everywhere.

"You're making him angry again," said Oliver. "He may not be the brightest…"

"Hey," said Tony.

"He may not be the brightest but he's the one holding the bat. It's time to get serious, Pinky."

"I don't know the combination."

"They're all the same this lot," said Tony, "probably can't even remember what boat she came in on."

Chloe was out of her seat. "What boat I came in on? What planet are you from?"

"What er, er, er jungle are you from eh?"

"Jungle? That smell must be coming from the shit you have for brains." Chloe decided at that point. She didn't care if she died, she wasn't giving a penny to this racist idiot. She spoke to Oliver. "You're obviously the organ grinder, keep your monkey in check or we are going to fall out."

She noticed the bat just in time and turned so it glanced off her shoulder. It still hurt like hell but it was aimed at her head.

"Can everyone please calm down?" said Oliver, "you know what we've come for and we're not leaving until we get it. You need to remember that combination and remember it quickly or somebody is going to get hurt.

Manuel was fighting back the tears from behind the boxes. He nearly jumped through the roof as his phone buzzed in his pocket.

Where are you? Get home now.

The message on Manuel's phone couldn't be clearer. His mother was in another one of her moods and as it stood, he would probably fancy his chances with the men with the baseball bats rather than dealing with her.

It buzzed again and he nearly dropped it. He peeked through the boxes and nobody seemed to have noticed.

Manuel??????

He quickly went into the settings and switched off the vibrating alert. He wasn't even allowed to have his phone on him at work but his Mother insisted on him being contactable twenty-four hours a day. If she couldn't get hold of him she would be at Shears in no time demanding to know why he hadn't replied.

He quickly typed a message and sent it to her.

Stuck at work.

That didn't put her off.

I don't care about your work. Get you backside home right now.

Any normal person would have alerted their mother as to what was going on so they could summon help. He wasn't normal and neither was his mother. She would find some way to blame him for the situation.

Manuel opened the camera on his phone, ensured that the flash was turned off and took some photos of the robbers. He didn't know why as their faces were covered and there was plenty of CCTV anyway. He just felt like he had to do something.

On examining the photos, he realised that he recognised something, the EDL hoody. These were the same two people he saw in Indy's store, the two whose description he had given to the police.

The phone started flashing, he jumped again. It wasn't the camera; his mother was ringing him. He had no alternative, he switched the phone off. He knew that it wouldn't be long before she arrived. This needed to be over before she did.

"Why won't you give them the money Chloe?"

Manuel was cemented to the spot with fear. He'd seen them hit Chloe with the bat and he still hadn't acted. He was ashamed of his cowardice. He tried his best not to cry, remembering his mother's words as he was growing up. *"Don't cry or I'll give you something to cry about."*

"Get out of the bloody way." Oliver had grown sick of Chloe and pushed her away from the desk in her chair.

Her shoulder was painful where the bat had hit her. She didn't think anything was broken but it would be badly bruised and she could already feel it stiffening. She resisted the urge to touch it as she didn't want to give them the satisfaction of knowing she was hurt.

Oliver and Tony busied themselves inspecting the safe. Just to Chloe's right, she thought she saw something. She looked through the gap in the boxes and saw Manuel staring straight back at her.

"Manuel, what the hell are you doing here?" she thought.

She raised her eyebrows in surprise and stared at him. He returned the look, his eyes pleading for some direction as to what to do. He was lost.

She looked over her shoulder at the two clowns checking the safe then back at Manuel. She shook her head. She didn't want him to get involved, she could handle these idiots. Once again, she faced Manuel and with the sternest look she could muster, she shook her head again.

Manuel slumped back against the boxes. His mother was right, he was a waste of a skin. He removed the ledger again and took a pen from his shirt pocket. A new entry was added and it was a big one.

Cowardice.

"How the hell are we going to get in there?" Oliver stared at the safe.

"That black bitch could give us the combination for a start," said Tony.

"I've warned you about that racist shit, cut it out," said Oliver.

Chloe glared at Tony. *"I'd love to take that bat off you and shove it right up your arse,"* she thought.

"What are you staring at?" said Tony.

"Not sure, they don't label shite these days."

Tony went for her again but Oliver dragged him back. "Leave her, we've got bigger things to worry about."

"Whatever, I'm having a smoke, my nerves are shot to bits." Tony removed a joint from his pocket and went to light it.

"You can't smoke in here." Chloe regretted it as soon as she'd said it.

"You're not in charge of me."

"Maybe not but as soon as you spark up, the smoke detectors will pick it up and an automatic call will go to the emergency services. Is that what you want?" She wished that she hadn't warned him but she wanted him to know that she was still in control.

"She's right Tony. Put it out," said Oliver.

"Fucks sake, will people please stop telling me what to do?"

"On second thoughts," said Chloe, "it might not be such a bad idea. Help yourself to a bar of soap and some washing powder from the store and with a bit of luck the sprinklers will come on and the shower will do you the world of good. Hell, why not go daft, get yourself some shampoo as well?"

Oliver couldn't help but laugh at that one.

"Shut your fucking mouth." Tony booted a box in Chloe's direction but it was full of cans and did nothing but injure his toe. He was now furious. He fumbled in his jacket pocket. "Who's laughing now bitch?"

Chloe froze. Oliver was speechless. Both horrified at the gun now pointing at Chloe's head.

"What are you doing, Tony?" said Oliver.

"She was asking for it."

"What the hell did you bring a gun for? Where did you get it from?"

"Never mind where I got it from. If you'd listened to me and we'd come in tooled up from the start we'd be long gone by now."

Chloe couldn't help but think that he had a point.

"I said no guns."

"Yeah? And where has that got us? You think that you're some sort of criminal mastermind just because you put some dodgy signatures on a few forms but you know nothing. I'm the real mastermind here."

Chloe couldn't help but laugh even with the gun pointed at her head. "Sorry, nervous laugh."

"You've got good right to be nervous. Now give us the combination for that safe or I'll blow your brains all over those baked beans."

"This isn't what we agreed," said Oliver.

"If you don't want to join her, you'll do as I say as well. What do you reckon Pinky, time to hand over that combination now?"

Oliver swiped at a pile of boxes with his bat. "What have you done? Why do you always have to fuck things up?"

"Things aren't fucked up, they are now back on track. I've warned you once Olly, you're either on my side or hers."

Oliver knew that he had no choice, nobody would believe that he had no idea about the gun. He was in with Tony all the way. All the way up to his neck.

"Give him the combination, love, we're not fucking about anymore."

"Christ," thought Chloe.

She knew her mouth would get her into trouble one day but she never expected it to be the sort of trouble that saw her staring down the barrel of gun.

"Okay, okay, okay. I'll give you the combination."

"See, that's how easy it is." Tony swung around to Oliver to make his point.

"Don't point that bloody thing at me. You've just made this thing one hell of a lot worse," said Oliver.

"How's it worse? She's going to open the safe, we're going to get what we came for and we can all live happily ever after."

"Apart from the fact that we'll now have armed police looking for us."

"Let's just get the money and get out of here and we can worry about that later."

"Fucking idiot," said Oliver.

"I've warned you Olly, don't push me."

Whilst they were arguing Chloe briefly thought about making a run for it. She had a chance of making it but the idiot with the gun was unpredictable. She stayed where she was. Then a thought filled her head.

"I was horrible to Hannah last night. What if that is the last thing she remembers about me?"

She didn't care what it took, she was going to get out of here alive. She needed to tell Hannah that she loved her. She needed to say sorry.

Another thought came to her and the fear gripped her.

"I can't remember the bloody combination!"

"Let's stop the fannying around, get the safe open love," said Tony.

"Best do as he says." Oliver was almost apologetic but he was resigned to the situation.

Chloe edged her chair over to the safe, took a deep breath and desperately tried to remember the four numbers that she needed. How difficult could it be? Impossible, that's how difficult. She had a complete memory blank.

"I can't, I can't remember it."

"Do you think we're going to fall for that?" said Tony.

"Come on, don't try that game. Don't think he won't use the gun, he's a bloody moron. God knows what he's capable of," said Oliver.

Tony glared at him.

"I'm not playing a game, I genuinely can't remember. Give me a minute, it will come back to me."

"You've been playing for time since we got here, don't think I haven't noticed." Oliver had begun to take charge again. "The combination, now if you don't mind."

"That bloody thing pointed at my head isn't helping."

"Take a step back mate, give the girl some space."

"I'm your mate now?" said Tony. "It was me pointing the gun at her head that got her to finally agree."

"Yeah but it's not helping now, give her some room to think."

"This is what happens when you give savages jobs. I bet a white bloke wouldn't have forgotten the number."

"Not this shite again," said Oliver, "can you please just open that safe so I can get Enoch out of here?"

"I'm trying."

"You're not trying hard enough. You've got five minutes then somebody is going to get hurt."

Manuel cowered behind the boxes, no longer feeling safe in his safe place. He had his ledger open in front of him, he was doing some calculations. He had messed up terribly and there was no way he could balance the books. His bad deeds, deliberate or otherwise massively outweighed his good ones. Not balancing the books made him feel physically sick, there must be a way.

"Please remember the combination Chloe."

"I'm getting sick of this," Tony was getting agitated.

"I'm trying my best, if I could remember the number believe me I would have entered it by now."

"That's just it," said Oliver, "I don't think we do believe you. You've been pissing us about since we got here."

"I'm telling you, there's nothing I'd like more at this moment in time than to give you the money so you will leave."

"Bollocks, you're probably sat there fantasising about hoying us in a big cauldron of boiling water and having us for your tea," said Tony.

"If I had a big cauldron of boiling water the only thing I would be fantasising about putting in it would be your clothes you smelly fucking cretin." Chloe knew this wouldn't end well but she didn't regret saying it.

Tony smashed the butt of the gun off her head. He was as surprised as anyone when the gun went off and shot out a ceiling tile.

Manuel let out a little yelp, Chloe crumpled onto the floor and Oliver looked on in disgust.

"At least we now know that it's loaded," said Oliver.

Tony had gone white. This was getting out of control. "Sorry, that wasn't meant to happen."

"If we're trying to get her to remember something, battering her around the head isn't going to help, is it? You could have killed her. You could have killed me."

"Sorry," said Tony again.

Chloe stumbled to her feet and back into the chair, a thin trickle of blood flowing down her neck.

"Don't die Chloe, don't die," thought Manuel. He couldn't bear to think how badly unbalanced the books would be if that happened.

"Give me that here." Oliver took the gun from Tony without any resistance and put on the safety. "Right this is your final chance, enter the combination now or somebody is seriously going to get hurt."

Chloe leant over the safe once again. *"Think, think, think."* She knew it was pointless. She had completely forgotten it and the blow to the head hadn't helped. She was going to die at the hands of two idiot robbers because she couldn't remember a simple four-digit number. And she hadn't had a chance to tell Hannah how much she loved her. Life was shit sometimes.

Tears streamed down her face, mixing with the blood trickling down her cheeks.

Then a voice from behind her.

"Maybe I can help?"

"Manuel?"

The rest of the day was as uneventful as it was depressing for Lynn with the only respite being the pie and chips she bought for lunch as she sat alone in the canteen at lunchtime.

She got the bus home, ignoring the looks of disgust from passengers who didn't want to sit next to her.

The cat was waiting for her when she got home. Whilst she wouldn't go as far as saying that Ruby liked her, she didn't hate her; yet.

She fed Ruby and headed straight for the freezer. Ice cream was the only remedy for how she felt. She ate a whole tub of Ben and Jerry's and cried through the ice cream headache.

"I don't care what people say, you're my cat and I'm not giving you up." Ruby rubbed against her leg. She put the empty bowl on the floor and let her lick the remaining melted ice cream from it.

Lynn felt sick and lay on the settee with her laptop.

She logged onto Facebook and browsed through everybody's perfect lives. She had numerous notifications but was trying to ignore them. The pendulum of support had swung firmly against her with only a handful of diehard cat fans still on her side. Some of the messages were downright nasty.

Could do with a dose of food poisoning yourself you fat mess.

Another double page spread in the Echo, it's the only way they could fit your picture in.

That's definitely the only pussy of hers anybody ever wants to see.

Her life was a mess, an utter shambles.

Then she saw the message. It was a picture of Neil Armstrong stepping from Apollo 11 onto the moon.

Every journey starts with one step, when are you taking yours?

Facebook was full of motivational messages but this one seemed to be aimed directly at her.

It was right. She was the only one who could change her life, she had to make the first step. She only wished she knew what that step was.

Her problems started a long time ago, she'd never been happy, even as a child. She'd always been unpopular but that was just life, she wasn't going to change for anyone else. The realisation was now dawning on her that she didn't have to change for anyone else, she had to change for herself.

She had multiple problems, unpopularity, over eating, lack of self-confidence but she'd always had them, why were things so bad now?

Was there one specific moment?

Things had briefly looked up. Darcy had died but that gave her the exposure in the Echo and hundreds of likes on Facebook, she almost knew what it felt like to be popular. But the tide had turned, she was more unpopular than ever. What had changed? Why had her problems intensified? She wasn't one hundred percent sure but she knew that they had escalated when she attacked Chloe from Shears. If she could speak to her, somehow make it right then maybe her life would change for the better.

The thought of going out of the house again wasn't pleasant but she had to make this first step towards redemption.

She grabbed her coat and headed for Shears.

"Where the fuck did you come from?" said Oliver.

"Manuel, what are you doing?" said Chloe.

"The reason she can't remember the combination is because she doesn't know it. She only knows half of it, I know the other half."

Chloe glared at him.

"Why would anyone give a weirdo like you the combination?" said Tony.

"I'm a weirdo? Chloe told you that she only knew half the combination but you two simpletons wouldn't listen."

"Simpletons, you do realise that we still have a gun."

"I am aware of that, yes. And what use is that gun to you? You can't shoot me as I have the combination, similarly you can't shoot Chloe as she has the other half. So, unless you are going to shoot each other or stick it up your bottom and blow your brains out, we can stop discussing the gun and I am going to tell you what will happen."

This was a new Manuel that Chloe hadn't seen before. Confident, in control and apparently completely unfazed by the danger he had just put himself in. She didn't have the faintest idea what he was up to or what his plan was. She prayed that he did.

"We're still in charge here," said Oliver pointing to Tony and himself.

"You may think that but you are wrong," said Manuel, "I have what you need and unless you do exactly what I want, you will never get it."

"And what is it you want?"

"After Chloe has entered the first part of the combination you let her go."

"And why we would we do that?"

"Have you not been listening, because I have what you need."

"But what's to stop her going to the cops?"

"Because you are still holding me hostage. Chloe wouldn't put my life in danger would you Chloe?"

She couldn't speak and just shook her head. She knew that if she'd given up the combination originally his life wouldn't be in danger now.

"I'm not having this little paedo telling me what to do," said Tony.

"Doesn't matter what you are having or not having, there can only be one outcome," said Manuel.

"What if we don't agree?" said Oliver.

"It's not for you to agree or disagree, there can only be one outcome."

"There can only be one outcome, there can only be one outcome, it's like arguing with a bloody robot."

"That's as maybe but there can only..."

"Yeah, there can only be one outcome we get it. I'm going to discuss this with my partner."

"Discuss all you like, there can only…"

"WE FUCKING KNOW MAN!"

Oliver and Tony walked to the far side of the office to discuss the situation.

"Manuel what the hell are you doing?" said Chloe.

"Saving you."

"I don't need saving, why didn't you save yourself?"

"I've got this under control."

"But you don't know the combination."

"They don't know that."

"But they will very soon, then what?"

"Then you'll be safe so it won't matter."

"Of course it bloody matters, you'll still be here."

"I know."

"What do you mean you know? Have you any idea how much danger you are in?"

"Yes."

"Manuel, you are worrying me. They have a gun. They are dangerously stupid."

"I am aware of the situation."

"Manuel, I want to throttle you sometimes. Dangerous men with guns, you know what that means?"

"Yes."

"Manuel, they are going to kill you."

Manuel mentally totted up the debit and credit columns in his ledger. The cats, the fire, the cowardice, the lies he had told Chloe.

"There can only be one outcome."

Oliver and Tony finished their discussion and returned to Manuel and Chloe.

"I'm not keen on the idea," said Oliver, "but as Mr Logic here doesn't appear to be budging, we don't really have any choice. We're going to let you go."

Manuel breathed a sigh of relief. Chloe didn't, she knew what it meant.

"I'm a reasonable man so I'm going to trust that you will keep your word and not go to the police as soon as you leave here. Remember that we still have your friend. Whilst I may be reasonable, I think we can all agree that my partner isn't." Tony looked hurt at the accusation but Oliver continued. "I can only control him for so long. If we get caught with a gun, we are both going back to prison for a very long time. We have nothing to lose. The first sign that you have broken your word and this won't end well for your friend."

Chloe nodded, her cheeks wet with tears. "Manuel?"

"Go before they change their minds, I have everything under control here."

"But…"

"There isn't time for buts, enter your two digits into the safe and get yourself out of here."

"My two digits?" She then remembered what was happening. "Yes, right." She headed over to the safe.

"Once you've entered your numbers, leave here and don't stop running until you are home. I'll give you ten minutes to get a safe distance away and enter the remainder of the combination," said Manuel.

"Hold on, hold on," said Oliver, "what's all this ten minutes business? We never agreed to this."

"I want to ensure that Chloe is safe."

"I don't want to be staying here another ten minutes."

"We can spend another ten minutes arguing about it if you like, I won't be changing my mind."

"Yeah, we know, there will only be one outcome. Jesus. Okay, enter your numbers and get out of here. Any funny business and I'll take great delight in killing him myself."

Chloe leaned over to the keypad on the safe. She racked her brains for the correct combination in the forlorn hope that she could save Manuel. Still blank. She entered two random numbers then took hold of Manuel's hands. She had never seen him look so calm and confident. Happy even. "You don't have to do this Manuel."

"I do, everything will be fine. The books will balance."

"Your ten minutes have already started love," said Oliver, "I'd be getting out of here while you still have the chance."

She kissed Manuel lightly on the forehead then ran for the door in tears.

Oliver patted Tony on the back, "In nine minutes' time, we are going to be rich men."

Oliver and Tony took a seat and watched the clock ticking down.

"What did she say your name was?" said Oliver.

Manuel didn't want to enter a conversation with them but decided that it wasn't worth antagonising them just yet, that would come soon enough. "Manuel."

Oliver and Tony both laughed. "Manuel?" said Oliver, "I wasn't expecting that."

"Manuel," said Tony, "are you another foreigner?"

"Another one?" said Manuel.

"Like your friend, the black lass."

"She's not foreign, she's from London."

"Same difference, so where are you from then?"

"High Barnes."

"We know you live in Sunderland now but your name's foreign, where'd you get your name from?"

"My mother gave it to me as a child, I believe this is customary in most houses."

"Is he winding me up?" Tony looked to Oliver.

"Unfortunately, I don't believe he is." He glanced at the clock, another five minutes of this.

"Right," said Tony, "I get that it was your Mam who gave you the name but why Manuel? Is your Dad a spick or something?"

"What's a spick?"

"Eh? A greasy Spaniard, you know like from Spain. Is your Dad a foreigner?"

"I don't know."

"You don't know where your Dad is from?"

"I don't know who he is."

"Well that's something we've got in common. If you didn't get your stupid spick name from your Dad, your Mam must really hate you."

"For the first time today, you may be correct."

"Eh?"

"Right enough of this nonsense," said Oliver, "Time's up Pedro, let's get this safe open and we can all go home and live happily ever after."

"Who is Pedro?"

"Pedro, Manuel, it's all the same to me just open the bloody safe."

"I can't."

"What do you mean you can't?"

"I don't know the combination."

"Not this shit again." Oliver stood up from his chair and booted it across the office. "How can you forget two digits?"

"I haven't forgotten them."

"What? You've just said that you couldn't remember them."

"I didn't."

"You are driving me insane here. Just enter the bloody numbers."

"I can't."

"Ah for fucks sake."

"The stupid spick bastard is taking the piss out of us." Tony launched himself at Manuel and slapped him hard across the face. Manuel smirked.

"Alright Tony, let's take a step back here and calm down. Let's give him one more chance and if he doesn't do what we ask he will be getting far more than a slap."

"Can you remember the combination?"

"No."

"You do realise that we're going to hurt you?"

"Yes."

"And will that help you remember?"

"No."

"Why not?"

"I never knew it in the first place."

Chloe sat on the wall opposite Shears with her phone in her hand, willing herself to phone the police. Her arm ached but it was nothing compared to the pain that Manuel would soon be in. She knew the robbers were unstable. She knew that Manuel was likely to get seriously hurt if not killed if they heard police sirens. She knew she couldn't phone the police no matter how much she wanted to.

"Why have you done this Manuel?" Tears dripped onto her phone.

She couldn't understand why he would put his life on the line for her. Sure, she'd been nice to him but was that any reason to give up your life?

Cars drove past, people wandered up the road, all of them oblivious to what was going on inside the store.

Chloe was oblivious as to what was going on inside Manuel's head.

All her psychology training couldn't help her control the robbers, couldn't help her to understand Manuel. She'd been wasting her time, she didn't understand people any more than the normal bloke on the street, she'd been kidding herself. And now Manuel was paying the price.

She was his friend, probably one of the only friends he had but would she put her life on the line for her friends?

She thought about this for a second then made a decision.

She typed three words into her phone and sent a text to Hannah.

I love you. xxx

She stood up, marched across the road and went back into the store.

Lynn got off the bus and headed towards Shears. She'd been trying to work out what to say to Chloe when she saw her. She'd said some nasty things online about her but she had been angry. She still had no idea how Darcy came to eat the poison but Environmental Health hadn't shut the store, maybe it wasn't their fault.

Her life had been bad before but ever since she attacked Chloe on Facebook it deteriorated rapidly.

She felt that she should apologise but didn't know where to start.

But what if Environmental Health were just taking their time? What if Shears was to blame after all?

Chloe had been mean to her as well. Maybe it should be her apologising.

"This is so confusing. Why can't anything be straightforward?"

Lynn had decided that she was going to give Chloe another piece of her mind when she got there but she was stopped in her tracks. She could see Chloe's bright pink hair up ahead. She was sat on the wall, she appeared to be crying.

"Probably girlfriend problems, those lesbians are so temperamental."

She watched her for a couple of minutes. Chloe seemed to send a message, dry her eyes then head back to the store.

"I don't care if she's had a lover's tiff with her dyke girlfriend, it's not my problem. She needs to be told."

Lynn stomped off up the road and, with great difficulty, ducked under the shutters and went into the store.

"What do you mean you never knew the combination in the first place?" Oliver's face had turned bright red.

"Why would anyone give me the combination, I'm just here to stack shelves."

"I don't believe the speccy little fucker." Tony slapped him again. "Look at him. Who wears a shirt and tie to stack shelves? He's management of some sort."

239

"I'm not sure what to believe any more." Oliver had his head in his hands, the gun still in his right hand. "Why the fuck would you come out of hiding and say you had the combination when you didn't?"

"Because you were going to hurt Chloe."

"But we're going to hurt you a hell of a lot more."

Tony ran across and drop kicked Manuel in the chest, sending him flying off the chair.

"So it would appear," said Manuel.

"Are you going to give us the fucking combination or what?" Tony aimed another kick at Manuel, this time at his head.

"I'm not sure whether it's your hearing or your comprehension that is at fault but I don't have the combination."

"Compry fucking what?" Another kick, this time to the ribs. Tony dragged him up from the floor. Manuel tried to straighten his glasses but they were broken. Tony swiped them off his face and pushed him against the wall. Manuel still had a smile on his face.

"Do you think this is fucking funny?"

"Not particularly, I've been punched, kicked and sworn at. You're not exactly Jimmy Tarbuck."

"Who the fuck is Jimmy Tarbuck?"

Manuel didn't have a clue who he was, it was just something his mother used to shout at him *"Do you think you are funny? Who do you think you are, Jimmy Tarbuck?"* It didn't matter now, he just shrugged and received another punch for his troubles.

Oliver walked across. "I don't buy this story, you're hiding something."

Manuel instinctively felt his pocket to make sure the ledger was still there. He regretted it instantly.

"Search his pockets Tony, let's see if the combination is written down somewhere."

Tony went into his trouser pockets first and removed his phone. He threw it to Oliver who switched it on. It started flashing as the notifications started streaming through.

"Somebody's popular. Didn't think you'd have so many friends."

Manuel knew who the notifications were from, Chloe and his mother were the only ones with his number.

"Looks like somebody has been a naughty boy," said Oliver, "Manuel here is late for his tea and Mummy is not a happy bunny. No wonder he volunteered to be beaten up by us, Mummy is going to give him a spanked bottom when he gets home."

The smile had gone from Manuel's face.

Tony removed the ledger from Manuel's shirt pocket. "What do we have here?" He sat back down. "Looks like we might have something here, Olly."

Oliver ignored the Olly comment and took the notepad from Tony. "Let's have a little look shall we."

Chloe had always wondered what was in Manuel's notebook but no longer wished to know.

The skinny, smelly robber was now punching him repeatedly, laughing as he did so. The other one looked on, possibly embarrassed but doing nothing at all to stop it.

Manuel still had a grin on his face, as if he knew something they didn't know. He certainly didn't know the combination, she still had no idea why he claimed that he did.

Manuel made another quip at the expense of the robbers. He received another backhander for his troubles. His eyes were swollen and blood trickled from his lip and flowed from his nose. He didn't seem to care.

"Stay quiet Manuel," she thought, *"stop winding them up."*

The skinny one was out of control now, he was enjoying hitting Manuel. She wanted to march in there and tell them to stop. But this wasn't Stacey and Alex squabbling over whose turn it was to make the coffee.

Of course, if she could remember it, she could just walk in there and hand over the combination but something stopped her. It wasn't fear, she was well past that. She sensed that Manuel did not want her to, sensed that he had a plan, no matter how ill thought out and he wouldn't appreciate it if the kicking he was taking was all for nothing.

She'd edged up to the door and watched Manuel getting the beating. It made her feel sick but she felt helpless. When she strode back into the store she didn't have a plan on how she was going to save him, she still didn't.

All she was doing was being witness to his torture, humiliation and possible death. She had no idea how to stop it.

"I need to do something."

The guys they were dealing with were idiots, dangerous idiots. There must be a way to trick them, fool them, but done in such a way that it wouldn't put Manuel in any more danger. Not that she was sure how he could be in any more danger than he faced now.

She started to look for some inspiration around her in the storeroom but felt a big presence lurking behind her. She was shocked when she saw Lynn looming over her.

Lynn went to speak but Chloe put her finger to her lips to quieten her. It had the opposite effect. "Don't you tell me…" Chloe's hands went up in desperation and she clamped one over Lynn's mouth whilst whispering the word "Please."

Chloe nodded to the gap in the door. Two men towering above the weird guy from Shears who was bleeding heavily and covered in bruises.

Lynn raised her hands in submission. Chloe removed the hand from her mouth. "Thank you," she whispered.

"What's this then?" said Oliver, "Is the combination in here?"

"It's a ledger," said Manuel.

"A ledger, so you're an accountant?"

"Sort of."

"Sort of? I used to work in finance myself back in the day, I haven't always been an armed robber."

"You can tell, you aren't very good at it."

Oliver slapped him around the head. "Less of your cheek. Am I going to find the combination buried away in this little ledger?"

"I doubt it."

"Am I really going to have to go through it?"

"I'd rather you didn't."

"You're going to tell us the combination?" said Oliver.

"Are we back to this again?"

"Look, we've knocked you about a bit but we're just warming up. It's going to get a lot more violent from now on. Wouldn't it be easier if you just gave us the combination?"

"It would be yes."

"You're going to give us the combination?"

"No."

"Why not?"

"I don't know it."

"Have we not been through this?"

"Yes, I'm confused as to why you keep on bringing it back up."

Oliver flicked through the ledger with a confused look on his face. "What the fuck's this?"

"A ledger, I thought we had already established this," said Manuel.

"A ledger of what though? Where's the baked beans, the milk, the daily takings? It makes no sense."

"It makes sense to me."

"But not to me, I've got financial qualifications coming out of my arse and I have no idea what this is. What the hell is it?"

"It's not meant to make sense to you, it's my ledger."

Oliver opened it towards the front and picked out an example. "Rude bus driver 1, carried pensioner shopping off bus 1. What is this shit?"

"A ledger."

"If you say ledger one more time I swear I'm going to shoot you between the eyes." Oliver raised the gun for the first time.

"I best stay quiet then as that's what it is."

"Is it a code, is that what we're looking at? Road Rage 2, Help cyclist who fell off bike 2. What does it mean?"

"I would have thought that was obvious."

Tony had started pacing around the room, he removed the joint from his pocket.

"You can't smoke that in here," said Manuel.

"I don't think that you're in any position to be telling me what to do."

"He's right Tony, remember what the girl said about the smoke detectors. We'll have the law around here before we know it. We need to crack this code and get this idiot to give us the combination. One way or the other, I'm not leaving here without the contents of that safe."

"I'd appreciate it if you didn't call me an idiot, Oliver," said Manuel.

"How do you know my name?"

"You and Tony have been using each other's names since you got here. I think it is fair to say that neither of you is the criminal mastermind."

"Fucks sake Ol...er Steve," said Tony.

"There's no point fucking changing it now, he knows what we're called."

"We're going to have to kill him."

"Kill him?"

"We have no option, he knows who we are. There's not exactly many criminal partnerships called Oliver and Tony. The Police will be onto us in minutes."

Chloe covered her mouth to stop herself from screaming. Lynn felt so ill that she may never eat again.

"Have you killed anyone before?" Oliver said to Tony.

"No, have you?"

"Of course I bloody haven't."

"There's a first time for everything."

"Look, let's worry about that later. We need the money first, let's see if the accountant can help us out and save his life so neither of us have to break our duck." He flicked through a few more pages. "What the hell is this? Killed fat girl's cat."

Chloe and Lynn exchanged a look of disbelief.

"It was an accident," said Manuel.

"I hate cats," said Tony.

"You killed a cat? How did you kill it?" said Oliver.

"Poisoned it."

"Doesn't sound like an accident."

"I never meant to kill it, just make it ill."

"Why the hell would you want to make a cat ill?"

"The owner is rude."

"Not surprised she's rude, someone killed her cat. Why on earth did you write it down?"

"To balance the books."

Oliver shook his head, "Stole old lady's cat. Why did you steal a cat?"

"To replace the dead one."

"Quite the little cat criminal, aren't you?"

"I'm not a criminal, I was just balancing the books." Manuel's voice had begun to get high pitched.

"Same here Manuel, same here. Now I think we can both agree that you wouldn't want this information becoming public. The fat lass whoever she is would probably flatten you if she found out."

Manuel didn't reply.

"Now this is what we're going to do Manuel. We're going to stop this charade, you're going to give us the combination and we're going to leave with the money and your little notebook. You are going to forget our names because if we get caught, you will be in the frame for the cat killing. If you don't agree, I'm going to hand the gun to Tony here and he is going to kill you. Do you understand?"

"Yes," said Manuel.

"Glad we understand each other. Now are you going to finally give me that combination?"

"No"

"No? Were you not listening? Tony is going to kill you." Oliver was exasperated.

"Give me the fucking gun and let's get this over with. He's not going to give us the combination. We're wasting our time and the stupid fucker doesn't care if you tell the world that he killed a cat. The bloke is fucking mental," said Tony.

"Manuel, are you mad? Are you happy to die to save your company a few quid?"

"I have to balance the books."

"Let's just kill him now, take what we've got and get the fuck out of here," said Tony.

"I'm not just killing someone in cold blood," said Oliver.

"He knows our names, he knows our history. He is going straight to the police when we get out of here assuming that his girlfriend hasn't already gone."

"She's not my girlfriend," said Manuel, "she's a…"

"Shut up, I'm trying to think," said Oliver as he held his head in his hands again. One hand holding the gun, the other holding the ledger.

There was a silence then Oliver spoke again. "I'm going to give you one last chance. If the combination isn't in this notebook I'm going to let Tony do whatever he likes to you. I'm past caring."

Manuel stared back at him without responding.

"And don't start the silent treatment nonsense because I told you to shut up. If you know something it is very much in your self-interest to speak now."

Oliver started thumbing through the ledger again. "What's this one here? Fire?"

"I started the fire at Indy's shop."

"That was you?"

"He was there, remember?" said Tony.

"I remember. What I don't understand is why you would want to burn his shop down."

"You hate the Pakis as well mate?" said Tony.

Manuel ignored him and spoke to Oliver directly. "It was an accident, I didn't mean to do it."

"It's always an accident with you, isn't it? You never mean to do anything."

"I did mean to start a fire originally but then changed my mind."

"How come the place burnt down then?"

"I've told you, it was an accident."

"But why were you going to burn it down in the first place."

"I didn't want the old woman to see her cat in the Echo."

"You do realise that we were going to rob the place? We wouldn't be here now if you hadn't burnt the place down."

"I don't feel so guilty now."

"You don't feel guilty about burning the poor bloke's shop down?"

"No, I don't feel guilty about giving the police your descriptions and saying it was you."

Chloe and Lynn were both in shock at Manuel's confession. Everything that had gone wrong this week was down to him. The cats, the fire, the robbery, everything.

And now he was going to die for it.

"He's grassed us up, the police are already looking for us," Tony stormed around the room kicking things.

"Why the fuck did you tell them it was us?" said Oliver.

"I couldn't tell them it was me."

"But why us?"

"You were there."

"But we hadn't done anything wrong."

"You were going to rob the place."

"But you didn't know that." Oliver was now pointing the gun at Manuel's head.

Lynn was crying.

"You okay?" whispered Chloe.

"It's all my fault."

"How do you work that out?"

"If I hadn't been nasty to you, he wouldn't have poisoned Darcy. Everything that's happened since then is because of that."

"You can't blame yourself. Manuel has gone mental."

"But it all started because of me. And it all started because he wanted to protect you. He's not a bad person."

As angry as Chloe was with Manuel, she knew that Lynn was right. Everything he had done, no matter how bad, had been done for the right reasons. At least it had according to his twisted logic. He'd offered up his life to save her.

"He isn't bad but he's very, very stupid. Think of poor Grace and Indy and how they've suffered."

247

"But he said the fire was an accident," said Lynn.

"Hold on. Fire. You've given me an idea. Wait here."

Despite having received the call saying everything went like clockwork at the docks, Dale was still nervous.

Only his top boys were on site today and they were on the lookout for anything unusual.

He checked his watch again, the lorry wasn't late but it didn't stop him checking. This was a massive step up and any mistakes could be critical.

Right on time he heard the airbrakes of the wagon and the shutters rattled open for him to reverse in. No Transit vans waiting this time.

The driver stepped down from his cabin.

"How you doing, Dale?"

"A lot better now that you're here. Everything go smoothly?"

"Couldn't be easier mate. The gobshite you stitched up fell right into the trap. They were waiting for him and I sailed through."

"And you definitely weren't followed?"

"Took diversions like you suggested. The only tail was your lads who watched me all the way in. We're in the clear."

"Let's see what we have then."

The driver unlocked the padlock and dragged open the back gates of the truck. He jumped onto the back and crawled through the pallets. "Give us a hand here."

Dale nodded to some of the lads and they climbed up and returned carrying a wooden crate with rope handles. Dale cracked open the crate with a crowbar and admired his delivery. Half a dozen semi-automatic rifles, the same number of automatic handguns, ammunition and enough grenades to take out half the city.

He picked up one of the rifles and looked down the sights. He'd been forced to use a handgun a couple of times but never anything as sophisticated as this. He didn't want to show himself up not knowing how to use it so put it back in the crate.

"Not trying it out boss?"

"Not here, I don't want any unnecessary attention. Get them hidden away for now and we'll move them later."

His two men took them away and hid them in a hole in the floor Dale had specially built.

"Think I need a drink," said Dale.

"Boss, Callum's here, says it's urgent."

Dale checked that the guns were gone, he trusted Callum but you couldn't be too careful. "Send him in."

Callum was thick set, shaven-headed and heavily tattooed, much like everybody else in the warehouse.

"Hi mate, what's up?" said Dale.

"Alright, Dale?" Callum shook his hand firmly and gave him a hug. "Tight security today, something up?"

"Just the usual tobacco but we're tightening up a bit, you can never be too careful."

They'd known each other since school, went to the gym together and had a handy little business arrangement. Dale usually taxed anybody with a criminal enterprise on his patch but he let Callum fence stolen goods and supply the odd gun without being taxed with one condition. If someone had done a big score, or was about to, Callum was most likely to know. If he knew, then he let Dale know. It was surprising that nobody had cottoned onto this little agreement but the criminal lowlifes they dealt with were too greedy to stop and think.

"Got anything for me?" said Dale.

"Not a great deal. Couple of break ins on industrial units, the usual suspects, not big earners. There is one that you might be interested in though."

"What's that?"

"Tony Hurbett."

"What's that smelly little twat up to?"

"Not sure, for once he didn't say much other than it was with that posh lad he was inside with."

"Oliver?"

"Aye that's him. Problem?"

"Could be, could be a very big problem in fact. You've no idea what they are up to?" said Dale.

"No, only thing I know is that whatever it is they are up to, they needed a gun."

"For fucks sake."

"Problem?"

"They're hardly Butch Cassidy and the Sundance Kid. Whatever it is they are planning, and I can guarantee that it will be some hare-brained scheme if that fuckwit is involved, will go massively tits up. And when it does, it's going to lead back to you because of the shooter and me because that stupid posh fucker has hold of my books."

"Fucking hell," said Callum.

"Fucking hell exactly. Come on, we need to get around there and try and dissuade them. At the very least we need to get the contents of that safe as far away from them as possible."

Chloe returned from the store with her arms full.

"I've got a plan to get him out of there but I'm going to need your help. Are you with me?"

"Count me in."

"Okay, this is what we're going to do." Chloe laid out the plan for Lynn. It was simple. It was risky but it might just work.

Chloe wrapped the cloths around the end of the broomstick and dowsed them in lighter fuel. She then lit it.

"Wave that under the smoke detector. As soon as the alarms go off, drop it on the concrete floor and put it out with the extinguisher. We don't want another incident like Indy's. I can take care of the rest." Chloe took her phone out of her pocket and sent a text.

Manuel's phone flashed on the desk.

"Looks like your Mam still isn't happy. I'm going to reply and say you are never coming home." Oliver picked up the phone and looked at the screen. "Chloe? What the hell is she texting for?" He clicked on it to read the message.

We're coming to balance the books.

"What the hell does that mean?"

Just then the fire alarms went off.

"Have you struck up that joint, you daft twat?"

"It's not me," said Tony.

Lynn dropped the broomstick and put out the fire as instructed. Part one of the plan complete.

Chloe took advantage of Oliver and Tony being distracted to burst into the office. Oliver turned to face her with the gun in his hand but she smashed him firmly in the face with the base of the second fire extinguisher. Part two complete.

The next step was easy. Grab the gun, point it at Tony and get Manuel and Lynn to tie him up until the police arrived. Unfortunately, the gun was now skimming across the floor and stopped right at Tony's feet. Part three fucked.

"Good try but maybe you should have stuck to chucking spears."

There was a scream from outside of the office, enough to distract Tony for a second as Lynn came barging in brandishing the fire extinguisher. She squirted the foam in Tony's eyes and he stumbled backwards. She then launched herself with an athleticism she didn't know she possessed and took out everything in her path, desk, chair, shelving and most importantly, Tony.

His ten-stone frame was no match for her twenty-stone mass.

"Get off us man, I can't breathe."

Chloe picked up the gun and handed the cable ties to Manuel.

"Can you do the honours Manuel? Best start with that one," she pointed to the bloodied and groggy Oliver. "I don't think the other one is going anywhere for a while." She winked at Lynn.

The fire brigade arrived moments later. They worked their way through the store seeing no signs of fire then they got into the storeroom and noticed the burnt rag on the floor. They then moved into the office and were quite surprised by the sight that greeted them.

Two men lying on the floor tied up. One bleeding heavily from his nose. Another man bloodied and beaten on a chair getting first aid from a black girl with shocking pink hair. Another girl stood beside them cradling a fire extinguisher in her arms. A gun lay on the desk.

"Think this one is probably for the police," said the fireman. "You take care of the fire yourself?" he said to Lynn.

"That and much more," she said.

"I do like a girl who can handle herself."

If she didn't know better she would think he was flirting with her. She blushed.

The police arrived shortly after and were equally shocked when greeted with the scene inside the office.

"Hello again, Manuel. Looks like you've been in the wars," said PC Sugden. He noticed Lynn in the corner. "Hello Lynn, you ended the boycott then?"

"Looks that way." She smiled at Chloe.

"Who do we have here then?" said PC Sugden as he looked at the two figures lying on the ground. "Branching out a little bit are we Oliver? You like the taste of prison food so much that you wanted to go back there?"

"Fuck off." He could barely speak due to his broken nose and missing teeth.

"And Tony Hurbett," said PC Sugden, "quite the partnership we have here. Dumb and Dumber." He opened Tony's denim jacket and saw the EDL logo on his hoody. "These the two jokers you saw at Indy's Manuel?"

Manuel nodded.

"You're not putting that shit on us," said Tony, "it was that little spick bastard."

"Of course it was Tony, of course it was."

"I can prove it."

"Save it until I've read you your rights."

Tony and Oliver sat facing each other in the back of the police van.

"Where the fuck did they come from?" said Tony.

252

"Where did they come from, where did that stupid little Spaniard come from? I thought you were watching the place. I thought you said that he had left," said Oliver.

"How's it my fault? You were watching the joint as well, you saw him leave."

"He only came back when you got that sodding gun out. So yes, I am blaming you."

"If you'd let me bring it in the first place we wouldn't be in this mess."

"Yes, it worked so well when you introduced it; fucking idiot. Don't think I won't tell them that it was your gun."

"It's got your fingerprints on it as well. We're both in the frame."

"I can't do another long stretch."

"Don't think we've got any choice."

"Fucks sake." Oliver banged his head off the side of the van. He wanted to wipe the blood from his nose but his hands were cuffed behind his back.

"Ah shit. Rizla's still in the car," said Tony. He started kicking the front of the van leading to the driver's section. "My dog, someone has to look after my dog."

"Shut up. We can't tell them about the dog, it's in a stolen car. We don't want that added to the list as well."

"But it's Rizla. Who's going to look after him if I am inside? He can't cope on his own."

"He'll probably cope better than he would with you."

"That's not fair."

"You're probably better off inside yourself. At least they'll force you to have a wash and clean your clothes."

"No need to be like that."

"There's every need. If I'd never met you I wouldn't be in this mess."

"You met me in prison, you were already in a mess."

"Fuck off!" Oliver tried to aim a kick at Tony and slid off the bench. He started to cry.

"Shut up you two," said PC Sugden in the front seat as he laughed at their predicament. "Now we're sending teams round to the shitholes that you two call home. Apart from them having to wear full anti contamination outfits, there's not going to be any little surprises waiting for them are there?"

"Shit," said Oliver.

"What's up?" said Tony.

"Dale's books."

"We could grass him up, reduce our sentence," whispered Tony.

"Don't be ridiculous," said Oliver, "he can get to us inside. Our sentence would be reduced considerably once he did. We're fucked."

Dale's BMW came screeching around the corner but he stamped on the brakes when he saw the blue flashing lights outside Shears. "No prizes for guessing who is responsible for that mess, absolute fuckwits. Come on, we'll take the scenic route."

He negotiated the back lanes, knocking over wheelie bins and various other bits of rubbish on the way. He would worry about scratches to the car later. This was an emergency.

They got to the end of the Oliver's street but were greeted with the same blue flashing lights.

"We're fucked Callum mate. Why did you sell a gun to that idiot?"

"Why did you give your books to that other idiot?"

Dale didn't answer and put the car into reverse. They drove in silence for a few minutes.

"Give the solicitor a bell Callum, looks like we're going to be in for a long night."

They raced back to the industrial unit, lifted the shutters and drove inside, pulling them down behind them. The men who he'd had on guard had gone, news must have travelled fast.

"Come on," said Dale, "we've still got time before they put things together and get a warrant we can move the guns."

The inside of the unit was in darkness. "Don't touch the lights Callum, we don't want to draw attention to ourselves." He switched on the torch on his iPhone and headed to the office to get the keys.

Callum stood at the door of the office as Dale worked the combination of the safe.

There was a dull thud behind Dale.

He swung his phone around to where Callum was standing.

A single gold tooth blinked back at him.

Barbara tried to get up the street but the police had cordoned it off.

"What the bloody hell has Manuel done now?"

Indy looked on from the police cordon. The flashing lights of the fire engines worried him. *"Not another fire, I hope Chloe is okay."*

Chloe, Manuel and Lynn gave their initial statements to the police and were told they would have to go to the station later to give official statements but they were free to go.

"Anybody fancy a pint?" said Chloe.

"I don't drink and my Mother will kill me," said Manuel.

"Manuel, you've just faced down two armed robbers. Are you really that scared of your daft old bat of a mother?"

"I guess if you put it like that."

"I'd love to join you but it'll have to be another time. I think I have a cat to return," said Lynn.

"Thanks Lynn," said Chloe, "for everything."

"Thank you, and I'm sorry about, you know," said Manuel.

"Don't worry about it." Lynn waved off his apology.

They left Shears and headed towards the Chesters. Barbara spotted Manuel from the police cordon.

"Manuel, come here this instant."

"Ignore her," said Chloe.

"I can't. I'll just be a minute." He wandered over the police tape. "Hello, Mother."

"Where have you been? Your tea has been on the table for ages."

"I've been a little bit busy at work."

"Why didn't you answer your phone? You know that the only reason I allow you to have one is so I can contact you."

"As I said. I've been a little bit busy."

"You're coming home right now."

"He's not, he's coming for a drink with me." Chloe was behind Manuel now.

"My son isn't taking orders from the likes of you."

"The likes of me? Would you care to enlighten us as to what you mean?"

A crowd that had gathered to watch the fire engines was now eagerly watching this exchange.

"You know exactly what I mean. Now Manuel is coming home with me so you can't corrupt him anymore."

"I'm not," said Manuel.

"What?"

"I'm going for drink with my friend after a hard day at work. It's what normal people do. I want to be normal."

"But you're not normal."

"Bye mother, don't wait up." Manuel and Chloe walked back towards the pub, pointing out Grace to Lynn.

Indy had been watching on. Grace had joined him. "Manuel your son?" Indy said to Barbara.

Barbara gave him a brief look of disgust. "Yes. Why? What has he done?"

"Saved me from a fire. He's a good kid."

"A lovely lad," agreed Grace. "Always happy to stop and chat."

This wasn't the Manuel that Barbara knew. "But he's, he's..." Her voice trailed off. She saw him heading to the pub with his friend. She knew that she had lost him. She had lost a son and a job in the same day. Quite an achievement, even for her.

"Are you Grace?" said Lynn.

"I am," said Grace, a little abruptly as she recognised Lynn from the protests.

"I think I may have a cat belonging to you."

"Really?" Grace put her hand on Indy's shoulder to steady herself. "You have Ruby?"

"It's a long story," said Lynn, "I'll tell you all about it on the way to mine."

As they wandered off, Lynn noticed Rizla shivering in the back seat of a car.

"And what are you staring at?"

Rizla looked back as if expecting something.

"Who leaves dogs in the back of cars anyway? People like that don't deserve pets." She tried the door and was surprised to find it open. She was disgusted by the smell and the way Rizla looked. "You're coming home with me, somebody needs to straighten you out."

Manuel and Chloe walked into the pub car park.

"You okay mate?" said Chloe.

"Yeah, I'm glad I've told her."

"Good man. Come on, let's get a beer."

"Chloe, I'm sorry. For everything, I never meant for any of it to happen."

"I know."

"It was all to do with my ledger," said Manuel. Then the realisation hit him. "The ledger. It's still in there, the police will have it. I am going to prison. I'll never survive prison. What would my Mother say?"

"Stop worrying Manuel. Have I ever let you down?" Chloe produced the ledger from her pocket. "Think we can all start with a clean slate now." She tore up the notebook and put it in the bin.

"The books are balanced."

The End

Acknowledgements

Susie, Monkman and Bill, your feedback has been as valuable as ever.

Iain and the rest of Holmeside Writers, thanks for all the encouragement.

Thanks to everyone who suggested names for the cats, especially Gemma for suggesting Ruby.

Thank you for reading Life In The Balance. If you enjoyed it, please leave a review.

You can follow Alan's website and blog at **www.alan-parkinson.com** and follow him on Twitter @Leg_It.

You may wish to read Alan Parkinson's other novels.

Leg It

Fifteen years since Peter Wood left school and disappeared, he returns.
Is he back to make peace or is he back for revenge?

Childhood in the eighties was fun for but nothing lasts forever.
Running away seemed like his only option; as did his return fifteen years later.
Will his old friends forgive him for going?
Will his enemies forgive him for coming back?
Will Pete win back the life he thought he had lost or will he Leg It?
A classic tale of love and friendship, revenge, gangsters and rubber pants.

Alan Parkinson's debut novel Leg It is set in Sunderland and mixes crime and humour in the style of Christopher Brookmyre and Colin Bateman.
Alternating between the lead character's schooldays and the modern day, it gradually reveals his reason for moving away and motivation coming back.
A fast paced comic thriller that will bring back memories for anybody who went to school in the eighties and will strike a note for anyone who ever wanted to put right what happened in their teenage years.

Available on Kindle, iBook and in paperback.

https://www.amazon.co.uk/dp/B004IE9Z46/

Idle Threats

Liam hates his job working for Phonetix Mobile. Fighting for every second and battling with every customer, he is close to the edge. Bumper's business is going under. His debts are rising, his drinking is getting worse and his wife has had enough. Jodie is unemployed and is desperate for work to give her son the life he deserves. Her mobile phone on the other hand, appears to have no intention of working.
They are all brought together by an armed siege that could change their lives forever.

The long awaited follow up to Leg It, Alan Parkinson's debut novel. Idle Threats, set in Sunderland, is a fast paced tale of guns, bombs, gangsters and sombreros.
Comic crime fiction in the style of Chris Brookmyre and Colin Bateman, Idle Threats will have you on the edge of your seat.
A must for anyone who has ever suffered either working in a call centre or spent hours on the phone to one.
Would you take it one step further and take a gun into a call centre to settle your grievances?

Available on Kindle, iBook and in paperback.

https://www.amazon.co.uk/Idle-Threats-Alan-Parkinson-ebook/dp/B013P6CCJC/

23280491R00153

Printed in Great Britain
by Amazon